SWITCHERS

by

CHRISTOPHER TALLON

DEDICATION

For Rachel—
the girl I met the summer before high school and
after hanging out with her <u>once</u>
started telling everyone I was going to
marry her someday.
I didn't know what I was looking for
but I knew it when I saw it.

PART ONE

CHAPTER
ONE

WHEN YOU KNOW you're about to die and your last thought is—
No, that's not the right way to start this. Okay, let's try this:
Boring and safe. That's how everything was.
Until the switchers came.

CHAPTER

TWO

I GUESS it all *started* on the last day of school, 1996, in Oakesville, Michigan. A small suburb near Lansing (the capital) and Michigan State University (go green!). Me and my friends—Andy, Dylan, and Birdie— were waiting for our last day of middle school to end. A buzz went through the entire school as the announcement came over the drive-thru quality speakers:

"All students report to the gymnasium at this time for an assembly. Bring your backpacks to the gym, as students will only, I repeat—only—be dismissed through the gym doors. Thank you."

After what felt like an eternity of listening to the principal and one of the counselors talking about summer safety in that hot, stuffy gym, there was less than a minute to go.

The rustling of kids gathering their backpacks grew louder by the second, like a wave rolling in. Mr. B walked impatiently to the microphone. "Ladies and gentlemen...remain *calm* and take your *seats*, please, until the bell rings." But it didn't put a dent in the sound. "And when everyone is seated, we'll begin excusing students row by—"

Despite having a microphone, Mr. B had to raise his voice over the growing excitement in the bleachers. He was still talking when the bell rang, but the mob of students stopped listening. They all ran to and out the gym's double doors, exploding out of the building like a pack of gazelles fleeing a lion. Birdie got split up from the rest of us immediately while he fumbled with his trombone case.

Mr. B gave up on the mic and jogged to get out of the way, scolding anyone within earshot as he did so. I wasn't sure where Dylan was, but Andy was just a few feet ahead of me. I kept my feet moving so I wouldn't get trampled, but in the sea of people, I was getting split up from Andy.

"Kurt!" Andy yelled. "Let's all meet up at the hole after dinner tonight, okay?"

"Yeah, okay," I said. The hole was our hangout spot in the woods behind the 7-Eleven. It was pretty common for us to gather there on Friday nights after dinner, heading home when it started to get dark.

I didn't realize Dylan was right behind me until he punched me in the shoulder and shouted, "Wuh-diddy say?"

"He said meet up at the hole after—"

Dylan got shoved from behind and turned instinctively—somehow managing to stop amid the flow of kids moving away from the building. It was a 6th grader. Well, technically a 7th grader at that point. Dylan pushed the frightened sixth-turned-seventh grader, causing a domino effect in that immediate area. The kids that fell by the door rolled or army-crawled to the nearest clearing to avoid the stampede.

"Dylan! Get over here—*right now!*" Mr. Bertrand had snuck out the side door and managed to catch Dylan one last time.

I'm pretty sure he heard me. If not, he'll figure it out sooner or later.

I finally made it through the ocean of sweaty, sour-armpitted kids to my bike, and went home to take care of some business before I met up with the guys.

I played Mortal Kombat 3 until dinner.

Then I ate and headed out on my bike to meet up with the guys.

CHAPTER
THREE

THE RIDE OVER WAS NICE—THE sun was warm, the breeze cool. After I rounded the first turn, the finished part of the neighborhood, as well as the sidewalk, ended. I rode past a block with close to a dozen houses on either side of the street in the process of being framed. The next block were only lots that had either just been cleared, or just had a foundation poured. From there, the route to the hole, which was behind 7-Eleven, was a narrow, single-track path shaved like a reverse mohawk into the tall field grass. There wasn't much around at that point, except a few old barns with chipped red paint and decaying white trim. A few farmhouses remained from a time before all the subdivisions, but most of them were vacant. Two or three were home to elderly farmers who retired when they sold their land to developers but didn't want to leave their homes.

The single track was on a wide shoulder of tall grass. The ground sloped down steeply from the shoulder into a forest of mostly pines. As I was getting close to the hole, I saw a large area of trees had been cleared to make way for more new construction. The dormant, mustard-yellow machines, dotted with scabs of dried dirt, were scattered about the scarred earth. The trees had been cut and cleared out, but the stumps remained, littered about like old gravestones. I was so distracted by all of it that I hadn't noticed Andy and Birdie standing on the shoulder ahead of me with their bikes between their legs. I grunted, white-knuckling the brakes. I managed to stop just short of running into the guys.

"Whoa!" they yelled. "Hey!"

"Sorry," I said.

Andy looked at me sideways, but knew I meant it. "Where's Dylan?" he asked.

I told them about Dylan's last dance with Mr. Bertrand, and that he might not have heard me. Andy dismissed it, saying, "Dylan's lucky it was the last day of school or he probably would've gotten a weekend detention." As we were talking about it, Dylan came into view. Birdie spotted him first. Dylan came in hot and made a hard stop like mine, but, unlike mine, he was *trying* to scare everyone. We were used to it and didn't flinch. Except for Birdie—he almost fell over.

Dylan started laughing. But when he saw what we saw, he swallowed it. "Aw, c'mon! What the hell, guys?"

"I dunno. Looks like maybe it's going to be a strip mall or something," Andy said.

"Oh, great," Dylan said. "Now you can see the hole."

"Just buy some new pants," Birdie mumbled.

We all giggled, except for Dylan. His eyes were on fire. Birdie's eyes went wide as an owl's, with his mouth open in a way that reminded me of the face you make when you pull a hair off your tongue. Birdie's joke missed the target, but his awkward-face pulled Dylan out of his rage. Even made him laugh a little.

Birdie looked at me and Andy, surprised we were laughing. He always looked surprised when people laughed at his jokes; he usually mumbled them under his breath. His sense of humor was one of his few traits that I appreciated, even if the delivery was a little weird.

"*Maaan*," Dylan whined. "Before the trees were cut down, the hole was completely hidden."

"You still can't *really* see it," Andy said. We all squinted and muttered in agreement.

"Maybe," Dylan said. "But it's not a great spot anymore. You couldn't even see the start of the trail from the road before. Now there's obviously a trail leading into the last part of the forest. And there'll be people around now."

"Yeah," I agreed. "But it's still way off the road."

"Well?" Andy said, sick of standing there. "Are we going or not?"

"I'm gonna ride through the stumps for a second," Dylan said. Then, through gritted teeth, he said, "*I can't believe they cut all this down!*" Then he rode off. Andy yelled out for him to wait up. Birdie followed Andy, as usual.

But I couldn't do a pity lap. Instead, I peddled straight, on what was left of the path, towards the hole, musing about the changes to come.

CHAPTER

FOUR

THE HOLE WAS STILL inside what remained of the dense forest. As far as the name goes, there's no mystery—it looked like a hole in the earth. I think Dylan was the first one to say, "Hey, let's go back to the hole and hang out." I would describe it as a crater like hole in the ground, maybe 30 yards across. There was a tiny "pond" at the bottom. Calling it that was a bit of a stretch since it was really more of a large, constant puddle. We used to throw rocks in it to make a splash, or, on dry spells, to hear the funny *SPLACK* sounds they made in the muddy banks. Mostly we hung out around the top edge, looking at comic books, baseball cards, stuff like that.

From one edge of the hole, I could throw a football to someone standing on the opposite end. Well, two-thirds of the time—I only tried it three times. The first two times the ball made it across no problem. On the third try I didn't quite get it all the way across. It hit the lip a few feet below the edge and careened down into the pond, making a dull *PISH* in the mucky water. Then, of course, I had to go down and get it, and almost lost a shoe in the process.

When I got to the hole, I set my bike up against the big tree we commonly used as a bike stand. I was four or five steps from the edge of the hole when I put one foot on the ground and started to swing the other leg over the crossbar. Then a strong wind blew through the trees just right, like the wind was *trying* to shove me over the ledge.

I lost my balance and did an awkward, one-legged lunge away from the bike. I closed my eyes, and yelled, *"Ah shit!"*

I curled into a ball to protect myself and waited to stop moving.

But I wasn't moving. *Am I okay?*

I grabbed at the ground as I opened my eyes. I was safe, but still reeling—breathing in sharp, shallow gasps while blood audibly swooshed through my head.

"What're you doing?" Birdie said, right behind me. My mind quickly snapped into focus. I stood and dusted myself off. I took baby steps up to the edge, looking for my bike.

"Your bike's over there," Birdie said, pointing. It had rolled behind a small bush, a few steps from the big tree. Once I took inventory of the situation, I was relieved, but quickly felt like an A-hole for freaking out like that. In front of Birdie, no less.

"Thanks..." I said.

"Yeah, sure," Birdie said, head down. "You alright, Kurt?"

"Hmm? Oh, yeah..." I said, still a little dazed. "Yeah, I'm fine. The wind blew really hard and..."

I couldn't think of an explanation, so I looked down and shrugged. Then we stood side by side, but I looked as far away from Birdie's eyes as I could.

"I can't believe we're high schoolers now," Birdie said, sounding almost like a question.

"I know—me neither," I said.

Then the conversation died, and we stood in silence. Birdie was a nice guy and all, just boring. And a little weird.

Maybe the guys ditched Birdie...

It wasn't totally unprecedented.

They're probably at Dylan's...

Ready to ditch him myself, I started moving towards my bike and said, "Oh dude. You know what? I forgot about—"

"Wait up," Dylan said, his voice sounded close, but I couldn't see or hear bikes.

"*Dude*, I'm not even pedaling hard," Andy shouted back.

"Ha..." Dylan said, followed by another, slightly weaker, "*ha*."

Birdie and I both chuckled. Every time we'd go somewhere on our bikes together, we'd pick a spot that was the finish line, and race each other to it. Kinda. Andy would win almost every time. Actually, he might've won *every* time—except the few times when he wasn't with us. For the rest of us, it was mostly a race to finish second. (Or at least not to be last.)

Andy rolled up, barely breathing hard, and said, "What's up, guys?" He leaned his bike carefully against the big tree we all used as a bike stand. He picked up a few stones and started throwing them into the hole.

Dylan straggled in on his bike with his entire body on one side of the frame, one pedal supporting his weight. He jumped off, ditching his bike in the general direction of the tree. Andy grimaced as the bike landed in a heap of crossed up brake wires with the handlebars pointed backwards. Ignoring everyone, Dylan walked to a shady spot and lay down on his back with his hands behind his head and knees pointing up in the air, trying to catch his breath.

While laying down, Dylan pulled a pink pack of gum out of his pocket. From that he pulled out a slightly bent cigarette. He sat up, taking a moment to straighten out the cigarette and catch his breath.

"You rode with that in your pocket?" Andy said.

"Did you want me to put it in *your* pocket," Dylan said, laughing at his own lame joke.

"Can you still use it?" I asked.

"Well, you don't *use* it, you smoke it. And sure, as long as it doesn't break." He stood up. "Even then, I could probably make it work." We watched as he inspected and gently did his best to restore it to near-original quality. "Yeah," he said. "It's fine. Who wants to go first?"

He pulled a lighter out of his shorts.

"Doesn't your dad notice when you take one?" Birdie asked.

"*Cigarettes?*" Dylan said. "He smokes a couple packs of these a day. Buys em by the box."

"Like...a *moving* box?" Birdie asked.

"Nah, not quite that big. Maybe more like a shoebox or something."

Dylan gave the cigarette and lighter to Andy, who tried to light the cigarette holding it straight up and down out in front of him like it was a candle. My parents didn't smoke, but I had seen enough TV and movies to know that while you light it, you had to put it in your mouth and hold your head at the same angle my dad did when he shaved the side of his neck.

"Here, let me try real quick," I said. He handed it to me, and I did it just like the bad guys in the mobster movies. I put the cigarette deep in the crevice of my pointer and middle finger, got it lit, and took a long, slow drag. I tried to think of a line from that Robert De Niro movie, but before I could even open my mouth to say it, I had a huge coughing fit. My lungs felt like they were being scraped from the inside with a hot, rusty rake. I held the cigarette out in front of me, as far from my face as possible. Someone grabbed it from me and kept things going. It went around and we all took two hits—enough to show that you could handle it—then gently rubbed out the remaining cherry. We all wanted to go to 7-Eleven to get the dry, stale taste out of our mouths.

We started for our bikes. Andy stopped us before we could push off and pedal on our way. "Hold on, guys." He got off his bike. "I'm gonna grab the rest of that and throw it away at the store."

Seizing the opportunity, Dylan yelled, "Race ya to the parking lot!" and sped off on his bike.

CHAPTER
FIVE

To my surprise, Birdie took off right behind Dylan. I yelled for Andy, who was fidgeting to get the cigarette butt into his pocket, to hurry up while I started pedaling towards the trail.

Dylan and Birdie got a decent head start, but I was better on the dirt than they were. My tires' first revolution spun dirt out behind me. The second time around, the wheels dug in, and I almost slipped off the back of my seat. Warm summer wind rushed over my body like shower water. I'd be able to catch Birdie in ten seconds. *If I get past Dylan, I might be able to hold off Andy the last few blocks!*

There was a quick rise in the trail—not quite big enough to get good air from, but enough to abruptly drop your guts into your lap—then a quick right turn on completely flat ground. I hit the rise as fast as I could. The floor fell out from under my heart. I took the right early, veering into the sparse field grass, so I could maintain a little extra speed. But the terrain wasn't ideal. I hit a rock or something that sent my back tire up in the air. The bike somehow managed to stay upright beneath me. My bike fishtailed and I almost T-boned Birdie, who was coming around the hard right turn. When he saw me, he went off the trail and hit the brakes, grunting something at me as I passed him. Once I reached flat ground, Dylan was maybe thirty feet ahead of me.

It would be close.

The strategy was to get close enough to make it a pure neck and neck sprint at the end. Under normal conditions, he might have a slight edge. But he just got done racing Andy and was the only one of us that took an honest puff of that cigarette. Hell, he took *two*.

Only two blocks to the store! Gotta catch Dylan!

Dylan stood to pedal at the base of the hill rising up to the side of the road. My bike had more speed than his, and it looked like I could pass him at the top. I doubted he'd have enough left over to catch back up to me.

Sure enough, I passed Dylan at the top, putting myself in the lead on the single track. But the single track didn't last long. Once on the sidewalk, it was a little less than a minute to get to the parking lot.

I heard Dylan scream.

Worried that my buddy had fallen and hurt himself I looked over my shoulder to see if he was okay. Dylan was fine. He screamed because Andy was passing him. Under normal conditions, Andy wasn't one to take these races too seriously since none of us were actually a threat to him. But this was different.

I looked forward and put my bike in the highest gear.

Less than half a block to go...

There was no need to turn around; I could hear the gears churning on Andy's bike, slowly getting closer and closer. It sounded like someone was flipping through a deck of cards right behind my ear.

Almost there...

I could feel the sensation of winning—the hair on my arms jutted out like porcupine quills—but as soon as it came, it was gone.

Andy passed me, getting half his bike ahead of me at the finish line.

CHAPTER
SIX

ANDY RODE, tall and triumphantly, into the parking lot towards the grassy patch on the far side of the store where we usually parked our bikes, I followed behind him

When he got off his bike, he wasn't even breathing hard.

As I came to stop, I couldn't look Andy in the eye. It felt like, on some level, I had betrayed him. In that moment I thought about being alone —not just in-my-room or walking-to-school alone, but left behind. Ditched. On that warm summer day, heart still working time-and-a-half, I felt very cold.

"Good one," Andy said. I looked at him. He meant it. That made me feel even worse.

"Yeah, I—"

Dylan came in, cursing between violent gasps. He sounded like a belligerent dragon, which made me laugh.

"Something..." Dylan struggled, "...funny?"

"Yup," Andy said, crossing his arms. Then we all laughed—even Dylan. Andy was the only one who could brazenly come at Dylan like that with no fear of revenge. Even Birdie was laughing as he gingerly rolled up behind us, even though he couldn't have known why we were laughing in the first place.

As everyone settled in, Andy's eyes wandered off and his smile melted away. All of us looked in kind. He was looking at the abandoned farmhouse behind the 7-Eleven. It was the divide between the big field next to the forest (and the hole) and the growing expanse off the highway. Now the old house was the only thing that stood between the past and the future. It was a small, red lunchbox of a house. Couldn't have been more than two bedrooms, maybe one and a half bathrooms, at the most. No garage. The front door was smack in the middle of the house with big square windows on both sides. Me and the guys spent many afternoons looking through the ancient yellowing windows. The carpet was probably a brilliant gold once, but by the time we started hanging around, it looked like a worn-out, hay-colored sponge. The walls and floors were dirty. The house smelled of dank wood and mildew. Time and disuse had turned the home's once bright red exterior the color of dried blood. The windows were all still intact, no small miracle with the number of kids that came and went.

But the house had something about it. It looked off, like it might, I don't know, attack. Its front windows were like the eyes of a mortally wounded animal with nothing left to lose. Despite my curiosity, I couldn't stand to look at it for very long. Andy, I noticed, was completely gone—out on his feet, mouth open, tongue practically hanging out—staring at the old house, as if those disturbed eyes, pretending to be windows, had him in a trance.

"Whatcha lookin at?" I asked.

"No..." Andy said absently. "I mean, I don't know. I'm..."

We all looked at him funny.

"Nothing," he said, shaking his head like he had water in his ears. He looked as though his brain was split in two, feeding him two different things at once, and he did not know which one to act on.

"Place gives me the creeps," Birdie said. He was standing behind us like an anxious lookout—head on a swivel, eyes jumping around frantically.

"It should," Dylan said. We all looked at him. He smiled an almost-not-there smile as his eyes stirred around, waiting to be sure we were giving him all of our attention. "The guy that lived here used to torture and kill people in the basement."

"Who?" Birdie asked.

"And why?" I added.

"I don't know who," Dylan said. "Don't wanna know, either. I wish I didn't know as much as I do."

"What're you talking about, dude?" Andy asked.

"Well...there was this guy. He was married and lived alone in that house with his wife, back when this town was just an old farming community. Him and his wife moved into this house to start a family. Time went on and they kept trying to have a kid, but nothing was happening. It was all either of them talked about. Most of their conversations became arguments, and one day the man snapped. He chained his wife up in the basement and tortured her for being such a bad wife—"

"For being a bad wife? He *tortured* her?" I said.

"Whadda *you* know about it?" Dylan said. I shrugged. "That's how people have been telling the story for years, okay?" He sucked his teeth and composed himself. "So anyway, he had her chained up, torturing her every day until she eventually died. Then he buried her somewhere. Some people say she's buried right under the 7-Eleven."

"Yeah right," Andy said.

"That's not even the worst of it!" Dylan shot back. "He liked it. The torturing and killing, I mean. So he started hitchhiking a few miles up the highway looking for rides. He'd get picked up and ask for a ride to his house right off the highway. And back then it wasn't well lit and there wasn't anyone around for miles. So he would get someone to drive him to his house"—the house creaked, sounding like the moan of a sad dog— "then he would hit them over the head and chain them up downstairs."

I couldn't resist saying: "That's a bunch of crap."

"Go in the basement, then. You'll see. There's chains on the wall. Chains with shackles on the end. There's even blood stains on the floor still. My brother saw it."

"I doubt that," Andy said.

"Alright then, know-it-all. Go in and tell me I'm wrong."

Andy and Dylan stood there staring at each other.

It was tense. Awkward.

"Before we do anything else, can we get something to drink first?" I urged.

"No, no. Let's take a look inside real quick," Andy said, not breaking eye contact with Dylan.

"Yeah, but—we're not going *inside* inside though, right?" Birdie said.

"No, no, no. No way," I said.

Then we heard footsteps crunching the twigs on the ground behind us. We looked and fell silent.

CHAPTER

SEVEN

Mike and Evan, the only kids to hold the title "kings of the bullies" their entire middle school careers, were standing behind us. They were a year older than us, and since they went on to high school, I had almost forgotten about them. Dylan's older brother was going into his senior year of high school and plays on the water polo team, so he's no pushover and he even said he wouldn't want to mess with those guys. Mike was always getting suspended for fighting, and word was Evan was expelled halfway through his freshman year, but no one seemed to know why.

Mike's arms were crossed, and Evan was drinking a Slurpee. Evan had the same look on his face as always. It was that of a simple child. A dimwitted smile—eyes that never seemed to focus on one thing very long, mouth always slightly open, and poor posture highlighting his doughboy frame.

Mike, on the other hand, was lean and muscular. He stared intently at us with a look of genuine contemplation: *Should I beat them up a little now and come back for more later, or go for broke and beat them bloody right now?* Evan never had a look on his face that showed a working brain. I pictured his diminished thought process looking something like a bloodlust horror comic where everything was wide-eyed evil grins and carnage.

Andy surprised me when he said, "What's up, Mike? Evan?"

Mike's head cocked to one side, squinting slightly. Evan slowly nodded at Andy with his strangely serene face, then looked to Mike to see what to do next. How Andy could be so cool and confident in that moment was beyond me. I was trying not to piss my pants.

"You tell me," Mike said, scowling.

Me, Dylan, and Birdie now looked eagerly to Andy, hoping he would save us from a world class ass-kicking. Andy said nothing. He seemed to be out of ideas—and possibly confidence. He must have felt the weight of our eyes on him. He shifted away from us, lowering his eyes first to Mike's feet, then his own.

"Damn," Mike said. "I was hoping you were tougher than that."

"What do you guys want?" Andy said, straightening up as he did.

"Ooooh..." Evan said. "He's trying to look *tough* in front of his little *girl*friends."

Mike ignored Evan's comment, still thinking, then said: "Looks like you're interested in that house. Feel free to go in and take a look, fellas."

Andy slowly moved himself between Mike and Evan and the rest of us. The gesture made me feel a little safer for a moment. Then I started to worry about what they might do to Andy. My mind was telling me to run, but I wasn't about to ditch Andy. Not again. Not when the situation was a lot more serious than a stupid bike race.

"No thanks," Andy said.

"Oh, I'm sorry. I can see where you were confused. That *sounded* like a question." Mike smiled for a second. Then it was gone. All business. "It wasn't."

The wind picked up and a chill swept through me. I looked up at the silhouette of the tree swaying in the wind on the other side of the store. That was when I realized that I couldn't see the sun anymore.

It was getting dark.

CHAPTER
EIGHT

MIKE AND EVAN began lurching towards us like bloodthirsty lions about to pounce.

"Come on you guys," Birdie pleaded with them. "I betcha we can get Dylan's brother to buy you guys cigarettes or something if you leave us alone. We'll go talk to him right now!"

"*Dude...*" Dylan said under his breath. Even though I appreciated what Birdie was trying to do, he was losing whatever itty-bitty shred of dignity someone in our situation had. At best, he was prolonging our beatdown—Dylan's brother would absolutely *not* help us, no matter the reason, and he might even beat Dylan up himself for being a wuss.

"How about this," Mike said, looking dead set at Birdie, "You go in the house, maybe I don't kick your ass. Or you don't go in and," faking a punch, "see what happens."

Birdie flinched hard. He turned back towards Mike slowly. Birdie stared at Mike, completely frozen, eyes and mouth stuck open as wide as they would go. He was too scared to blink or breathe, let alone speak.

"I heard you talking about the psycho that used to live here," Mike said. "I heard the same story. There's actually a lot of truth to it. But you forgot to tell them that the house is haunted by that weirdo, along with all the people he tortured and killed."

"Heh-heh. Yeah," Evan said, taking a drink of his Slurpee.

"Don't worry, you'll probably be fine," Mike said, grinning like a deranged clown.

Mike walked up to Birdie, sidestepping Andy, and grabbed Birdie by the scruff of his shirt collar. He dragged Birdie up to the front door of the miserable house and opened the ratchety screen door. As he was pushing Birdie in, Andy ran towards them. Mike turned when he heard him coming. Just as he did, Andy dropped his shoulder square into Mike's chest, sending him flying off the front steps, landing on the seat of his pants, and sliding into the first half of a backwards somersault in the process. It was awesome—until the reality of the situation kicked back in. And just like that, Evan descended on Andy, holding him in a full nelson like some tangled-up marionette.

"Oh-ho-ho," Mike giggled incredulously. He stood, not dusting himself off, and stared hard and deep into Andy's eyes. To Andy's credit, he didn't blink or shy away, even as the first punch, an overhand right, connected on his cheek directly below his left eye.

Bullseye.

After the punch, Mike held out his hand with a strained look on his face, like his hand was turning into a lobster claw before his eyes, but quickly put it down at his side, clenching his jaw. As if his hand were reacting to an intense electric shock, his fingers were tensely spread apart and his whole hand was shivering.

In my mind, Andy went from being a cool friend to the biggest badass of all time. Without throwing a punch—hell, just by *taking* a punch—he put a hurt on the most feared teenager we'd ever encountered—maybe even broke his hand.

With his face!

Badass or not, however, Andy was definitely looking like he had gotten the worst of it. An explosion of dark bluish purple had spread from his cheek, covering most of the left side of his puffy face from his eyebrow to just above the edge of his mouth. Dylan whispered, "Holy crap, Kurt. Lookit him—his parents are gonna think he stuck his face out into traffic."

Using his undamaged hand (the one he used to punch Andy hung limply by his front pocket), Mike grabbed Birdie, who was still frozen in shock, by the back of the neck and tossed him through the entryway of the house. Then Mike turned, and using a pistol-whipping motion, hit Andy again square in the center of his bruise. Andy groaned and briefly shuddered. Mike turned back to Birdie and said, "Get in that basement! Then, once you're down there, holler up and we'll send ol bruise-face down for you."

Birdie took a few baby steps farther inside the house, then turned back with a pleading look on his face. Mike hit Andy again with the same pistol-whip pound on his rapidly darkening cheek. It made Andy's knees buckle. His chin began to wiggle as he was trying to stifle a whimper. A few tears gathered around the swollen crevice of his bruised eye while a steady stream dripped from the other.

Birdie's mouth quivered. He was quick to tighten his lips. Below his constricted mouth, his chin was covered in lines and dents. As a warning, Mike put his hand up as if to hit Andy again. Birdie looked at Andy quickly—almost mournfully—before turning to run to the stairs. He hung a right and disappeared.

A few seconds of near-total silence passed, except for the faint sound of Andy trying to control his agony with rapid, shallow breaths.

"You down there yet?" Mike shouted.

Nothing.

Dylan and I looked nervously back and forth from Andy, to each other, to the house, and on and on. There was nothing.

Dylan nudged me in the ribs with his elbow. "Dude, what if he's hurt?"

Mike overheard and looked questioningly at Dylan.

"Seriously," Dylan pressed, now looking at Mike. "What if the stairs were rotted out and broke or something. He might've broke his arm or leg—"

"Or his neck," Evan said. Mike's head swung towards Evan. Evan's grip on Andy had loosened visibly. Andy broke free with a violent jerk. It startled an already shaken Evan, who jumped back. Mike took one full step towards Andy, but Andy was staring him down with his one good eye—which now made *him* look like some sort of grotesque comic book villain—and stopped Mike's advance mid-stride.

"Okay!" Birdie yelled. "I'm downstairs!"

"Birdie! Are you alright?" Andy yelled back.

"Yeah..." He said he was alright, but his voice wavered. He didn't sound in pain, just shaken up. Or, as Birdie's mom described herself when Birdie didn't come home before the streetlamps came on, scared *you-know-what*.

"See?" Mike said. "He's fine. Go get him, tough guy."

Andy and Mike stared each other down. Neither giving up any ground, nor making a move.

"Andy?" Birdie called.

Andy looked at me and Dylan, then walked quickly into the house. By this time, the sun was all the way down, the edge of the sky was burnt orange, blending into a thin layer of purple before meeting the empty blackness. I lost sight of Andy before he made it to the top landing of the stairs. I heard the clomping of his feet and the creak of the stairs.

It was quiet for a moment.

Then there was a shriek of terror.

CHAPTER
NINE

BIRDIE CAME RUNNING up the stairs at full sprint. He shot out of the house and right through all of us before we knew what was going on.

"*Something happened!*" Birdie yelled, then screamed again as he got on his bike and started pedalling off.

When I looked around, I saw Evan's dumb face had gone blank. He looked at Mike who started backing away, anger and confusion twitching back and forth on his face.

"What's going on, Mike?" Evan said.

"I...uh..." Mike babbled incoherently.

"Andy!" Dylan screamed, but he didn't move towards the house. In fact, we had all started backing away from it. Evan continued to stand there, eyebrows raised. Mike barely whispered, "Let's get outta here." And when I looked away from the house, they were gone.

"Andy!" I screamed.

Nothing.

Dylan and I each took turns yelling, trying to get some kind of response, anything, from Andy. The urge to move had become overwhelming, but I didn't know whether to run to the house or away from it. Fear may motivate, but it doesn't help with decision-making.

"Come on, Kurt—let's get some help," Dylan said.

"We can't just leave him down there."

"*I'm* not going in there. Even if we *did* go in there, what if he's hurt? Are you gonna put him over your shoulder and ride him home on your bike?"

"I...*no*."

"What if there's someone—or some*thing*—else down there? I'm not..." He trailed off, shaking his head.

"Okay," I said. "Let's go in the store and call 9-1-1."

"Yeah. Okay, yeah—that works," Dylan said. We nodded at each other in agreement. We took half a dozen steps before we stopped at the sound of someone walking up the stairs.

"Andy?" we said in unison.

I watched the door over my shoulder—my toes pointed towards the front of the store, my legs crouched (*on your mark, get set...*), allowing me to look easily behind me so I could be ready to run away from whatever was coming up from that basement.

Slowly, a shadowy figure materialized inside the doorway. Dylan yelled to whomever it was, but it stopped moving. Said nothing. Then it laughed. As it did so, the shadowy figure came out and turned into Andy. But he carried himself differently than he had moments ago. It was hard to say how. Like, maybe, he stood more upright, or moved at a subtly different speed, or...something.

Thinking the same thing as me, Dylan said, "Dude, is that Andy? What's he *doing*?"

Andy was looking around, observing the sky, the house behind him, the store next to me. He was smiling—not a happy smile per se, but one of a man that had just been released from prison—and started laughing again. It was eerie.

"*Fellas*," Andy said, hands out low, palms up. "Good to see you."

Good to see us? It's been, like, a minute since I saw you—if that.

Andy walked past us to his bike, made a few adjustments to the seat and handlebars with the quick-release levers, and got on.

"Let's ride, boys," Andy said.

Was he faking how hurt he was before, or did something happen when he went in the basement? And what did Birdie mean when he said *something happened*? I couldn't say what it was, exactly, but something was off.

CHAPTER

TEN

ANDY WAS ON HIS BIKE, one foot on the pedal the other tiptoed on the ground. He was looking at us expectantly. Dylan started to get his bike up from where he had carelessly tossed it.

"Hold on a sec," I said.

"What?" Dylan said, stopping before he had his bike all the way righted. Andy's face didn't change, his one good eye fixed on me but not really looking at me.

"Birdie said something happened. Are you okay?" I said.

"Besides this big-ass bruise on my face? Yeah, I'm great, thanks. Let's go." He started pushing the bike slowly with his grounded foot.

"Wait!" I said, which caught Dylan by surprise, dropping his bike completely.

Andy came to an abrupt stop with his head down between his outstretched arms, clearly annoyed. He sighed loudly; the damaged part of his face was all I could see. "What is it, Kurt?"

The flood light shone from the front corner of the building, filling up part of the darkness with a too-bright yellowish glow. The deep tones of the light seemed to amplify the bruise on his face. It was absolutely hideous—he must've broken something (besides Mike's hand). I lost my train of thought and found myself unable to turn away from the bruise, even though it gave me a sick feeling, like an elevator coming to settle.

"Birdie said something happened," I said numbly.

"Did he say what?" Andy asked.

"I don't know. After you went down there it was quiet for a minute, then he came running out like he was being chased, screaming," I said waving my hands mockingly, "'Something happened!'"

Andy laughed. "That's what he came up with? Genius. Listen guys, whatever you think is going on—you're wrong."

"What? What does that mean? What happened?"

"Nothing," Andy said. "Not yet."

"What does that—"

"Hey," Dylan said. "Wait up!"

Andy had started pedaling away. *What's his deal?* He didn't race out, I could have jogged and caught up to him. He was just leading us out.

"Where we going?" I yelled.

"Tell ya when we get there, buddy. Hurry up!" Andy said. Dylan was on his bike already, watching me stand there shrugging my shoulders.

"*Dude*, let's go," Dylan said. He started pushing himself forward with his foot, but he waited until I had my bike under me before he went to catch Andy.

CHAPTER
ELEVEN

WE RODE until we were back in our neighborhood. We must've made good time; Dylan and I were struggling to breathe. Andy had very slowly, very methodically increased the pace from normal cruising speed to one where we could hardly keep up. While we sucked air, Andy told us—without breathing hard—that we were going to Birdie's house to check on him, make sure he made it back alright.

We made a couple of quick turns off the main road, through the dark streets, to Birdie's house. There were a few lights on inside, and the garage door was open. Andy slowed down and stopped one house short of Birdie's. There was a big bush between Birdie's driveway and his neighbor's. Andy got off his bike and knelt behind the bush. Birdie's neighbors weren't home or had settled in for the night; their lights were out. When Dylan and I caught up to Andy, we set our bikes down next to his. He motioned us over to the bush and we crouched behind it to stay out of view.

"I'm gonna make sure he got back alright. You guys stay here and don't let anyone see you. Alright, Dylan?"

"Yeah, okay."

"Cool. Kurt, you alright? I see smoke coming out of your ears."

"Huh? Yeah, I'm fine. It's just...why don't we all go?"

"If his mom sees me, it'll be easier to talk to her by myself," Andy said.

"Why?" Dylan asked.

"His mom and my mom are cousins."

"*Seriously?*" Dylan said.

"Yes," Andy said. He looked at Dylan and sighed. "Why are you making that face?"

Dylan's upper lip was drawn back in exaggerated disgust. I laughed. Andy's mangled face twisted.

"Just stay here," Andy said. Then he got up and walked to the front door.

"Dude, I didn't know they were related," Dylan said. "I think I lost a little respect for Andy."

"Right? Not about losing respect for Andy—that's messed up. But how did we not know they were related?" I said.

Dylan made that grossed-out face again and I spat air in a giggle-fit. This really didn't seem like the time to be goofing around, but it made the situation a little less uncomfortable.

"Dude, *shut up*," Dylan said. Andy was at the door. He peeked inside the window by the door.

"What's he doing?" I said.

"I dunno."

"Why doesn't he just knock or ring the doorbell?"

Andy looked at us. Then both ways down the road. Satisfied no one was around, he looked through the tall window next to the door one more time. It looked like he was standing watch, making sure no one was going to come out.

After a minute, he walked in a crouched position, crossing under the big living room window. When he reached the corner of the house, he ran over to us. He took a knee in front of us and started talking quickly in our little huddle.

"He should be back any second," Andy said. "We just need to wait a minute."

"For what?" I asked.

"Get your bikes," he replied. Andy grabbed his without waiting for us and ran it between Birdie's next-door neighbor's and next, next-door neighbor's houses. "*Hurry!*" he said over his shoulder.

Dylan and I looked at each other, clearly puzzled. Then we heard the sound of Birdie's bike coming down the sidewalk.

"Get your asses over here!" Andy hissed.

"What's your *deal*, man?" Dylan asked as we rushed over.

"Quiet." Andy looked around the corner of the house. "Once he's back, I'll have a little chat with him. Then the three of *us* will get going," Andy said.

"Get going?" I asked. "Where?"

He said nothing, just pushed through Dylan and me as he ran towards the driveway to intercept Birdie. We watched from around the corner of the house. Birdie got to the driveway and stopped, got off his bike. Birdie had his backpack on, which meant he'd gone back to the hole for it. I'd completely forgotten we left them there.

Birdie stopped his bike near the end of the driveway and looked at Andy reverentially, like he was famous or something. Andy walked up to him very calmly. He didn't say much, but Birdie ate it up, nodding with his mouth open. The last thing he said to Birdie looked like a question. Birdie dropped the backpack off his right shoulder and started to open it as it hung across his body. Andy stopped him from opening the backpack, saying something to Birdie with a very serious face. Birdie looked down and nodded. Andy bent his knees a little, moving his head down to force eye contact with Birdie. Birdie looked at him. Andy asked something again. Birdie looked him in the eye and nodded. Andy pointed at Birdie's watch. Tapped it a few times, then pointed at the backpack. Birdie nodded one last time. Andy patted him on the back and walked away. Birdie disappeared into the garage. A few seconds later, the garage door came down.

A moment later, Andy was by us and we were all looking at the big bay window. Birdie walked inside. His face was blank like he was in shock either from what happened at 7-Eleven, or because of whatever Andy said. Inside the house, his mom ran up to him and hugged him like she hadn't seen him in years. Then she held him at arm's length and looked him over in a panic. He grabbed her by the hands and went through the old I'm-*fine*-mom routine. And it seemed to be working. More or less.

"Okay," Andy said. He stood and walked to his bike. "The next thing is to address the situation from earlier." He touched his cheek and winced. Then he moved his jaw around like he was trying it on for the first time. "So, here's what we're gonna—"

"Address the situation?" Dylan asked.

"Yeah, what does *that* mean?" I added.

"What do you think I mean?" Andy said.

"*Mm*-mmm?" We shrugged.

He sighed. "That's because you didn't let me finish. *We don't have time for this.*" He closed his eyes and took a deep breath. "OK, listen— Mike and Evan should be out by the lake a while, yet. We can go a more comfortable speed this time. Ready to go?"

"Are you seriously telling me that we're going to go and find Mike and Evan right now?" Dylan said, but I was thinking it, too.

With a humorless chuckle, Andy said, "Yup."

CHAPTER

TWELVE

IT WAS FULL DARK. To the west, you could barely see a small blanket of light coming from the college and the city. The neighborhood was pretty new and, at nighttime, sparsely lit. Birdie's house was near the end of the only row of completed homes. His street was done, and all the yards had grass and fresh new trees held upright with little wires. It was hard to imagine that someday they would have full, shade-providing branches. (Or that the houses behind them would soon literally be shells of themselves.)

"We're going to go where *they* are?" I had to ask. I couldn't believe it. *Either he isn't right from that knock on the head, or I missed something.* Dylan didn't say anything, but the look on his face conveyed the same feeling.

"Yeah, but you don't have to do anything," Andy said. "Don't worry. I just need you to be...a presence. And it's not gonna work unless you two try not to look scared."

Dylan and I stood there looking at Andy the way Evan looked at Mike when things started to go south.

"Come on," Andy said, getting on his bike. "I'll explain on the way."

"On the way where?" I asked.

"Crighton Lake."

The street behind Birdie's house had a few lots that were cleared for construction —flat, desert-like ground with posts and little flags dotting the barren landscape. One or two foundations were already poured, piles of wood flanking them for framing the new houses. All of the houses in the neighborhood looked more or less the same. The only real difference was the yards, and even then it was bizarre to see them at night, lit only by the pale moonlight. With only blues and grays showing, they looked like mausoleums.

We rode easily through the soft summer breeze, but I was shivering in my damp clothes from the sweaty ride to Birdie's house. I don't know how Dylan felt, but my legs were useless. I really had to dig into the pedals—which sent a dull ache through my body—just to get the wheels turning. Once I got moving a little, I shifted to the highest gear so I wouldn't have to push the pedals so hard. Even then it was an effort to keep going. I had to keep counting down from fifty, telling myself we'd be there the next time I reached zero. When we came to the big hill, I closed my eyes for a deep, thankful breath and happily let gravity take over. But then I remembered: the big hill meant we were almost to Crighton Lake.

CHAPTER
THIRTEEN

CRIGHTON LAKE WAS A GROSS, man-made abomination. The original idea, as I heard it, was that the developers wanted a lake so they could build around it and charge more for the waterfront lots. So they made this recreational lake for people in the soon-to-be neighborhood. But immediately, they realized it was impossible to keep it clean. They tried having several companies come with different plans—chemicals, adding different biological elements (fish, plants, snails, etc...), and always promising that next summer would be the summer. Of the half dozen houses or so they had built around the lake, one was sold, but no one lived in it yet, so the lake went largely ignored. There was a dirt trail that ran along the swampy, unbuildable side of the lake. About halfway down, there was a small area that was completely blocked by trees and dense brush. This was, Andy surmised, where Mike and Evan would be.

"A:" Andy said, "It's summer and they probably don't go home until late; and B: They're probably avoiding whatever consequence might lie ahead for pounding on a younger kid's face. So, our targets should be—"

"*Targets?*" Dylan said, but Andy spoke over him with a perturbed, authoritative voice.

"—*SHOULD BE* by the lake. Probably lighting fires and hitting each other with sticks or whatever they do. With the three of us standing up to them together, I see no problems."

"Can you tell us *why* we would want to do that, Andy?" I said. "They looked really freaked out, man. I mean, your face is...*Messed. Up.* Play it up like it hurts worse than it really does, and I bet we can get those guys in lots of trouble."

"Yeah, dude," Dylan added. "I mean, c'mon. What if they come after us? I don't think I can take either of those guys. If they quick jump one of us, then it's one-on-one, and then..."

"Heh," Andy said, biting his lip. "That's a good point, Dylan. I'm glad you're thinking through all the possible scenarios. That's exactly what you should be doing right now." Dylan looked at me like he just won a prize. I still wasn't sure.

Andy continued: "Here's the plan. I'll talk to Mike. His hand is pretty messed up; something broke when he landed that punch. I remember how his hand crunched and practically molded around my cheek. If I remember right, I'm pretty sure I saw him pull up gimpy after the fact. That's why he only hit me with the butt of his other hand."

Andy laughed like he suddenly remembered an old joke. "You guys stand right next to me. One of you on each side. If Mike comes at us, you two take him. He won't be able to throw more than one punch with his right hand, and if he tries to use it at all, he'll have plenty of pain to show for it." Andy slowed down to ride between me and Dylan. "Trust me. The *two of you* can take one one-armed guy. I'll take Evan. He can't be much stronger than me and I'm definitely in better shape.

"It shouldn't take long before Mike is ready to retreat, and Evan will try to do what he always does—follow Mike. I, however, am not going to let him. That is the most important part: we cannot, I repeat *not*, let Evan get away. I've got a few things he needs to hear. You guys just help me with Mike. Got it? Any questions?"

"Should we get Birdie?" I asked.

"No. He's already doing his part," Andy said.

"Yeah, but," I had to pause to collect and organize my thoughts. Everything was happening too fast to keep up, and none of it made any damn sense. "Why wasn't he freaking out when we saw him at home?"

Dylan interjected, "Or how do you know that he didn't tell his mom what happened? She might be calling *your* mom! Moms are *always* talking to each other."

"Which is another good point," Andy said, nodding in a strangely condescending way. "We need to hurry so you guys can get home before your parents start to worry and try to ground you or something," Andy said.

Dylan squinted as he tried to make sense of it all. Then said, "So... even if your plan works, won't Mike and Evan just come after us later?"

"And if it *doesn't*," I added, "they'll kill us. You might be as big as a high schooler, but me and Dylan are way smaller than those guys. Broken hand or not, I'm not sure—"

"*They* aren't the ones you gotta worry about," Andy said. But before I could ask what he meant by that, he stopped his bike and said: "We're here."

I completely lost sense of time while we rode, talking about the improbable plan Andy proposed, and found myself wishing for more time.

I'm not ready for this...

I needed more time—time to think this through.

But there was no more time.

"Let's leave the bikes here," Andy said. "It'll be quieter."

There we were at one end of the trail, the way to school was at the other end, and Mike and Evan were somewhere in the middle. I went over our seek-and-destroy plan in my head, but the more I thought about it, the harder and faster my heart beat.

I dropped my bike, sweating and shaking. At that point, I stopped thinking. Had to. If I gave even one more second for this madness to stew in my brain, I would've had a full-blown panic attack. The scary thing about it? I wasn't even aware of my brain's switch from thinking to autopilot. It was as instinctive as blinking. A part of my mind, normally under the radar, pulled the manual override. No more thoughts, just a feeling of melting into my surroundings.

Dylan said, "If everything works like you planned—"

"It will," Andy said.

Dylan stared him down for interrupting. "Yeah, well what if Mike and Evan aren't even here. Or what if they're watching us now and they're just waiting to sneak up on us, or they're going to grab our bikes and throw them in the lake? Or *take* them?" Dylan was nervous, crossing into totally-losing-it territory. I noticed but didn't think about or react to it. It was just happening around me at that point.

"Great question, Dylan," Andy said, clapping Dylan on the shoulder. "I'm impressed. You've really given this some thought. Not bad."

Dylan calmed down and beamed with pride.

"Okay," Andy continued. "We'll push them out in the opposite direction, towards the school. And, just in case, we'll stick our bikes inside the tree line over there. They won't see them in the dark. Anything else? No? Alright, let's do this, fellas."

Andy walked with a smile on his face. In the back of my mind, I was still worried, and not just about getting beat up. I was worried that something was wrong with Andy. He was always confident, but never one to start a fight (let alone a vengeful manhunt). And Dylan—he suddenly seemed all too eager to follow Andy into battle. This wasn't our thing. We weren't goons. The idea of winning this fight was almost as troubling as losing it. But all those thoughts were a whisper in the background.

Andy started walking, Dylan right behind him.

I—now acting without thought—followed.

Part of me wanted to tell Andy and Dylan, who was right on Andy's heels, to stop and go home. But that part of my brain wasn't in control anymore. Even though I knew better of it and wanted to bail, I couldn't. There was an invisible train. Andy was the conductor, Dylan was shoveling coal into the fire, and I was the little caboose at the end.

The stars were out. More than I was used to seeing. Our steps through the sparse grass on the trail were quick, each stride sounding like two pieces of paper rubbing. The light reflected off the lake to my left, but the moonlight didn't seep past the tree line to my right where, in the darkness of the swamp, I heard crickets, frogs, and toads singing a cacophonous, droning melody. Taking in the enormity of the darkness, I found myself following close on Dylan's heels, like he was doing with Andy.

My heart was beating faster than normal, but with each step we took towards Mike and Evan, my heart became calmer, steadier. My thoughts went from racing at top speed during our initial descent into the dark trail, to a singular, calm stream. Not even a stream, just blankness. I saw what I could see, heard what I could hear, and allowed my senses to adapt to my surroundings without my brain getting in the way. It was confusing to feel a rush of adrenaline and have such a calmness of mind simultaneously. It reminded me of the old saying: the calm before the storm. Then I was pulled back into the moment when Andy said: "Why'd you guys take off so soon?"

Take off? I didn't—

Oh...he's not talking to us.

CHAPTER

FOURTEEN

THERE WAS a brush-lined area that was invisible from the road. That's where Mike and Evan were momentarily camped around the light of a fire—a small teepee of twigs, no more than a foot in height or diameter. Mike stood behind the fire, facing us. Evan was squatting near the fire with his back initially towards us, but he turned and stood quickly at the sound of the unexpected noise. Mike's injured hand was supported under the wrist by his good hand. It had swollen noticeably to the point I couldn't see the knuckles at the base of his fingers.

"You shoulda known better than to come back here," Mike said.

"Why?" Andy asked. "Are you going to break your other hand on my face?"

Mike put his hands down, trying to conceal the damaged hand behind his hip.

"I'll break a lot more than that if you don't get out of here," Mike said. "*Now.*"

"I don't doubt it," Andy chuckled. "See, the thing is, you got a free shot on me while your little friend over there held me down. Way I see it, that type of unwarranted aggression is how you start a war. And seeing as how you and I both took damage, I'll have to call it a draw—"

Mike said, "Getting the entire side of your face—"

"—but there's no such thing as a draw in war," Andy continued, his voice raised like a football coach giving a pep talk, or a police officer giving commands to a suspect. "War demands a victor. A winner. And, unfortunately for you boys, a loser. This requires a blood sacrifice.

"Last time we met, you had the element of surprise. And hey, good for you." Andy offered a short little golf clap. "But this is Act Two, which is the final act for you, Mikey."

Evan stepped forward. "You—" he started.

"When I want *you* to talk, you'll know it," Andy said. His tone, mixed with the way his bruised, swollen face contorted as he spoke, scared the hell out of me. It was so foreign. I felt—though his body language indicated fully that he was addressing Evan—like he was letting *all* of us know.

My heart felt like it was the size of a football, pounding mercilessly against my ribs. I actually felt my blood—almost as if it had turned to tar—stickily dragging its way through my neck and chest. The pressure built to panic-inducing levels. I started to get lightheaded.

Andy waited for Evan—whose mouth was wide open but silent—to stop moving, which he did. In the silence of the night, I could hear Evan's heavy, strained breaths. He didn't dare blink his eyes, let alone move.

Mike's eyes were cold. Bitter. Angry. Andy turned back to face him. They must've been standing about ten feet away from each other, but Andy stood like he was right in Mike's face—leaning forward, shoulders down and back, with hands over his hips, looking ready for a quick-draw shootout. Mike's eyes had softened. He still looked angry, but nervousness was in the mix now, too.

"Right now, you're probably wondering, *Did I make a big mistake?*" Andy said. "And the answer is yes. Yes, you did. And I can see by looking at you, you know it. Let it sink in. Really let it take over. Because this is what happens, Mike. You choose a violent path, you have a violent journey. Oh, Mike." Andy clicked his tongue. "We've all got to learn our lessons, don't we?"

Before any of us knew Andy had finished his speech, he charged Evan, spearing him in the gut with his shoulder, driving him into the ground with a hard *thud*. Mike moved towards Evan and Andy, but, in the blink of an eye, Dylan jumped forward and blindsided him, sending him to the ground. The instinct to brace his fall did Mike more harm than good as he fell onto his damaged hand and began convulsing like a worm getting run through by a hook. Mike, in a struggle against his own pain, incidentally broke free from Dylan. Dylan lay on his side curled up clutching his stomach.

"Kurt!" Andy yelled. "*Get* him!"

Mike was getting up slowly, carefully cradling his broken hand by his chest. I walked up to him as he was getting to his feet, still trying to roll his body up over center, and hit him in the face as hard as I could.

It stung my hand as bad as the time Dylan dared me to take a full-on high five from him without flinching. With that and the sharp sound that cut through the night, I realized I had slapped him—hard. He fell backwards on his butt but rolled over and got up to his feet quickly. He looked at Dylan, who was getting to his feet with a wheezing cough, and me. Then he looked at Andy and Evan.

Evan was on the ground, arms pinned under Andy's knees. Andy had Evan's shirt collar in one hand, pressing Evan down, and a softball-sized rock in the other hand, held fully extended over his shoulder. He had the kill shot all lined up. Mike made a pitiful moaning sound. Andy snapped his head, exposing Mike's sickening handiwork in the pale gray moonlight. Mike's eyes moistened and he started walking backwards. Dylan took a few quick steps, blocking the part of the path to make sure Mike didn't go out towards the bikes. Mike looked once more at us, then Evan and Andy. Then he turned and ran full tilt down the trail. Dylan walked over and stood next to me. We watched in silent disbelief of what we saw—our friend Andy, the nicest guy we knew, getting ready to murder a kid with a rock. A mean kid, sure, but still just a kid. And still *murder*.

"I don't need you guys for this next part," Andy said. We looked at each other for a moment. My eyes pleaded for Andy to stop, but my voice remained silent. Andy didn't move a muscle. He looked like a baseball card of a pitcher midway through his delivery. As scared as *I* was, I tried but couldn't imagine what was going through Evan's mind.

A wildlife show described how an animal, once its neck is in the lion's jaws, stops struggling and accepts its inevitable fate. That was the only connection I could make.

"Get the bikes ready," Andy said. We didn't move. He looked at us with rage in his one good eye. "*Hurry up!* This won't take long."

Dylan started to say something, but the words caught in his throat. His helpless face looked at me, then Andy.

"It's *fine*," Andy reassured him. "Everything's going to be fine. *Go!*"

Dylan's shoulders slumped as he turned. He and I walked to the bikes, not looking back, not saying a word. I felt the pressure of my shoelaces against my feet, but everything had gone numb. My mind included.

The walk back to the bikes felt like the longest walk of my life. It was like I could see the end of the trail, but every step I took made it drift a little further away. There it is, there it goes.

I stopped at the end of the trail and picked up my bike. Dylan did the same. We stood for some time, bikes in hand, not saying anything to each other. It felt strangely similar to sitting outside the principal's office, knowing that whatever was about to happen was not good. I couldn't tell what Dylan was thinking because I couldn't bring myself to even look at him. I also couldn't bring myself to think about what might be happening down the trail. The whole thing was like a bad dream you wake up from but can't shake right away.

"Alright," Andy said behind us. "That's taken care of."

CHAPTER

FIFTEEN

"*What the hell was that?*" I shouted at Andy. "What happened back there?"

Andy picked up his bike and smiled at me. He looked like two different people—the Andy I had known most of my life, and the one I met at sundown. The one who was one of my best friends in the world and, at the same time, the one with a face that made my guts shrivel.

"Don't worry," Andy said, unreasonably casual about all of it. "It's not as bad as you think."

"Uh, *yeah*. It *is*," Dylan said. "You can't just kill people, dude."

"Oh, no. I didn't..." Andy laughed. "He's fine. I just needed to scare him. That's all."

"It would've been nice to know *before* I thought you were going to bash his face in with a rock!" I said.

"I know—"

"Seriously, dude," Dylan said. "I was all for giving somebody a black eye or something, but that was going too far. I was about to stop you, and not in a nice way."

Andy was shaking his head at the ground, letting out a few breathy chuckles. "No—you weren't." It didn't sound threatening or annoyed, just matter of fact.

Dylan looked away from Andy and our eyes met. Dylan flashed me a dirty look and stomped away from us with his bike. He mounted his ride, said a quick, "See ya later," to me, looked at Andy and muttered a few obscenities under his breath, and pedaled off.

I started to worry that my parents were going to be waiting up and worried. I usually made it home, at least to check in, before the last bit of sunlight disappeared. If nothing else, to get something to eat really quick. I hadn't talked to them since breakfast, and now the stars were on full display. Then I thought, *If I'm gonna be in trouble, I don't want to see how Andy's parents react after they see his face. They'll probably take him to the hospital and file a police report and the police will want to talk to my parents and I'll get in even more trouble—*

"Are you still worried about Evan?" Andy asked.

"Kind of..." I wanted to trust Andy the first time he said Evan was alright, but something didn't feel right. While I was talking to Andy, it felt like I was talking to someone else, a stranger. Maybe it was the knock on the head, or maybe it was his face. When I saw him from the side, looking only at his swollen, purple face, he was unrecognizable.

"Relax, Kurt. Evan's fine. And I can tell my face is bad by the way you keep looking at it, but trust me, I'm fine. Just breathe, man. You're going to hyperventilate."

"No, I'm not." (Yes, I was.) "I'm fine, it's good, we're good—"

"Look," he said. "I'm sorry you guys got freaked out. I saw it on your faces, and I also saw how Evan reacted to how freaked out you were. I went with it, I had to."

"Why?" I asked.

"It's hard to explain, Kurt," he said.

"Try."

"I needed to make a strong impression on him."

"So he won't mess with us again?" I didn't expect him to say anything that made the way he acted excusable. But what he said next totally threw me.

"No—kind of the opposite, actually," Andy said.

"*What?*"

"You'll know what I mean. Ask me more after it happens."

46

"After *what* happens?"

"Trust me," he said. "You wouldn't believe me even if I told you what was about to happen. Just wait until it happens. Then you'll be ready to hear what I have to tell you."

"OK..." I said. "I still have no idea what I'm looking for, or what you're talking about."

He looked far into the distance, squinting slightly with his good eye. I couldn't tell if he was thinking of the right words, or if he didn't want to say (or if he was BS-ing me and was trying to keep a straight face).

All he said was: "You'll know it when you see it."

CHAPTER

SIXTEEN

I DON'T REMEMBER the ride home. I guess my body sort of went home on autopilot. One minute I was talking to Andy, the next I was at the end of my driveway—stopped, bike under me, and both feet planted down. I stood there looking at my house, feeling weird. A little lightheaded, maybe. *Shake it off and get in bed.* I put my bike away in the open garage, took my shoes off, and hit the button to shut the door.

From the garage, I walked in through the kitchen and beelined straight to my bedroom.

Had my mom looked at me, I'm sure she would've immediately started in with, "What's wrong? Something looks wrong." But, to my relief, my parents were watching TV on the couch in the living room. When I came in, they didn't turn their heads. Without diverting her eyes from the TV, my mom called out something to the effect of, "How was your day, hun?"

"Hi, Mom. Hi, Dad, it was fine," I said. I closed the door at a steady, very intentional pace, trying to sound calm, and I walked to a very deliberate beat. Not a sprint, but not tiptoeing. I didn't want to appear as though I was sneaking past my parents, though I most certainly was.

Walking up the stairs with no intention of stopping or looking into the living room, I said, "I was riding around with the guys. I'm really tired. Just gonna head up to bed."

"K. Goodnight, sweetie," Mom said.

Sweetie? Ugh. I'm not five, Mom...

"G'night, buddy," Dad grunted.

As I closed my bedroom door, I yelled goodnight to my parents through the narrowing gap. Methodically, I shut the door. Not hard enough for Dad to get pissed and lecture me about how doors were meant to be closed, or too softly to pique Mom's curiosity.

I fell face first into bed and didn't move. Before I drifted off, I slid my socks and pants off and crawled halfway under the sheets. Then my body went limp. But not for long. As tired as I was, lying there I could only toss and turn whenever I closed my eyes. Horrifying images from that little scene by the lake were charred into the backs of my eyelids. I think I might have actually fallen asleep with my eyes open. One second I was looking at the shadows on the ceiling...

CHAPTER
SEVENTEEN

...THE NEXT I was lying on my stomach with a wet drool patch edged up to the corner of my mouth on my pillow. It was late morning when I woke up—or maybe early in the afternoon. Probably afternoon: my stomach was doing somersaults, making sounds like a creaky old wood floor. By the time I got out of bed, my parents were probably well past that first part of the day where you stand around looking busy while you drink coffee and talk to people (at least that's how my uncle described "the workday for the well-dressed").

My eyes were still blurry from sleep when I waddled down the stairs. The first thing I noticed through my blurry, squinting eyes was how intensely the sunlight exploded into the house. My room was almost completely dark except for a ring of light that glowed around the edge of my curtain. However, in the rest of the house, the sunlight melted in like a river of magma. There didn't seem to be even a sliver of a shadow in sight.

I looked into the living room. There was an old clock—I guess you might call it a *family heirloom* or something—on the mantle. It was ticking loudly. A hard, mechanical, almost echoey sound. But the second hand didn't advance with each heavy click of the gears. It just jiggled in place. My shoulders slumped and my head fell back.

Great, Mom's going to think I broke it throwing a ball in the house or something.

I dragged my feet to the kitchen to call my mom. The way I figured, calling her right away instead of letting her see it when she got home might improve my chances of being acquitted. However, on the way to the phone, I noticed that Mom had made pancakes for breakfast. She put a few on a paper plate by the stove and covered it with the cheap clinging wrap that isn't quite a hundred percent clingy.

Doesn't matter. A quick zap in the microwave will make it taste fresh again. Just a few seconds, then I'm going to destroy that stack of pancakes before it knows what happens.

The broken clock was a time-sensitive thing, but a hollowed-out stomach on a growing boy takes precedence over pretty much everything, so I figured I'd kill a few pancakes before I delivered the bad news. Might as well go out on a full stomach.

I removed the wrap and took the pancakes to the microwave. I stood in a square puddle of concentrated light on the floor. It was warmer than the rest of the floor, like sticking your feet in warm water.

Bing!

I grabbed the plate and went to my usual snacking spot—resting shoulder-first in the entryway between the living room and kitchen. The TV wasn't even turned on, but I watched the dead, gray screen out of habit while I grabbed a pancake, folded it in half like a gigantic slice of New York style pizza, and crammed it into my mouth. While staring at the lifeless TV screen, I chewed my pancakes and zoned out, allowing my eyes to adjust to the early summer sun.

With dread, I looked at the clock again. But I was stunned to see the clock was working fine.

CHAPTER
EIGHTEEN

I CHECKED the time on the clock in the kitchen and it was within a minute of the broken one. *Well, previously broken...ish.* I happily discarded the clock business, figuring my eyes were playing tricks. They hadn't finished warming up all the way, after all.

As I stood around—eating pancakes in my boxers—I couldn't help but think about the previous night.

About what was said.

What happened.

Replaying it in my mind, now in the safety of my house and the light of day, did not make me feel any better than it did the night before in the sweat-soaked, cold, bitter darkness. The fear and confusion, so tightly aligned with those memories, was difficult to shake. A chill ran down the back of my neck.

What's going to happen the next time I run into Mike, or Evan, or Mike and Evan? What am I going to say next time I see Dylan or Andy, or even Birdie? How do you move past something like that?

I thought it over, brushing away bits of sleep crust from my eye with one hand while continuing to shove pancakes into my mouth with the other. Taking a deep yawn, the kind that brings you to your toes, I decided it might be best for me and everyone involved if I stayed home all day. Just shut it out. All of it. Everything. *There are plenty of movies to watch and video games to keep—*

BOOM!

A crash of thunder cut through my thoughts. My knees bent and my hands dropped halfway—almost a gunfighter's stance. The plate of pancakes fell to the floor.

How is there a thunderstorm in the middle of a sunny day?

CHAPTER

NINETEEN

I LOOKED OUT THE WINDOW, oblivious to the pancake sticking out of my mouth, and saw an almost completely clear and bright blue sky. *That's weird.*

Another crash of thunder. Louder this time.

I ran to a window on the other side of the house. Nothing. Hardly a cloud in sight.

Andy said *something* was going to happen, but he didn't elaborate— I would know it when I saw it for myself. Was this what he was talking about?

No...

Another crash of thunder.

No?

Another crash of thunder. This time the house shook a little, rattling the dishes in the cabinets and jangling the keys hanging by the garage door.

I ran to the living room. From there I could see out the big window overlooking the front lawn and the street. In the time it took me to get to the window, a few people had already begun lining up on their porches and in their driveways, looking up at the sky for the source of the mysterious noise.

Another crash of thunder shook the house, violently this time. I had to let my knees go soft to keep my balance, like when you land funny on a trampoline. Something fell to the floor in another room of the house. I ran past the front door and up the stairs, using the banister to complete a full-speed, ninety-degree turn onto the stairs and up to my room. I quickly threw on some clothes lying on the floor. They weren't the clothes I wore to school yesterday, but they were on the floor by my bed. *Meh, they smell clean enough.*

Once dressed, I started back for the front door again. A few steps out of my room there was another crash of thunder. The ground shook even harder than before. The lights in the hallway went out and I heard things falling to the floor in different rooms throughout the house. As the shaking subsided, the earth bellowed a demonic growl.

Once the shaking stopped, I moved as quickly as I could, unlocking and exiting the front door. Absentmindedly, I left the door open behind me and stepped out onto the lawn. Looking towards the sky, I spun to get a three-hundred-sixty-degree view. Off to the west, thick black streams of smoke were rising angrily into the blue midday sky. The sound of a hard wind rose from behind me, but I hardly felt it blowing. Then the sound rose almost to a scream.

"What's going on?" a voice yelled in panic. It came from up the street. "Someone tell me what's happening!"

The wind got steadily louder until I had to cover my ears. It sounded like a blender amplified through stadium speakers.

This isn't the wind...

The sound became intolerable. It was accompanied by a rumble that made the skin on my arms and neck shrink intolerably tight.

Roughly half a dozen military jets were coming our direction in a widespread formation. As they passed overhead, they split like a school of fish in different directions, turned completely around and regrouped heading west again towards downtown, in the direction of the capitol and Michigan State University.

Trying to decide what to do next, I looked around, watching everyone else. Their dumb-struck and slack-jawed faces were turned to the sky, watching the planes. Looking at the others, I realized my mouth was hanging open, too. ("Better shut that trap before a bird flies in there," my uncle would say.) We all watched in silence as the planes, now regrouped, started dropping things from their undersides. These things fell with a strange, serene quality, like a leaf falling from a tree. Then they fell below the obstructed horizon. And then another crash of thunder shook the ground so viciously my feet gave way and I fell to my hands and knees.

"We're under attack!" someone screamed. And I mean *screamed*—I couldn't even tell if it was a man or a woman. And just like that, panic overtook order.

CHAPTER

TWENTY

PEOPLE WERE SCREAMING AND RUNNING. Some into their houses, others out, a few running back and forth, more or less stuck in place like the monkey in the middle. I guess most folks who were screaming were calling out to their loved ones, but quite a few were screaming for some kind of explanation of the circumstances. And some were just screaming —nothing intelligible, just shrill, panicky, loud noises. They all blended together in a chorus of terror.

As all this unfolded, I got up off my hands and knees, stood, and slowly turned myself again, this time my eyes looking straight out in front of me, to see it all. My mind went blank; logic and reason were foreign ideas. I stood there like a background extra in a movie, thoughtless and emotionless. Nothing seemed real.

There was another loud crash, followed by another and another. People started crying. Adults grabbed their kids—picking up the littles and dragging the not-so-littles by the arm—and went inside or crammed into their cars, as though the airstrike was a tornado they could drive away from. In a moment like that, I guess...what do you do? No one prepares you for an all-out attack. There's calling 9-1-1, just say no, stop drop and roll, but surprisingly little for end-of-the-world scenarios such as this.

CHAPTER
TWENTY-ONE

IT WAS FRIGHTENINGLY obvious that *no one* knew what to do. With the few available options, there seemed to be no majority collective action one way or the other. Across the street, the MacKenzies were loaded up in their green station wagon, pulling frantically out of their driveway, running over their mailbox in the process. Ms. Mora down the street was screaming while she clung onto her fluffy white cat as it clawed wildly at her. She cried a repetitive series of, "ah," and "oh," but looked determined to get the cat into her gray Volvo with her. Next door to her, the Kesten kids were scooped up by their college-aged babysitter who brought them inside. At first, she ran them towards her car parked along the curb, but a few steps from the passenger door, the MacKenzies' station wagon smashed the front corner of the car and she thought better of it.

In the midst of the unfolding chaos, old Mr. Miller caught my attention. He lived on the same side of the street as me, one house from the corner. I noticed him—in his usual jeans with suspenders and VFW hat —because he was the only person besides me who wasn't running or screaming. I only ever saw him outside when he came out to yell at speeders and "no-giving-a-shit kids." Mr. Miller had set up a lawn chair at the mouth of his garage. I watched him pull a lighter from his jeans, then a cigarette from the pack in the chest pocket of his gray t-shirt. He lit the cigarette and took a long drag as he replaced the lighter and lowered himself onto the lawn chair. Then he picked up a rifle that was lying on the ground beside the chair and laid it across his lap. One hand on the cigarette, the other resting familiarly on the stock of the rifle. I was stunned to stillness and silence; Mr. Miller seemed unshaken, like he was at home, in his element—the only person in view not taken completely aback by everything. The kids in the neighborhood always thought he was crazy, but now I knew he was.

This doesn't happen here. This is the United States. This doesn't. Happen. Here. Nobody messes with us. Not like this. Right? Surely the good guys will swoop in any second.

I watched the sky. Listened for new sounds. Waited for something to change. But time went on and if anything changed, it was for the worse.

I've got to get out of here. What do I do?

It was obvious that driving in this torrential crapstorm would be way too dangerous. Not that I had a car anyway. Panic-crazed people everywhere were driving recklessly in search of safety. The MacKenzie's mailbox and the babysitter's car were the tip of the iceberg. At almost even intervals I could hear the sounds of cars banging and crashing, metal against metal, windows breaking, eruptions of people shouting at one another.

Reality set in. I no longer allowed myself to merely exist in this land-scape. I knew I had to do *something*.

CHAPTER
TWENTY-TWO

MY CHEST BEGAN to ache and tighten, snapping me out of my daze. *I'm too young to be having a heart attack.* I put my hand on my chest. My heart was beating hard—alarmingly and painfully hard—but not all that fast. It felt like coming up after being held underwater a few seconds too long. I had to remind myself to breathe.

In...

Out...

In...

And out...

The air passing through my nose had a steely after-taste and stung enough to make my eyes water. I took another breath and held it in until it began to feel like a solid object in my chest.

Finally, my breathing returned to normal. As a result, thoughts that made sense started flowing between my ears again.

It's all going to be alright. This has got to be almost over. Everything will be set right. My parents will be here. Everything's going to be fine.

The whine of emergency sirens screamed through the air. One at a time, fire trucks, ambulances, and police began rapidly approaching. That is, if they hadn't already been there and I was just in shock and hadn't noticed.

Planes flying in the distance—this time moving parallel to my street —unleashed another flurry of thunder, shaking the ground once more, followed by another set of cars crashing into one another. Then two sets of gunshots: a series of *tchu-tchu-tchu*s followed by and mixed with a set of *pft-pft-pft*s. Then there weren't any more shots—not for a while. Only distant sirens and horrified screams.

I walked backward towards the house, turning around where the grass met the pavement to trot more quickly into the kitchen.

The phone! I'll call my parents.

Then planes flew almost immediately overhead. There was more thunder—the loudest yet. It shook the ground so fiercely that when I grabbed for the phone, I nearly ripped the whole thing off the wall. I held it in my hand with my fingers frozen over the dial pad.

No, I'll call 9-1-1 first, I thought, but immediately decided against it. *No, every emergency vehicle in the siren'd fleet is already responding to, well...everything.*

I took a deep breath and let thoughts come to me: *Mom's closer—call her first, then Dad.*

I put the phone up to my ear and began dialing. But there was no switch in the earpiece from dial tone to soft purrs as my finger punched the buttons. I pressed the hang-up button several times, but my ear wasn't met by the old familiar dial tone.

Only silence.

CHAPTER
TWENTY-THREE

When I reached to put the phone back in its cradle, I missed. I didn't see, or even feel that I had missed it—only heard the gravelly swish of the receiver dangling against the wall. I went to the living room to get the clock, thinking: *The exact time doesn't matter, but if I need to take shelter in the basement or something, I can bring the clock with me. I'll wait twenty...no, thirty minutes and...I dunno...see what happens.*

As I rounded the corner into the living room, I saw the clock wasn't on its normal spot over the fireplace. It had fallen during one of the rounds of bombings and now lay face down in front of the fireplace. I got on my knees and turned it over like I was about to give it CPR. Before it fell, the glass was pretty cool—crystal clear, lined with silver and cut with angular edges, almost diamond-like. Surveying the damage after the fall, the glass was mostly cracked to the point it looked like the foggy center of an ice cube. Or—in a few remote, little spots—it was completely missing. The TV remote was face down on the couch. I grabbed it to bust out the glass .

Another crash of thunder, followed in quick succession by *boom-boom-BOOM!* The earth shook; the house groaned in protest. Dust and chunks of drywall fell all around and on me from the ceiling. The big window in the living room cracked from the vibration. I quickly cleared the clock's face of the obstructive glass remains and saw, thank God, that it was still working.

Okay, good. Maybe I'll give Mom and Dad five, no ten minutes to get here. Then I'll—

"Kurt!" Andy yelled from the entryway.

TWENTY-FOUR

HE RAN OVER TO ME, but I paid no attention. I was looking at the clock. Checking the time, so I could start my five, no...*ten*, ten-minute timer.

"We gotta go, Kurt," he said.

"Hold on." I didn't look at him; I had to watch the clock. Ten minutes—no more, no less.

Andy huffed a little. Then there was a brief but tense silence, during which something must have dawned on Andy. With a tone of sudden awareness, he said, "*Actually*..."

While I kept my eyes on the clock, he walked off. I heard his carpet-muted footsteps fading down the hallway, disappearing into a different room. The clock ticked and tocked. And the seconds, thank God, marched on. *Almost one minute...*

I watched as two more minutes went by. Then I heard footsteps coming up the hallway. Andy said, "Hey, c'mon man. That clock's too big, anyway. I found you a wristwatch in your parents' room."

For a split second it bothered me that Andy went into my parents' room and pillaged their stuff, but all things considered, it was too trivial a thing to give anything more than a fraction of a second's thought to.

"Alright," he said. "I only have a few more things..." he trailed off. As he ran upstairs, he yelled, "*Hey! Get yourself ready to go.*" Then he stopped near the top of the stairs. "Right now, Kurt. Like—right *now*, right now."

But I kept looking at the clock. He gave up and went looking for whatever.

Time kept moving and Andy had stopped stomping around. He got what he needed, and he came downstairs with a loaded up backpack.

My backpack.

Andy stood in front of me and took a deep, calming breath. As he was about to speak, another series of booms and mini-earthquakes interrupted him.

"Dude, I've got to wait for my parents. Just a few more minutes," I said.

"You know what? *Fine*," he said. "But that clock is gonna stop moving in—"

He paused a little to check his watch. Then a little more to, I don't know, make it more dramatic. Then he counted down: "10—9—8—7—"

"What're you doing, man?" I said.

"4—3—2," then silently pointed at the clock at almost the exact moment the second hand got stuck. *Tick-tock-tick-tock-tick-tick-tick-tick...*

I didn't know what to say. I looked at Andy. He was showing me his watch *and* the watch he took from my dad. They were both doing it, too.

Completely unable to think, I slowly looked up at Andy.

"Every time this happens," he tapped his watch, "it's going to get worse out there."

"How do you—"

"I'll explain later. We have to go. *Now*."

CHAPTER

TWENTY-FIVE

ANDY GRABBED me by the arm and dragged me out of the house like a parent dragging their child to timeout. With the frenzy of things happening outside, I didn't want to leave the house, but fear ("the Great Motivator," as my uncle calls it) didn't allow me much of an ability to reason, so, once he had me moving, I was easily herded off.

We stopped at the entryway rug. The corner of it kicked up and stuck under the door when Andy came in. I was facing him, or my body was, but my eyes were drawn to the cracked window, where the nightmare was taking place.

It had been a few minutes since I'd heard bombings, or even planes. But now they were gone. Like they had never been there in the first place. When the planes stopped flying over, the blasting jet engines and roars of explosions were replaced with car alarms, crying, shouting, screeching tires, car accidents—screaming.

Gunshots.

The weird thing is—I think I was less afraid of the planes.

CHAPTER
TWENTY-SIX

THE BOMBING SEEMS to have stopped.

I'm not sure I really believed it, but at that moment, I needed to. It was hard enough trying to accept what had already happened, so expecting more of it would have been unbearable. I couldn't take any more of it.

It has to be over, it just has to. Maybe it's over. Sure, the Army or whoever is probably shooting down those planes right now—if they haven't already.

Everyone within sight and earshot had turned into frightened animals. Screaming. So many different voices screaming. More cars crashing, things breaking.

More gunshots.

Geez, at this rate they won't need to bomb us anymore—we might finish ourselves off.

"Get your bike and meet me outside under your big tree. Got it?" Andy said.

I nodded absently.

"Look at me," he said. While others panicked, he seemed very clear-headed. Focusing on him and his relaxed demeanor helped calm me down. "We're going to be fine. The guys are going to be fine. But I need you to listen to me very carefully, alright?" He looked patiently but also expectantly into my eyes and waited a moment. Then he said, "Say something, Kurt, so I know you heard and understood."

"Get my bike. Meet you over there."

"Right—just over there, under the tree. Hurry up, alright?" Without giving me time to reply or acknowledge him, he was gone. I don't remember him leaving, just being gone.

CHAPTER
TWENTY-SEVEN

As I was about to step outside, two cars, less than two-hundred feet away from me, narrowly missed hitting each other. Tires screeched like fighting cats as the cars took evasive action. A gray hatchback swerved and smashed its headlight to pieces as it uprooted a mailbox post. The other car, a gold Buick, swerved uncontrollably and went over the curb, past the sidewalk, and fishtailed to a lawn-destroying stop in the middle of Mr. Miller's front yard. The gray hatchback continued on like nothing happened. Mr. Miller jumped out of his seat and ran—impressively fast for an old guy—beyond the stupidly idling car in the middle of his green, green grass. In one swift movement he knelt on one knee and lifted his rifle. He took aim quickly, lined up, and fired one careful shot at the gray hatchback.

Immediately following the shot was the sound of shattering glass, then the sound of a bellowing car horn. Impulsively, I ran to the middle of my lawn to get a better view. As Mr. Miller slowly stood, a satisfied grin hooked its way across his stubbly face. The driver lay slumped over the wheel, pressing against the horn. The horn continued to protest until the gray hatchback plopped over the curb. The driver's body heaved up, bounced off the steering wheel, and the horn gave one final squeak before the driver's body slumped over the shifter.

I looked around.
Andy was gone.

CHAPTER
TWENTY-EIGHT

AGAINST MY BETTER JUDGEMENT, I trusted (or wished) that Andy was waiting for me, so I ran back into my house, heading straight into the garage. The noise seemed muted in there. I could hear it, but it didn't seem real, like standing in the hallway of a movie theater.

Why am I in here?

I couldn't remember. I walked over to the fridge in the corner and opened it. It took me a few seconds—looking around at the cans of RC Cola, my dad's beer, and the stuff that my mom was going to use to make dinners this week—before I remembered what I was there for. My bike was up against the wall next to the garage door. I walked over to my bike, grabbed it by the handles, and looked at it for a second. Then I heard the mechanical buzz and whistle of jets flying in the distance.

I did not want to be alone with a front-row seat for another performance of this hellish circus—I knew I needed to hurry. *But where are we gonna go?*

CHAPTER
TWENTY-NINE

THE GARAGE DOOR was useless with the power out. I had to roll my bike out the side door, which was hard to get open. We never used it, and over time, it had become practically impossible to open. Seriously, it was stuck shut so bad we didn't even keep it locked. I had to turn the knob and ram the entire side of my body into it with as much force as I could without hurting myself. It did not budge with the first hit. The second time, I hit it harder and saw the door started to open. The third time, I hit it as hard as I could. The top of the door was free, but the bottom was stubbornly wedged into the doorframe. I turned my back to it and kicked it twice with the sole of my shoe until it finally budged.

CHAPTER
THIRTY

I RAN my bike over to the side of the yard by the tree where Andy said to meet him. I crouched down, kneeling beside my bike. A second later, Andy ran up with his bike and took the same position. There under the shade of the oak tree—the same one we used to climb and eat popsicles in—Andy was looking patiently towards the sky.

"I hear them, but I don't know where they are," I said.

"They're close, listen. Did you see how they were flying?" he asked.

"Whaddya mean?"

"In relation to each other. They're actually using an old Air Force formation: the combat box," he said.

"Huh?"

"There are four groups of planes. Each group consists of three planes in a triangle. Those four groups combined make a diamond shape when you look from below or above, but each group is flying at a different height. This way they can stick together to bomb bigger targets, or the groups can separate to spread out and hit smaller targets."

"Yeah, I saw them separate, but they came right back together."

"But I didn't see any other planes flying around," he said. "Did you?"

"I don't know. I don't think so. All I saw were the ones that were bombing."

"That's right."

"So?"

"So that means that they aren't worried about other jets engaging them."

"Okay..." I said impatiently.

"That means that no one is fighting back, Kurt."

"Maybe someone is on their way."

"No, don't count on it. This isn't a fight; it's an invasion."

"No, this stuff doesn't happen. We don't get attacked unchallenged. Someone hits us, we hit back."

"Unless it's not someone *else* hitting us."

I shook my head. *What is he talking about?*

"They flew the combat box over the capitol and the university, then they split to hit the smaller cities. But they can only carry so many bombs, and they bombed the piss out of this area once already. Now they're coming back with another payload, but where did they get it?"

"I don't know. A ship or a base?"

"Right. And for them to get back this fast means that they landed, got more ammo, took off, and are back to blow up more stuff. Seems like they did that pretty fast, doesn't it?"

"Yeah..." I said. "But how are they—"

"Those aren't foreign planes, Kurt. Those are ours."

"What? No—that's not possible."

"It is, and that's exactly what's happening." I stared incredulously at Andy. He continued: "And it's happening *everywhere*."

"No..."

CHAPTER

THIRTY-ONE

"They're going to come back around soon."

"Are we gonna die?"

"Only if we don't get moving."

"How are we going to get far enough away on our bikes? People are going crazy. I heard gunshots on the main road, and Mr. Miller is crazier than we thought. So there's going to be people like that all over the place. And even if we take a car, I can't drive, and the roads are probably all backed up, and—"

"Whoa, whoa. Calm down, Kurt. I need you to trust me on this— we're going to the hole. Everyone is going to be there, and it'll be safe. There's nothing around it so it won't get hit directly. If we stay in the hole, we should be safe from the blasts. They're not dropping nukes, so we just need to be far enough away from anything that could be a potential target, and a pond in the woods isn't likely to be a target. That said, it's not going to be comfortable for us when we're there, but we'll be able to walk away from this when they stop."

After taking a second to *try* to think over what he said, I told Andy I was ready to go. I heard the faint sound of explosions in the distance. The sour scent of the explosives carried in the wind. Again, I felt my blood surging through my neck and hands, but was surprised that, with the pandemonium, my heart wasn't beating a mile a minute. The sound of the frenzy around us intensified, and a new series of shouts and sounds of reckless drivers erupted.

"Alright then," he said. "Let's get going."

"Wait a second. Is *this* what you were talking about yesterday?" I asked.

"*Yester*day? Oh...yeah. Yeah, this is what I was talking about."

"You *knew* this was going to happen?"

"Yes, Kurt. I knew."

"How?"

"I'll explain later, when we aren't on the move."

"Hang on, hang on—why didn't you say something besides," in a mocking voice, "'*You'll know it when you see it*'?"

"You wouldn't't've believed me."

He was right. I knew it, but I still had to unclench my jaw and take a deep breath before I could say another word. What is it about other people being right that has the ability to piss you off so badly?

"Alright," I said. "I'm listening, and I'll believe just about anything at this point. Go ahead. *Please* tell me what's really going on."

This time Andy closed his eyes and took a breath, clearly trying to push aside his own frustration. "They're going to kill anyone in their flight pattern, which will be all the people who didn't have advanced knowledge of their attack—whoever isn't one of *them* basically—and push any survivors out of the metropolitan areas and take control of the cities."

"Who? Who's doing this?"

"That part's gonna require a longer explanation than we..." the sound of jets cut Andy off mid-sentence. His eyebrows spiked up and his eyes went wide. "*COVER YOUR EARS!*"

CHAPTER
THIRTY-TWO

HE COVERED HIS EARS, the look on his face was urgent, intense. I covered mine, but it was a little too late. There was a series of blasts. After the first few I couldn't tell how many there were exactly, but they shook the ground and I screamed as loud as I could until I ran out of breath, and still the ground shook. When everything stopped again, Andy shook me, and I opened my eyes. My ears were ringing, but I could still hear Andy's voice saying that we had to go immediately.

CHAPTER
THIRTY-THREE

WE RODE THROUGH THE NEIGHBORHOODS, keeping as far away from the main roads as possible. We cut through backyards that edged the well-maintained facade of suburban landscaping, occasionally veering from a straight path in favor of tree coverage unless there wasn't any. We came to a stop. To get out of the neighborhood you had to cross a street. There was maybe fifty or sixty feet of absolute open space from one sidewalk to the next, with trees on both sides of the road. But that open space was littered with wrecked and abandoned vehicles of all makes and sizes in the lanes, on the shoulders, and spilled out over parts of the sidewalk. The real problem was the cars that wrecked and went off the street entirely. They cut off any path around the blockages in the road. No emergency vehicles could get through even if they wanted to.

"What do we do now?" I said, looking at the frozen river of steel.

"Pick it up," he said.

"What?"

But he had already picked his bike up and put it over his head like one of the sand people in Star Wars. "Let's go," he said.

"Right," I said as I grunted and threw my bike up like I was hoisting a trophy—a heavy, wiggling trophy, with an odd center of gravity.

"*Whoa!*"

The bike went up and over my head, but I couldn't stop its momentum. I let the bike fall behind me while I dropped onto my butt. Andy laughed while I pushed myself off the ground. I dusted my butt off and picked up my bike, hands more squarely planted on the frame and put it up more like a weightlifter.

"Squeeze through where you can; climb over where you can't."

"Okay."

We wiggled a little more than halfway through the wreckage before we had to climb over anything. It seemed that there had been an accident ahead to my right that caused one lane of traffic to have a long chain of read-end collisions. All the cars smashed together front to back like that formed what looked like a long, hard, dead worm like you see on hot summer days after an early morning rain. We climbed over the mechanical corpse. Standing on the other side of it, both of my feet on the yellow line, I heard a helicopter.

Andy immediately hurled his bike, then mine, as far away from the road as he could.

"Get under a car. *Now!*"

I did. As fast as I could. All the cars had been abandoned. I could hear people in the distance, but no one was lurking around the by road. No sooner had I stopped moving, completely enveloped in shadow, when wind from the helicopter blew dust in my face. It only lasted a few seconds before the tatter of the rotor blades began drifting away.

When it was little more than an echo in the distance, we crawled out and ran to our bikes. The acrid scent of burnt explosives was stronger and I could see dark plumes of smoke in the direction of the college and downtown Lansing, where the capitol and government buildings stood. Or used to stand.

As we rode, I thought about what was happening and how little I knew: the whos, the whats, the whys, the hows. I trusted Andy and followed him. But what he said back at the house was playing on a nonstop loop in my head:

They're going to kill anyone that didn't have advanced knowledge of their attack—whoever isn't one of them.

But *Andy* had advanced knowledge. Should I be worried about him?

CHAPTER
THIRTY-FOUR

I TURNED that one over in my mind for a minute, but wasn't able to land decisively on yes or no. *As long as I'm with him, and he doesn't get killed, I should be alright.*

All I could do was trust and follow. That and be on guard until things—something, *anything*—started making sense and people stopped killing each other in between other people attacking them. I looked suspiciously at Andy, who was focused straight ahead, then at the scenes of destruction around me. Where there used to be rows of houses, there were stumps—similar to the tree stumps in the field that had been cleared near the hole—of what used to be homes next to houses that remained intact but with burn marks, busted windows, and torn-up roofing and siding.

As we rode through the chaos, I scanned around me for whatever attack might be coming next—or *whomever* it might be coming from.

CHAPTER

THIRTY-FIVE

"Do we still need to ride through the grass, man?" I pleaded. "My tires are kinda flat," I gasped, "so it's kinda hard," I gasped again, "to pedal."

Andy's chest fell into his handlebars while he screamed with laughter and said, "*I just filled em up at your house yesterday!*" He stopped laughing, but only after enough time had passed to allow my embarrassment to turn to anger. Seemingly unaware of my reaction, he throttled back a bit, spinning his pedals backwards—creating that high pitched spinny-grinding noise—until I caught up. As he began pedaling again, he said, "We can slow down a little, but we need to stay away from roads whenever possible, and travel under the trees at *all times.*" I didn't agree so much as I accepted it as the terms of my surrender. Hey, anything goes so long as I don't have to try to keep up with Andy at full speed on a bike.

Rather than making a straight line through the neighborhood, Andy led us around every cul-de-sac, far away from the road, through a brush-filled "shortcut" to the park. I got a few scratches, and about a dozen mosquito bites. It wasn't very long through the brush, luckily, before I could start to see the top of the water tower, which meant we were near the park.

Instead of riding *through* the park—the hole was essentially straight across to the other side of the park from where we were—we stayed a few yards from the mowed grass line, opting for tree cover instead of a smoother, easier ride in the open area. As we were about to pass behind the bathroom building by the edge of the playground, Andy took a hard left, through a waist-high thicket of more brush and tall grass, deeper into the trees. I had never gone into the woods this way and wasn't completely sure where we were going.

We rode on for a few minutes until the brush and forest abruptly gave way to a long, wide, unnatural clearing. We came to a stop just shy of it.

"Where are we?" I asked. Andy was looking at something intently and only put up a finger in a not-right-now gesture. The smell from the explosions hit me again. That vinegary, hot metal odor. Teetering flames crawled up out of a crater upwind, blurring the sky with dust and smoke. That crater was barely touching one wall of a square perimeter of chain-link fence. Adorning the top of—but at a forty-five-degree angle to—the fence were three strands of braided barbed wire. Inside the fencing were lots of metal pipes and coils at the base of several fifteen-foot-tall stanchions. From those stanchions, electric cables divided to meet one of two large towers standing side by side. Those cables then connected to a long series of sets of similar twin towers. I had seen big, long groups of electric cables near the highway before, on long drives to see family, but not around here. I suppose there's a lot we don't know about familiar things.

We stood about halfway between two sets of towers. The third and fourth sets from the tattered electric grid, to be exact. Most of the towers looked normal, except the set closest to the grid's fenced area. They were completely knocked over, lying like two people who bumped into each other on ice skates and collapsed into a shared pile of knees and elbows. The next set leaned under the tension from their fallen comrades. The third set wasn't completely upright, but you wouldn't notice if nothing else was out of place. We rode along the edge of the clearing towards the downed lines.

I said, "Hey, I don't think it's a good idea to go—"

"It's *fine*. The power's completely knocked out," he said, not bothering to slow down. In my hesitation, I had briefly stopped pedaling, so I struggled to get back to full speed. We crossed the clearing between the last two sets of standing towers. I listened for it, but there was no electric hum. The silence was somehow horrifying.

"When the planes came through, they didn't drop bombs randomly," Andy said.

"Hmm," I said. "I guess not."

Besides the route being painfully roundabout, it was also difficult terrain and there was no momentum to be gained. It ripped my muscles to shreds. Eventually, it caught up to a trail that I didn't know existed. It wasn't the smoothest trail, but it was a million times better than what we had been riding on. This trail took us towards the hole.

Andy—like it was an impressive accomplishment—jumped off his bike and said, "And we only had to cross one street."

"Uh-huh," I said flatly, sweating and grimacing.

I looked around and was quite surprised to find we were not the first ones there.

CHAPTER
THIRTY-SIX

NOTHING WAS MAKING ANY SENSE. It felt like watching a foreign movie without subtitles. My head started to spin a little, like when you read for too long in dim light. Suddenly it was as if the reality that bound everything around me kind of disappeared, like part of my brain had fallen asleep, and everything around me was nothing more than a lucid dream. I absurdly noticed that, besides the bombings, it was a beautiful day outside. The hole was slightly elevated and gave a halfway decent view of its immediate surroundings. You didn't really have to look up, so much as out, to see the sky. Beyond the lazily drifting smoke, there were only a few small feather strip clouds in an otherwise endless blue eternity. Back at the open space around the electrical towers, the smell was strong and awful, but the trees at the hole thankfully served as a good buffer from the wind that carried those smells. The nearby highway usually provided a drone of traffic noise, but what sounded like some seriously awful wrecks must have caused traffic jams that made the lanes, shoulder, ditch, even the median, impassable. Forget the zoom and swish noises at that point, I could barely hear any running engines. Only some horns and people yelling. The tone of the yelling seemed to have shifted—originally scared, then confused and angry—to something more melancholy. Sad. Empty. Regretful, maybe.

I guess Andy had said that the guys would be at the hole, but I half expected him to be wrong. I almost felt like I *needed* him to be wrong. How could he be so calm during all of this? So calm, so sure, so certain. I wasn't sure, right up until we got there, that *we* would even make it. Despite Andy's cool demeanor and strange certainty about our safety, I couldn't stop thinking about Mr. Miller—and all the other Mr. Millers of the world—just waiting for an excuse to kill someone. They could be anywhere, and what was I going to do—throw my backpack at them?

All the gunshots I heard were the other Mr. Millers out there using this as an excuse to go full-blown crazy.

Though, to his credit (if you can really give any) he didn't pick a random person to exact his years of accrued frustration caused by, as he called them, "fast-driving, no-giving-a-shit kids." He saw that little hatchback driving in such a way that someone else probably would have gotten hurt or killed, so he simply eliminated what he saw as the negative from the equation. Perhaps even chaos has some order to it, screwed up as it may be. But that's assuming that the person who *thinks* they're the good guy actually *is*.

CHAPTER

THIRTY-SEVEN

TO CLEAR MY MIND, I took a moment to focus on my immediate surroundings. A few steps away from me, Dylan was pacing back and forth in front of Birdie, who was sitting, legs crossed, back up against a tree. Dylan's face was that of a worried parent. Birdie's, however, was easy and unchanging, like he was in a trance—body, here; mind, a million miles off.

"Guys!" Dylan said when he saw us. He ran up like he was going to hug us, and for a second, he looked like he was strongly considering it. But instead, he smacked me and Andy uncomfortably hard on the shoulder a few times. While he did that, I noticed something weird— there were more bikes on the ground than there were people at the hole. *Me, Birdie, Dylan, Andy. That's four. But there's one, two, three, four, five, six, sev—*

CHAPTER
THIRTY-EIGHT

I BROKE AWAY from Dylan with a sharp forearm push and looked all around. But no one else seemed to be there. I closed my eyes, for a very brief moment, and listened between rushes of wind for the planes. They all seemed to be gone.

For now.

The orchestra of devastation continued in the distance: crying, cars crashing into and scraping against one another, sirens, yelling, and the occasional gunshot. It was impossible to focus on one sound; each sound eerily harmonized with one another, blending in a horribly perfect way. The only other noise was the wind passing through the leaves. Like waves lapping the shoreline, I listened to how it rose and fell in gentle rhythms.

...but, who rode those bikes?

THIRTY-NINE

NOT MOVING AT ALL, not even to breathe, I opened my eyes and cautiously scanned the area. My mind was racing too fast to keep up with everything. Birdie sat calmly, like this was no big deal and, in fact, he could maybe stand a little catnap before the party really got going.

"Who-else-is-here?" I said in one quick breath.

"Kurt, calm down," Andy said. He was looking at me like the guy on the *Clockwork Orange* movie poster in Dylan's brother's room.

"No, someone else is here, man!" I managed to somehow yell and whisper.

"You didn't tell him?" a girl's voice said.

"*Who is that?*" I said. "*Where is she?*"

I looked but didn't see anyone besides the guys. I spun wildly like a wounded animal snared in a trap.

"Down here, tough guy," she said, standing almost at the bottom of the hole. She was a few steps from what we called the pond, which could easily be mistaken for nothing more than a large puddle.

I looked down and saw a girl wearing shorts and a barely sleeved t-shirt. Her hair was pulled back, showing her face in its entirety. I was so stunned, I couldn't help but stare at her. I didn't realize I was staring for a long—and retrospectively uncomfortable

—moment until she said something to me. Then I noticed two things: first, my mouth was open; second, she had locked eyes with me, making no effort to look away. A wan smile edged up on one corner of my mouth. She met my nervous little half-smile with a full-out scowl.

"Quit staring at me, kid," she said through her teeth.

"Oh...uh, sorry," I said. I turned my face, but my eyes were drawn back to her in a hopefully subtle sideways glance.

"Uggghhh!" she growled, rolling her eyes dramatically. "I knew you guys were gonna be annoying."

She walked halfway up the lip of the hole towards Andy, shifting her stance noticeably away from me. When she came to a stop, she crossed her arms and tilted her head to the side. The scowl was now laser-focused on Andy.

"Did you tell these guys *anything*?" she asked.

"Only what they needed to know," he said.

"Oh yeah? And what was that?"

"Something was going to happen and I'd explain the rest after it did. I didn't exactly have time to give them all the specifics."

"Okay. So, in the time between our arrival and an hour ago when the invasion began, you didn't have time to tell them?" she said in what sounded like a reasonable tone. But the look on her face told the truth— it was the same face my mom wore when my dad came home with a surprise purchase. ("Okay, Phil. You didn't take the kids to a movie because 'the price of popcorn at the theater is *ludicrous*,' but you don't mind spending $800 on the new golf clubs. Does that sound about right?")

"They wouldn't have believed me," he said.

"*Ugggghhh!*" she turned away from him in disgust. Then she turned back to him, rubbing her forehead, eyes barely closed under raised eyebrows. "Boys—they really are *so* dumb." She looked and sounded like this idea was a universal certainty, and also caused her a great deal of physical pain.

Dylan stood and said, "*Hey...*"

"Not now," Andy said, putting his hand out like a crossing guard.

"No, that's messed up. This *girl* can't just come into our place and—"

"This *girl* is going to kick your hairless ass in two seconds if you don't *shut...UP!*" She took a second to calm down, to breathe. Then she looked at Dylan, her eyes wide open, and told him, "Sit down and be quiet." She pointed to the spot he had come from.

Aside from his older brother, Dylan was not used to people speaking down to him. Not without an overblown response, anyway.

The fact that a girl had just done it... Well, he stood there in shock, mouth open with whatever words he was going to say frozen on the tip of his tongue. He looked at me like I was supposed to press his reset button. Poor guy stood there, not sure what would hurt worse: swallowing whatever he was about to say on his own or say it and have it force-fed back down his throat. Or up his...well, you get the point.

I shrugged back at him. *Hey, man. Don't drag me into this.*

He looked at her. She raised her eyebrows as if to say, *Go ahead, little boy. You got somethin to say?* Dylan cycled through a few sets of spasmodically squeezing and releasing his fists. She didn't move except to blink. And she even did that with authority. Her body language radiated strength and confidence. And, at that moment, rage.

In a matter of seconds, Dylan's eyes started to betray him. They seemed to water, but not quite to tears. His face swirled in little bursts and pops, going from rage and contempt one moment, to fear and embarrassment the next, until finally landing heavy on the latter.

Andy stuck his lower lip out a little and gave him a reassuring nod as if to say, *There, there now—it'll be alright.* Dylan looked confused and defeated. It was strangely satisfying.

CHAPTER
FORTY

SHE STOOD THERE, waiting for Dylan to sit down, with her hands on her hips and chin stuck out like a boxer taunting their opponent, until he— I'm not sure how to describe it—slowly meandered, I guess, over by the rest of us. She turned her head back, studying the area behind her.

What is she doing?

After quick consideration, she yelled, "Come out here a second, ladies." Two girls came out from behind a pile of medium- and large-sized branches and tree trunks that had fallen into and bunched together near the hole. One of them—the one who came out slowly, like a suspect surrendering herself after getting surrounded with no way out —was wearing a light, summery dress. The other girl came out quick and confident, like a model on a runway. She wore athletic shorts and a t-shirt with the girly, extra short sleeves showing off her muscular arms and shoulders. *Geez, this girl's got better arms than me.* (Which wasn't really saying much.) *Dang—she's even got better arms than Andy.* (That *was* saying something.)

"I was talking about you too, genius," the bossy girl said.

Who is she talking to?

My eyes went begrudgingly from the bossy girl and her friends back to the pile of wood. I couldn't believe it. If I thought this might be a trap before, now I was sure of it.

"Hey," Evan mumbled weakly.

CHAPTER
FORTY-ONE

HE REGARDED US TIMIDLY, looking towards us, but shielding his eyes with his brow so as not to look any of us directly in the face.

"What the hell is *he* doing here?" Dylan asked, mirroring my thoughts exactly.

"I'm not sure. He was here when I got here," the bossy girl said. "Which was well before you did and *waaaay* after I explained everything to those two," nodding towards summery dress and sporty girl.

"Come on, now," Andy said with an irksome grin. "I told them enough."

"You didn't tell us anything," Dylan said. "Did he tell you anything, Kurt?"

"A little, just before we came over. But I still have no idea what's going on."

"Unbelievable," she said. "Alright, kid. What exactly did he tell you? And you," she snapped her fingers several times, "*Evan*. Get over here while we straighten this out. I want to make sure we don't have to go over this again."

Evan inched up to a reasonable listening distance—still keeping as much ground as possible between himself and us—as I recapped it as best I could. The bossy girl laughed humorlessly at several points in my summary and cut me off before I was finished.

"Okay, here's what's happening," she said. Andy gave her a look of protest and began to speak, but she stopped him. "Oh no, you had your chance. I got this now." She waited for him to regain his composure and give her the floor. Then she said: "My name is Patricia. Andy and I are switchers."

"*Switchers?*" I said.

"Yes. We're from the future—approximately twenty years in the future, to be specific."

"But—"

"Yes, time travel is possible, but it's not like *Back to the Future*. The 14-year-old me and Andy are now in our"—she pointed at herself and Andy — "adult bodies. We switched places with them. Hence the name —switchers."

"Bullshit," Dylan huffed.

"*See?*" Andy said, smiling proudly.

"Okay, then." She walked right up to Dylan, close enough to hit him. "You can go this on your own. Would you rather do that?" Dylan shifted uncomfortably under her stare. When it was obvious that he got all his interrupting out of his system, she continued. "Yes, to answer what you're already thinking, time travel is possible, but, like I said, it's not like *Back to the Future*. The consciousness of my and Andy's teenage selves are now in our adult bodies and vice versa. And it's not just us. There are a lot more switchers—like the people piloting those planes, for instance."

"And all the others around the world," Andy added.

"Right. This is not an isolated event. This is not one or two countries. It's not country versus country, nation versus nation, government versus government. It's past versus present. Well, to you guys, it's present versus future. And it's a worldwide thing. People from our point of origin have been, and are as we speak, switching. Not everyone is switching, but everyone who is has a role. Some on the front line, others are hiding now and getting ready to take over the cities when all the switchers are in position and everyone else has been flushed out. So before you think about where you can go, know this: the idea of running to safety is not a realistic option. Not long term, anyway."

"What do we do then?" I asked.

"He's always been like this, huh?" Patricia asked Andy.

"Pretty much," he said, laughing softly.

"*We*," she said motioning at herself and Andy again, "are going to try to help *your* cause. You are going to get out of the way and not do anything stupid."

"Okay," I said. "So we just follow you?"

"Oh my—" She held her temples. "I changed my mind. You got this, Andy. I can't do it," she said. Then she walked back to where the girls were standing.

CHAPTER

FORTY-TWO

"WHAT'S HER DEAL?" I asked Andy.

"Long story. But right now—just worry about right now. You guys are going to switch soon." He saw the concern on our faces. "Don't worry, you'll be fine. It feels a little weird, but it doesn't hurt. You will be sedated when you get there, but that's just to help you adjust to your surroundings. So don't worry if you feel like you're stuck in first gear; it'll wear off soon. You'll see the Andy who *actually* got punched in the face. You should recognize him; he'll just be bigger and older. He'll look like a different person, but you'll get used to it. He's in the same boat you're in."

"We'll be on a boat?" Dylan asked.

"No, Dylan. No, you won't. It's a figure of—never mind. It's better for now that we keep it simple. You're going to travel through time via a body swap, more or less. You'll wind up in your own body. It's just in a different time, aged to the time that you're traveling to; you're going to sound, look, and feel older, but it'll be you in there. Remember that, Okay? Don't do anything stupid while you're in our bodies and the people from my point of origin, or PO, will take care of everything. But if you get in the way or screw things up for us, it's not going to help your situation. Now get outta here. Everything you need is waiting for you when you get there; relax and know you're taken care of. And keep your mouth shut. Ask no questions. If anyone asks you anything, play dumb."

"Hey! Hey!" Birdie said. He was tapping his watch—that I had never seen him wear before—like a miniature drum. "It's doing that thing again!"

Forget that it was the first thing I heard him say since we got there, it was the first time he had moved so much as an inch since we got to the hole. At some point during the conversation, Birdie had gotten to his feet.

FORTY-THREE

"WHAT'S GOING ON?" Evan interrupted.

I couldn't believe that he wasn't getting it.

"We're totally screwed and there's nothing we can do about it, except go hide out in the future as gross, old people," I said, muttering a few of my dad's favorite swear words under my breath—you know, for good measure.

"I know that you *moron*," Evan said, strenuously pinching his eyes shut. "Just because I don't believe what they've said so far, doesn't mean I don't understand it." He turned back towards Andy and Patricia. "*Why* are...us from the future...attempting this type of hostile takeover?"

"This *whatnow*?" she said, almost sounding more like a declaration than a question.

"It doesn't make sense that people would want to go backwards through history to a time that isn't *that* great anyway. Not unless there was some compelling force twisting their collective arm."

"The...*what*?" she said. She blinked a few times—her eyelids seemed to stick together each time—as if she were trying to focus her eyes. She regained her composure quickly. She studied Evan's face for a few seconds, with a look of disbelief. Then she beelined straight to Andy and punched him (hard, too) in the front of the shoulder.

"What the hell?" he said.

"Are you messing with me right now? What did you tell them?" she barked through her teeth.

"Nothing. Only what little Kurt here recapped," Andy said, a grin on his face and his hands up by his shoulders in mock surrender. "This guy filled in the rest on his own. He's smart. Even as a kid, follows the grown-up conversation pretty good, huh?"

Evan? Smart?

"Do you even know where he is, who we'd be switching out for?" she asked.

A short but acrimonious silence followed, and Patricia grew increasingly irritated by the nanosecond.

"No," he admitted after some hesitation.

"Great. So, what are we doing with him?" Patricia asked.

"I don't really know," he said with an amused chuckle.

"You think he's a genius?" she asked. "Why, because he was able to figure out some vague idea? Look at him—he doesn't even know he figured something out, let alone *what* he figured out."

Andy looked at Evan, then back at Patricia. "Sorry, I got distracted. What did you say?" Andy said, obviously trying to push a few buttons. Patricia looked like she was ready to go Mr. Miller on Andy.

"He is—a genius, I mean," a new voice said.

CHAPTER

FORTY-FOUR

Patricia looked at her, obviously not expecting anyone from her camp to join the conversation.

"How do you know, Katie?" Patricia asked. At this point, I think everything she said sounded kind of bossy to me—whether it was or it wasn't—but she also sounded genuinely intrigued, if not somewhat concerned.

"I take advanced math classes at Michigan State. So does he," she said, nodding at Evan. "At least he *did*—for a little bit. Most of the year he went to Michigan State with me once a week, but after we took this test, they pulled him out and had him start taking graduate classes. He stopped going to school with us completely."

"Yeah, cause him and Mike got expelled," Dylan said.

"No," Evan said. "*Mike* got expelled—right after I told him I wasn't going to school anymore. He, I don't know, decided he didn't want to keep coming back anymore and finally got himself kicked out."

"Seriously?" I asked. "You've been taking classes in college? How?"

"I took a test to get in. Then I took another test, and my professors said there was nothing left they could teach me, and Michigan State offered me a free ride on the spot to study some theoretical math. I haven't spent as much time with Mike since then."

The other girl spoke up, the one with the dress. "Why'd you ever hang out with that guy in the first place? He's so *mean*."

I knew her from school, but I didn't really *know* her. She seemed like one of the cool kids. Not in a bad way, like some people say it, but just— I don't know—cool.

"I guess because we live close to each other. Before I moved here I didn't have any friends. Neither did he. Other kids, for whatever reason, stayed away from me because I'm smart. He didn't get along with anyone because he's always so angry. His parents fought a lot, and his dad is mean. His mom is mean, like she says mean stuff, but his dad, like, beats him up a lot."

"So you're friends with him because you don't make friends easily, his parents aren't the greatest, and your houses are close together. That's a pretty stupid reason to hang out with someone," she said.

"Reas-*ons*," he corrected her under his breath. "With an S."

"Oh my..." Patricia's shoulders swayed angrily. "Boys—I swear, even the smart ones are dumb."

Evan looked at her—kind of. His eyes were closed when he began speaking again, but he was facing her. "He was nice to me when we first met," he said. "And when someone like that is nice to you, everyone else stops being mean."

"Is *that* supposed to be your excuse?" Dylan asked. "That's why you hang out with a psycho future serial killer?"

"Listen, last night was way different," he said. "I don't know what got into him. I've never seen him like that. His parents were fighting really bad. Like breaking stuff in the house, yelling, and really trying to hurt each other. I was outside with him and could hear things breaking and stuff hitting the walls between screams. Finally, it got really quiet for a few seconds before his mom screamed her lungs out, in pain or out of fear, or maybe both. He ran inside to try to stop his dad, then his dad went after him.

"He wasn't in there very long before his mom came running out, got in the car and drove off. She yelled several things, but the main idea was that she wasn't ever coming back. His dad started yelling at Mike, telling him this was all his fault, and calling him every terrible name you can think of. Mike came out of the house bleeding from his nose a little and shaking. He got on his bike and started out without me. I followed him. Eventually I got him to calm down a little bit and we went to the 7-Eleven. He was using the Slurpee to ice his face when we saw you guys. I'm not making excuses for him or what he did, just letting you know...why I hung out with him, and why he's the way he is.

"Maybe it wasn't a problem for you guys, but I always got made fun of for being fat, or smart, or for having to shave at the beginning of middle school. Everyone looked and laughed at me. I hated it. But when I started hanging out with Mike, everything changed. The kids that used to pick on me and laugh when I walked by—when they saw me coming, they got out of the way." He looked right at Dylan. "I don't like holding kids while Mike punches them." He glanced at Andy after he said it. Then he closed his eyes, still facing Andy, and said, "Sorry about that, by the way. I don't think I said that yet. But I am. Really."

"I'm over it," Andy said. "You didn't actually hit *me* anyway. If it was *me*, I would have—"

"Yeah, yeah, we get it, tough guy," Patricia said. "How's your shoulder?"

Andy looked like he was about to scream at her, but turned his head down, almost like he was smelling his armpit. Then he brought it back up, eyes closed, face serene. As he let out an audible breath, he opened his eyes and focused them on Evan again.

"Hey," Andy said—Evan's head was still lowered but he raised his eyes to meet Andy's. "Sorry I scared you, ya know, with the rock."

"It wasn't that bad," Evan said.

"Bullshit!" Dylan yelled. "I saw your face—you looked like you were gonna have a heart attack!"

Evan's face twisted and his body tensed—a little bit of schoolyard bully was still in there. Dylan noticed and shifted his weight uncomfortably, despite trying to look tough. The silence was painful, almost as if the silence itself was creating pressure on my eardrums. Neither one had anything to gain from fighting, but Evan seemed to have the most to lose—he was surrounded by a group of friends that already took it to

him once, and if he wore out his welcome now, he'd be on his own out in that surreal, nightmarish merging of worlds.

It wasn't long before everyone looked uneasy. Andy played the part of the old-timey, Wild West bartender—standing uncomfortably in the potential crossfire, a mere heartbeat before the gunfight breaks out in the saloon. The girl in the dress looked stunned by the comparatively minor (all things considered) violence about to take place, and Katie, the girl with the muscles, for some reason looked calm, confident she could hold her own if the fists actually started flying.

Patricia waited until the tension had built itself fully. Then she waited just a *little bit* longer. I wanted to say something but feared breaking the silence would provoke someone's hostility. Patricia, on the other hand, didn't care about any of that.

"Well done, you've proved you're both a couple of timid idiots. Both of you stand down," she said. And wouldn't you know it, they listened to her—*without hesitation!*

"Okay," Birdie said, eyes down on that new watch of his. "It's back to normal."

CHAPTER
FORTY-FIVE

"I'm sorry, but when is this *switching* thing supposed to happen?" Summer dress asked.

"Good question, uh..."

"Elizabeth," she said.

"Okay, Elizabeth," Andy said. "Should be anytime. We don't have a direct, or even efficient means of communication with our people. We had a directive to find all of you—"

"*Most* of you," Patricia corrected him, staring a hole through Evan.

"—and bring you to a safe location." He looked at his watch. "When the watches start doing that funny little thing again, then get ready to go. Speaking of which, you should probably be on solid footing. Switching has a disorienting effect and the," he fumbled for the right words a moment, "older version of you might lose their balance and give you an unnecessary ding, should they fall."

"Don't want anyone falling into the bowl," Patricia said.

"It's called the *hole*," I said. I wasn't trying to be rude, or anything like that, but thought she might want to know the proper name for this place.

She did not.

She stared at me and shook her head.

"Okay, then let's get ready for it," Andy said. She gave him a sarcastic smile before she and the other girls went back to their original hiding spot.

Andy said, "Alright, fellas—"

"Tell them about their watches!" Patricia interrupted.

"Thanks, hon," he said sarcastically. "I brought watches for you guys. He reached into his backpack and tossed each of the other guys an analog watch—ones with hands instead of a digital face. "You'll have a short heads up when a switching window is about to open; the watch will keep ticking, but the hands won't move forward until it's done."

"*Oh...*" I said.

"Yeah. Now get down on a piece of level ground, plenty far away from that ledge."

I went over by Birdie who had gone back to ignoring everyone. I sat next to him against the big tree.

FORTY-SIX

"WHAT'S UP?" I said.

"Not much," Birdie said.

"Well *that's* not true." I tried to say it funny.

"Yeah..."

"Why aren't you going to switch?"

"They said I can't," he said, looking down.

I couldn't believe it. It took me a few seconds to figure out where to go from there.

"Do you, uh, know why?"

He shook his head. "They didn't tell me."

I tried to think of something optimistic to say but couldn't think of a positive ending to that story. *Did he die sometime between now and twenty years from now?* Then I felt terrible for always treating him like a tagalong. For all I knew, I might never see him again. I kind of felt like crying.

"Listen, man," I started. But he was looking at his watch.

"It's doing it again!" Birdie shouted.

I could hear Patricia telling the girls, in a stern but calm voice, "Everything's Okay, it's gonna be okay."

I looked at my watch. It was stuck in place, same as the mantle clock when all this started.

I looked up to try to say something to Birdie, just in case this was the last time I would see him. He was watching Dylan, standing a few feet away, with a great deal of concern. Dylan, who had been sitting with his arms wrapped around his knees, went into an extremely short, jerky convulsion before he fell over sideways.

"Here we go!" Andy said.

Dylan got up on one arm and looked around cautiously. Then he looked at his hands and felt around on his face, arms, and body.

Dylan looked at me and asked, "Everybody make it okay?"

I looked at him strangely, then at Andy, but my vision was getting blurry. It felt like an explosion went off in my chest, sending a frightening shockwave through my body.

Then I heard someone—sounded like one of the girls—scream, right before everything went black.

PART TWO

CHAPTER

ONE

As my eyes opened unevenly, they were met by a thick, yellow, swirling light. My tongue was dry, and it stuck weakly—like an old peeled-off Band-Aid—to the roof of my mouth. I fought to get my head clear, but it didn't seem to help. It was like waking up for school after playing video games all night, tottering along that tightrope between dream and reality.

After a few minutes, I realized I was sitting in what felt like a reclined La-Z-Boy. There was movement. People were scurrying around, making various noises. But the noises and movements in the room didn't quite seem to sync up. The movements people were making didn't have a linear quality. It was more as though they were in front of a fritzed-out strobe light. I tried to push up on my elbows to look around, but my limbs were stuck in place. Unlike most La-Z-Boys, this one had arm and leg restraints on it.

Hmm... That can't... That isn't... This isn't very great...

Lifting my head as best I could, I looked to my right and saw a group of medical looking people. They had scrubs, stethoscopes, and studious faces. Or eyes anyway; they all had masks covering their faces from the bridge of the nose down. They stood around some other chairs, which I assumed were the same style as the one they had me strapped into. But the other chairs looked less like La-Z-Boys and more like those you'd sit in at the dentist's office. Only these were thicker, sturdier. The seats were covered in leather, or, more likely, fake leather. *Pleather,* my uncle called it.

The medical staff didn't seem too interested in me or the chair to my left. Beyond that chair was an unpainted gray cement wall. Pushed against it were carts with various machines and instruments one would expect to see lining the halls of a hospital. I squinted my heavy-lidded eyes at the person in the chair. It looked like Dylan—same hair and nose —but I wasn't completely sure. The hair was different, a little longer, more wild looking. The face, minus the stubble, was generally the same. I noticed a difference in the skin around his eyes, too—bags under the eyes and the tiniest hint of a little wrinkle forming on the outside edge. He actually looked a lot like his dad, just without the beer gut.

I couldn't see who occupied the row of chairs to my right. The doctors or nurses or whatever were blocking my view. They had made a tight wall, encircling one of the chairs. They were moving quickly, checking vitals and reading monitors, handing things to the person in the center of the action. They almost sounded like they were yelling at each other—not in anger, but like they were in a big, big hurry. It was all coming out too fast for my brain to register. I could hear the words. I could recognize the words. I could not, however, seem to comprehend the meanings of the words as they were strung together.

"...coding..."

"...get the defibrillator..."

"...stand back..."

A flurry of voices cascaded into my eardrums, all echoing and bouncing off one another. Finally, another team of people appeared out of my peripheral vision and quickly carted the chair and its occupant out of the room. I closed my eyes—mostly out of frustration at the way I was reacting to the drugs—and moaned.

"Oh, great..." a man's voice said. "This is just perfect. Go check on Stephens."

"I'm actually right in the middle of something at the moment," a woman's voice replied. "You'll either have to wait a minute or take a look at him yourself."

There was an audible gasp. At this, I opened my eyes as wide as I could until they felt like they might fall right out of my head, and focused as best I could, ignoring the drool dripping down my cheek. The entire group—a half dozen people or more, in lime-colored scrubs, masks, safety glasses, surgical bandanas, and gloves—stopped and looked back and forth while he stared at the woman. She simply lifted her eyebrows, tilted her head, and gave a sideways nod towards me. He looked at the group. They looked away. He sighed and walked out, shaking his head. The remaining spectators giggled amongst themselves, but she narrowed her eyes and the room went silent.

Then the woman looked over towards me, then some machines near me, and said, "He's fine. But he probably doesn't need to be awake right now."

Someone quickly walked towards me, adjusted one of the contraptions by my side. I blinked.

Once. Twice.

But, despite my physically draining best efforts, the third time I blinked, my eyes wouldn't reopen. I thought I heard music rolling in faintly, which happens sometimes before I nod off while reading myself to sleep. I shook my head violently until I was able to pry my eyelids apart. Leaning my head back, I looked at Dylan (or whomever). Or tried to, anyway. Before I got my head spun all the way back around, I fell back headfirst into blackness. The sounds of the room melted into oblivion, giving way to dreamless sleep.

CHAPTER
TWO

I woke up—who knows how long after my arrival—still in the chair, but to a slightly different surrounding. I was in a small room. All cement, no windows. No one else was around. My first impression was that we were in a prison or something. Then I noticed, *hey, the restraints are gone.*

"Welcome to the future, time traveler."

My head jerked to see a man in the corner of the room. It took a few seconds, but I quickly recognized him as Andy. He was sitting on a stool wearing all black—a t-shirt, baggy black cargo pants, and military-style black leather boots. The boots looked particularly worn down, with the steel toe jutted through the leather exterior like a protruding broken bone. He was looking at me with the same eyes, but without the bruise. He had no facial hair and a very short, well-groomed haircut. He must've been at least six foot two, maybe more. It was hard to tell for sure while we were both sitting, but he definitely looked bigger than the Andy I had seen...*twenty years ago?* This Andy looked more like a professional athlete.

"How ya feeling, man?" he asked.

"Strange."

"Right? They give everyone medicine to keep us from freaking out when they first get here."

"What kind of medicine?"

"I dunno. Some kind of sedative. You know, to keep you calm. When they gave it to me, I just felt really, *really* relaxed. Still a little freaked out, though."

"Yeah, this whole thing is...it's crazy," I said, referring to both Andy's anecdote and to seeing myself for the first time in the mirror that hung from the wall over his shoulder. He said something else, but I missed it. Every movement I made startled me—I couldn't believe my face and body looked so old. I had to look away, I couldn't stand the sight of my eyes in a stranger's head. It was too much like something from a scary movie.

"—you know?" he said.

He had been going on about something, but I totally missed it.

"Huh? Sorry, I'm still a little out of it," I said.

"Yeah, I get it. I was saying that you can imagine what it was like for me when I got here without any kind of heads up."

"Oh, right. How much time have you spent here? Is time different here or " I wasn't sure how to finish that sentence.

"No, it's the same, I guess. But I don't know for sure. They said I've been *here* the same amount of time other me switched to our time."

"In the basement of the old house?"

"Yeah," he said, nodding solemnly.

We spent a few more minutes reminiscing like old friends who hadn't seen each other for a while. It hadn't been long but, at least on my part, with the extreme changes in our appearance (I went from a thin-armed boy to a slightly less thin-armed man with a five o'clock shadow), it felt like weeks had passed since we'd seen one another. An uncomfortable silence settled in the room. But it didn't last long.

CHAPTER
THREE

I was relieved and startled when someone came up from behind us and pulled open a large curtain I had previously failed to notice. I was in a room with three solid cement walls and one curtain. It seemed more like a hospital than a prison at that point. *Or maybe an infirmary* in *a prison.*

The woman appeared to be in her late twenties or early thirties. She also wore scrubs and was holding a clipboard. She had light brown hair, pulled sloppily up into a messy bun. Strands had broken free here and there, which she pushed hastily back behind her ears. I couldn't see her eyes as they were glued to the clipboard. Figuratively speaking —obviously.

Andy, as good as it was to see him, wasn't much help figuring things out. This woman had a clear sense of purpose. She was, by far, the person in the room with the most knowledge of what was happening outside of it.

"Kurt Stephens," she said, not asking a question, but making it clear she was talking to me. I didn't respond, just straightened up and looked at her. I faintly recognized her voice from before—the woman who told off that man earlier. Looking at her didn't help me figure out if I was supposed to say something because she was focused solely on the clipboard clasped in both of her hands. She spoke again, still looking at the clipboard: "Kurt Stephens—yes, no, don't know?"

"Yes," I said.

"Are you asking me or telling me?" She looked up for the first time.

"Tell...telling."

She looked back down at the clipboard, her expression never changing. "Do you understand where you are and what happened to you?"

"No, and not really," I said, which drew a little laughter from Andy. He recovered quickly as the woman in the scrubs stared at him. It was the same look teachers gave students when they spoke out of turn; the same look she gave to the other medical folks when they were laughing.

I figured I had better try to get some answers before she could go on with whatever she was doing, so I used this interruption as an opportunity.

"I know what I was told—I switched with my older self. But I'm a little freaked out and still not sure I really know what's happening right now." I continued before she could ask another question. "Where am I? Not when but *where*? And where's Birdie?"

"Excuse me? What makes you think I would know who that even is?" she asked.

"He was with us when we switched."

"I don't know anything about that. Now, I'm sorry but I have to ask you a few more—"

"Well, what about Evan?"

"What *about* Evan?" she said. "Look, I don't know a Burly or an Evan. Now, please—"

"*He*," I said, pointing at Andy, "brought them both with us to the place where we switched. Said that *Birdie*—not Burly—wasn't *in* the future and that Evan might be useful. He almost got in a fight with that bossy girl about it."

"Bossy girl," she said, putting the clipboard at her side and making hard eye contact with me. "You mean Patricia?"

"Yeah. Right?" I asked Andy. He shrugged. "Oh yeah, you weren't... doesn't matter. Yes, I'm pretty sure that was her name. Andy basically insisted they bring Evan along and, for whatever reason, brought Birdie with him, too."

"*Really?*" Her eyebrows went up to match the rise in her voice. Something had clearly piqued her interest, and she began scribbling furiously on the clipboard. I couldn't guess what it was at the time.

If I had known, I wouldn't have said anything.

After a few seconds of her pen relentlessly scratching at the clipboard, I said, "Um—yes."

"And you're sure it was *Andy* who brought them along?" she said. The clicky end of her pen pointed at grown Andy, but her eyes were on me, imploring me to answer.

"Uh...yeah. Why?"

She mumbled the names under her breath as she wrote. When she finished, she asked, "Who else was there?"

"Err...Katie...Elizabeth...Patricia...Dylan, me and Andy—obviously—and Birdie and Evan."

"No one else? You're sure?"

"No. I mean...yes."

"Okay," she said, folding her arms and shifting her weight, "which is it?"

"Yes, like, that's it. That's who was there."

Her eyebrows went up with a sharp inhale as she bent her head to scribble one more quick note. As she was turning to leave, she said, "Okay, thank you, Mr. Stephens," while continuing to write. Then she disappeared behind the curtain.

"Wait!" I yelled. But she was gone.

CHAPTER

FOUR

I GOT up to follow her—or tried to. My legs didn't feel completely under my control, and no sooner than I tried to stand, I started to fall over. Andy stopped me and eased me back into the chair.

"Whoa, slow it down," he said. "The stuff they sedated you with makes your legs a little shaky. Besides they'll bring you back in here and strap you down if you do go out there. Trust me."

"What the hell is going on?" I asked Andy.

"I don't really know. I came in same shape as you're in now. They didn't explain much to me until a few hours ago, before they brought you guys over. When they said they were bringing you guys in, they asked if I would talk to you. Help you ease into the transition, I guess."

"What did they tell you to say?"

"Nothing really—just to talk to you. Keep you calm until you got more comfortable."

"What about you? Who talked to you?"

"They had a video of *me*," he gestured at his face with both hands like a flight attendant.

"Nothing about Birdie?"

"No. Why? What did my switcher say about him?"

"Switcher?" I asked. He made a look like, *what else would I call him?*

and spun his pointers around each other to keep the conversation going.

"Oh, right. Uh. okay, back at the hole, right before we came here, I heard that Birdie wasn't going to switch. But future you—your *switcher* —wouldn't say any more about it. Birdie seemed to know something. He was acting strange, very quiet and disconnected from everything that was going on. Your switcher and him talked about it, I think, before everything got weird."

A strange look swept over Andy's face. "Got weird?" he asked.

"After you left," I said.

"What happened after I left?" he asked.

Then it hit me for the first time. He didn't know about any of it. The bombs. The chaos. The screams. The gunshots. Mr. Miller.

None of it.

He leaned in and looked at me, curious and clearly unaware of anything that happened after he switched. I didn't know where to start. Thinking about it in my head, it didn't seem like it actually happened, but instead it seemed like a distant memory of a movie or something.

I figured I'd do my best to give the straight play-by-play starting from the moment he came out of the house. "Well—"

But before I had hardly got going, the lights went out and a low wailing siren went *wh-o-o-o-o-o-p—wh-o-o-o-o-o-p—wh-o-o-o-o-o-p— bap-bap-bap-bap-bap—wh-o-o-o-o-o-p—wh-o-o-o-o-o-p—wh-o-o-o-o- o-p—bap-bap-bap-bap-bap* over and over.

CHAPTER
FIVE

I CLOSED my eyes and braced for more bombing.

Nothing.

Just the alarm and lots of shuffling feet. The nurse, or whoever, returned, this time empty handed, and threw the curtain back hard. It flew up in the air as much as it slid out of the way. She came in looking a bit dazed and panicky but quickly composed herself. Over her shoulder I saw dozens of people speed-walking, sidestepping, and shouldering through walls of even more moving people in a large hallway.

Andy rose to his feet when she came to a stop in the center of the room. She looked from him to me and back. I was still sitting. She said to Andy, "You can walk. I'll push him in the chair. This is important: We have to move now and we have to move quickly."

"Yeah. Fine," he said. But he sounded a little flustered by our new situation, stuttering slightly on the Yeah before his voice kicked in.

"What's going on?" I said.

"We temporarily have to move you gentlemen to a more secure location. For the time being you'll be in...less comfortable quarters," she said.

Birdie would've probably said something like, *oh, you mean like a cat's butthole?* and for the first time in my life, I actually missed that kid.

"Why? What's happening?" Andy asked.

"Possible contamination," she said in a long, sighing exhale. To me she didn't sound nearly as concerned as one should while saying something as ominous as that in a place as creepy as the mausoleum-inspired, windowless bunker we were in.

"What does that mean?" I asked Andy. But as he was offering a clueless shrug, the nurse replied, with only the tiniest hint of tension in her voice, "It means you need to get to safety if you want to avoid an unpleasant death. This evacuation is standard procedure and it's fairly common. Most of what we do in response is overkill, I'll grant you, but we can't afford *not* to be too careful."

"What do you mean?" Andy asked.

"No time. We need to get to the secure containment area. *Immediately.*"

She wheeled my large chair out of the triage or recovery area or whatever it was. There was one central desk in the form of a circle with no real front to it. Around it were lots of other little rooms, like mine, with three hard walls and a curtain.

We went down a long network of seemingly identical cement hallways. There were numbers, letters, and arrows stenciled on the walls, but not many, if any, whole words. We eventually came to the end of a line that was moving quickly, but constantly getting longer even so. It reminded me of the screening area at an airport, only the people doing the screening were in the same black uniforms Andy had on—all black, sort of a military-meets-safari-style outfit. The woman pushing my chair kept her eyes forward while taking incremental steps towards the head of the line. As we got closer, I saw a rotating door behind the five people at the front checking people in. It was a surprisingly brief amount of time, given the level of stress the situation appeared to be causing everyone, before we made it to the front. All the people had constipated looks, but were mostly calm, so they were able to pass through quickly.

When we got to the front, the woman presented a badge and answered a few standard questions: who are you, who are they, where'd you come from, and so on. She flipped through the chart from earlier. She had put it in a basket, or something, affixed to the back of my chair.

As the conversation was coming to an end, another man in black walked up and whispered something into the screener's ear.

"You sure?" he asked.

The man nodded.

"Alright. This one's coming through," he said, pointing to Andy. "And this one," he said, pointing to me, "is going back to the lab."

"What?" the nurse practically screamed. "I'm not going anywhere but the containment area."

"That's fine," the screener said. "We'll take him from here. You can move through with your other patient."

She didn't hesitate, grabbing Andy by the arm after giving me a little shove to the side of the screening area. Andy said something indistinguishable in all the chaos, then he was led through the rotating doors.

And he was gone.

CHAPTER
SIX

SOMEONE in the growingly familiar black fatigues started wheeling me away from the screening area. From the waiting line, a mass of concerned faces watched me getting wheeled off. I could feel their stares on my skin, like crawling spiders. None of them said anything, only continued flocking to the containment area. I looked back towards the revolving door, but Andy was long gone.

Taking me back to the lab? What's going on? Is this some sort of concentration camp? That would make sense, wouldn't it? Bombing, abduction, getting processed into some awful place, and now being taken to some kind of lab.

"Hey," I said over my shoulder. "What's going on here?"

The man pushing me was breathing quickly but steadily enough to answer me—he simply chose not to.

"Come on, man," I pleaded. "I switched and no one told me what's going on. Where are we going? Am I going to die? I am, aren't I? *Oh my God!*"

He looked for a moment like he was going to say something but took notice of all the people watching us and bit his lip. With renewed conviction, he fixed his eyes a thousand yards straight ahead of him, clenching his jaw. I tried to stand up, but he pushed me easily back into my seat without breaking stride. I hollered a few more requests for information as the lights and sirens flowed through the canals and caverns of this action-movie-bad-guy lair. Every time I did, people looked at us with panicked, confused stares.

"Someone said I'm going to the lab. Is that bad? Am I contaminated or whatever?" I was quiet, waiting for a response that wasn't coming. "Please!"

"You're being kind of a bitch right now," he said quietly, still staring ahead.

"What?" I was stunned.

"Just calm down. You're not going to die."

"What is everyone running from? Where are they going?" I asked.

"*Shhhh!* The alarm means conditions outside *may* lend themselves to a possible parasite contamination. It's like when the weather person says the conditions are right for a tornado—doesn't mean we're gonna have one, but we very well could, so..."

What is he talking about, parasite contamination?

"This is basically the equivalent of everyone holing up in the basement until the storm blows over, but I wouldn't worry—we haven't had any incidents since we established this community."

"But—" was all I got out before he cut me off. Technically he was still speaking, I guess.

"In the meantime, you might want to mentally prepare yourself. Take a few breaths. Close your eyes. Think about what you remember from your PO before you switched."

"*PO?*"

"Point of origin. The point in space and time from which you originate."

"O...K..." I said. "Why?"

"Because you might still be there. And you might not be alone—or amongst friends. Most people do a really stupid looking face dive. The first time," he grinned. "But it's like jumping off a swing. Get ready for it, do it, and do your best to land on your feet. Or at least, not bust your ass."

"But—"

"And be ready to run."

Why would I need to run?

"Wait," I said. "I still don't get it."

My head felt a little funny—lighter than usual and working slightly below normal capacity. I clenched my eyes shut for a second, trying to shake the feeling. "I think it's this medicine they gave me..."

"Listen," he said sharply. "This body feels it, not your—whatever you wanna call it—higher consciousness. When you switch, you'll feel whatever's going on with the body you're in at that moment. The way your meds make you feel now will be gone the *second* you get back to your PO."

"PO?" I said. "What's that even mean?"

"Not the best listener, huh? PO: Point of origin. The place you came from, where you were before you got here, that's your PO. The place your switcher came from, right here, right now, is his PO. And when you switch, the older you will feel the effects of whatever they gave you. That probably sounds good now," his voice took a warning tone, "but you never know what you're switching into. Running and out of breath, sunburned, gunshot wound, you name it."

"*What?!*"

"Whoa, easy. That's a worst-case scenario."

"That's not funny!" I shouted.

"No—it isn't." We rounded one last corner and he said, "Here we are," as we rolled to a park in front of a door with no handle. By the door was a small panel that had three columns of numbers like a touchtone phone.

1	2	3
4	5	6
7	8	9
*	0	#

I continued to protest, trying to make some rational argument for staying out of the room that lay beyond the metal door. He wheeled me to a stop next to the pad, not trying to conceal the code from me, and finished before I was able to really say much of anything.

The door whirred with a heavy drilling sound for a second before it clicked loudly. A little green light lit up next to the numbered panel. There were, again, about a half dozen people in the room with a small pushcart and an extra La-Z-Boy/wheelchair like the one I was in. The pushcart looked a bit like a rolling gray toolbox you might see at a tire shop. It had several thin shelves and one large one. But the top of the cart was flat with high edges like the cart the lunch lady puts the milk cartons on. Everyone was wearing surgical garb—heads, mouths, and eyes covered.

"You can leave him in that chair, but kindly put him in the center here," one of the doctor-types said—I couldn't tell which.

"What am I supposed to do when I get there," I asked while he pushed me into place.

But he didn't respond.

When I came to a stop, the medical people were all staring at me, but I couldn't discern who spoke. The drab lighting glinting off their protective eyeglasses and the masks and head covers made it impossible to make out any facial expressions. But I could tell something from their body language. They all looked like a hungry mob waiting for Thanksgiving dinner.

Someone had taken over on the wheelchair at some point, moving me slightly before locking the wheels. The guy who pushed me in was nowhere to be seen. Hands were on me immediately. Someone was checking my blood pressure with an inflatable cuff. Someone was looking into my eyes with a flashlight. Someone was getting stuff out of the cart while someone else was untying the neck of my hospital gown. Then someone started putting little suction cups on my chest and temples. I still had the IV in, but they were getting out bags of something else to put in it. Then they started strapping me fully into the chair—wrists, upper arms, chest, waist, thighs, and ankles.

"Why are you strapping me down?"

"It's procedure," a voice said. Again, I couldn't tell who.

"What're you gonna do to me?"

"Nothing," a voice said, "now stop wiggling." I didn't even realize I was squirming in my seat until I was told to stop. I tried to slow my body and mind, surprising myself in the process at how easy it was to do so. Maybe it was part of being in an adult's body. More likely, it was the drugs. "We're sending you back to your point of origin, temporarily."

"Switching?" I asked.

"Sure," someone replied with no interest or sincerity.

Something was going to happen here no matter what; I resigned myself to whatever lay ahead. Then Dylan, of all people, came in.

CHAPTER
SEVEN

LIKE ME, he was escorted by someone in black fatigues; unlike me, he was up and walking on his own. Medicine must only be for switching.

"Kurt, you okay man?" he asked.

Now that I think about it, I don't remember seeing a gun on the guy who pushed my chair in, but the guy in black fatigues with Dylan had a gun on his leg, just below the hip, in a holster that started at his belt and ended with a strap that wrapped around his leg, just above the knee.

"Yeah, yeah. I mean, I think so," I said, staring at the gun.

"Alright, man. So listen," Dylan said, looking nervously back and forth between me and his new friend. "You've gotta, like, check in, be helpful if they need your help, or whatever. Otherwise just stay out of their way."

The man in black had been staring into some unknown point in space. His eyes met Dylan's. He tipped his head faintly.

Dylan responded by quickly adding, "And tell them there's a change of plan. You have to tell Andy these exact words:

"They had to pull one from each unit—" Dylan's voice trailed off on the last two words.

"Are you *asking* me or telling me?" This was something our teachers liked to say, and we lifted the expression, knowing full well that using it pissed off the person you said it to.

"Shut up, man. *Dang.*" The man in black fatigues cleared his throat. He was really starting to give more of a prison guard kind of vibe. "Okay," Dylan said, though more to himself than to me. "And tell them their suspicion has been confirmed."

"What does that—"

"*Just tell them!* Pull *one* from each unit. Suspicion *confirmed!*"

He made me repeat that a few times, until I snapped. "Dude—I've got it!"

Dylan didn't look satisfied and looked as though he were going to take me through it once more. I tried to think of something that would make Dylan shut up, but I came up short.

It didn't matter. Before Dylan could say anything, the guard spun him around and thudded him between the shoulders with a flat palm to corral him towards the exit.

My chair was laid back. I lifted my head to see where they were taking Dylan while I tried to get a read on what happened. My head was pushed down, and a strap was thrown unevenly over my forehead.

"Ready," a hollow voice said.

"Ready?" I said. "Wait, wait, wait, wait. Ready for what? No, no, no..."

Everything went black, and a fit went through my body. It started at my head and, like a whip, waved through my body all the way to my feet. At the end it felt like someone was digging through my head with an ice cream scoop.

And then it was all gone.

CHAPTER
EIGHT

HAVE you ever been so tired laying down that you blink your eyes only to find you slept for hours when you opened them again? It was kind of like that, I guess—I blinked, here one second, and somewhere completely different the next. And if that sensation wasn't odd enough, the immediacy of going from fuzzy headed to sober, like a flick of a switch, sent uncontrollable shivers through my body. It only took a split second to fully appreciate how clearly I could think, but that appreciation disappeared quickly as I realized I was falling—face first to the ground.

It's like jumping off a swing...

Just before I hit, I was able to stick my arms out and ran a few steps on all fours before I would have otherwise smashed headfirst into the ground. Once it had sunk in that I was back where I was supposed to be —in my PO—I had to think about what else the guard, or whatever he was, told me about taking stock of my surroundings. Don't want to stand still in the crosshairs.

I took a knee on the ground and looked around, fingertips still touching the earth, looking like a sprinter getting set on the blocks.

I was outside. In the woods.

That's not helpful. Not without a little more to go on...

I kept scanning my surroundings. Looking for anything. Listening for anything.

It was quiet.

Everything seems right. No one's dropping bombs and, hey, I'm not strapped into a chair in somebody's dungeon.

"Kurt!" Elizabeth yelled. "What's the matter?" She must have been close already, she knelt beside me with a gentle hand on my back as I was getting up to stand.

"What happened? Is he alright?" Patricia said. It was a different tone than I had heard from her before—she sounded genuinely concerned, the way a friend would.

"I'm fine, I think," I said. "They're not still bombing, are they?" Elizabeth took her hand off me and briskly stood up. I stood up, too, and said, "I feel a little weird. Is that just part of switching?"

When I got to my feet, I saw all the faces of the group staring at me, like the ones back in the lab, only not covered. It appeared that everyone was still here and intact.

Well, that's good, I guess.

With everything that happened after I switched the first time, I hadn't really thought much about the group I left behind—the ones borrowing our bodies. At least a day must have passed since I left my point of origin. The sun was near the center of the sky but still in the east. On a backpacking trip in Michigan's Upper Peninsula, I learned that moss always grows on the north side of a tree. From that I could lay out which way was east, west, and (obviously) south. And the group was hiking east, into the sun.

When I looked back at Patricia, her upper lip was quivering in anger and her eyes were narrowly fixed on me. I wasn't sure what I had done to piss her off in the first place, but I must have done it again. I took a few steps back, worried she might come at me. Then she looked at Andy the same way. He shrugged and gave the classic *don't-look-at-me* face in return. I cautiously surveyed all the other faces—everyone else was looking back and forth between me, Andy, and Patricia, not sure what to make of our situation. Then all eyes collected on me.

Uncomfortable in the spotlight, I shrank back a little more and looked to the only people I really knew now—Evan and Birdie, who were standing in the middle of a semicircle of switchers. Evan looked surprised to see me, as did Birdie, but Birdie—unlike Evan—looked happy to see me. Like he was about to smile.

"What's up, guys?" I said.

"Hey, Kurt," Birdie said casually. Evan bent his arm up, leaving his elbow against his side, and briefly raised his hand in an awkward, short wave.

"What are you doing back here?" Andy asked. He was standing by Patricia. Elizabeth backed up slowly to join them.

"I'm supposed to tell you: the people at your...what was that dungeon-looking place, anyway?"

"A base," he said. "Go on..."

"Like, a military base?" I asked.

"Sure, like a...we don't have time. What's going on? Why are you back here?"

"Oh, uh..." I couldn't remember. When the drugged-out feeling faded, the information kind of went with it.

"Seriously?" Patricia said, not so much angry but very much annoyed.

"Yeah, sorry," I said. "The drugs they gave me when I switched still hadn't worn off yet and...and they had Dylan tell me, like, two seconds before they switched me back here..."

Patricia and Andy started bickering at each other, and then it came to me: "They needed to pull one from every unit. That's what they said."

"Did they say why?" Andy asked.

"No."

"Did they say anything else?" His voice sounded normal, but he had a slightly worried look on his face.

"Uh...*yes*, they did. It was, um...that the suspicion is confirmed. Something like that."

Elizabeth's mouth opened in surprise, but—after a sharp look from Patricia—she put a normal face back on.

"What does *that* mean?" Andy asked Patricia.

She shrugged.

"Okay, fine." He was angry. Not at me, but in general. "Was there anything else? *Anything?*" he asked.

"No. And I didn't get a chance to ask, between how fast it all happened and the drugs they gave me. I'm surprised I could even talk, let alone think."

"That's because they gave you too much," Elizabeth said. "Drugs, I mean. I told them before we left—drugging you people out of your minds was a bad idea. Better to give too little and up the dosage as needed, *if* needed."

"Alright," Patricia said. "Might as well get over it. Nothing we can do about it now. We'll ask Stephens what's up when he gets back. Until then, we've gotta keep moving."

"Yeah..." Andy mumbled, biting his thumbnail. He remained lost deep in thought, then dropped his hands to his sides with a thud. He mumbled a few unintelligible words under his breath and started walking.

CHAPTER
NINE

WE GATHERED OUR THINGS, which didn't take long at all, and headed out, still moving east and a bit north. A few minutes into our hike, Elizabeth came over by me. "Hey, little Kurt. Is there anything else that's come back to you, you know, that might be helpful to us?"

"Like what?" I said.

"I don't know. We don't know why they sent you back, or when they're switching you again."

I wasn't sure what point she was trying to make, if any, but she was right—there's no reason why they're sending *me* back and forth instead of Andy or Dylan. Or one of the girls for that matter. They all seemed somewhat perplexed to see me return to them, the exceptions being—using the term I heard in the lab—the people from my point of origin.

"Well, an alarm went off. I was in the hospital part of the base, I think, when it happened," I said.

"Do you know what the alarm was for?" she asked.

"Something about contamination, but the medical person who took me to the safe area said that it was no big deal. That it happened all the time."

"Is that it?" she asked, putting a hand on my shoulder.

"I went to the line to get into the safe area and people in black uniforms came to get me right when I was about to go in. They took me to the lab, told me to tell you those things, and then I was here."

"Don't you guys think we should tell him everything," Katie said. "He might as well be in-the-know. Especially if they've decided to make him a carrier pigeon.

Andy considered it for a moment. He looked at Patricia and asked, "You wanna tell him?"

"No," she said. "You should've done it in the first place. Go ahead—fix your mistake."

Andy looked at Patricia—biting his lower lip and smiling with the rest of his mouth—and began slowly nodding his head up and down. Without stopping he turned his head over his shoulder to talk to me. The bruised side of his face was all I could see, and it was still awful looking. The bruise had gone from a dark bluish purple, to varying shades of pale purplish brown. Before he looked like a victim of a brutal attack. Now he looked more like a battered comic book hero. When he spoke, he sounded like the voiceover on an educational film.

"The universe as we know it is malleable—it can be bent without being damaged. Temporarily. The theoretical limits to this are far beyond where we are with what we call switching. Switching is really just the beginning of our understanding. We believe that with advances in our current technology, we will be able to move into different parallel worlds outside of our timelines. For the time being the most we are able to do—effectively, efficiently, and at a massive rate, anyway—is travel within our own lifetimes.

"That means that all the people who have switched were, at the very least, alive in our point of origin, approximately twenty years from the time we're presently in. The pilots doing the bombing and the soldiers on the ground were tracked down in different VFWs and other similar groups easily. The rest are people like us, us being the youngest to be recruited into these efforts."

"What efforts?" I asked.

"The invasion effort, I suppose you'd call it," Andy said.

"But why are people from the future coming back and harming

people from their past—versions of their own people? It doesn't make any sense," I said.

"Well," he paused. "People don't see it the way you do when they are pushed into a corner, as Evan said earlier. Remember?"

"Something about something in your point of origin forcing your people out of their...proper place."

"Exactly. That was right on. There is a really nasty, and I mean *really* nasty, parasite attacking humans in our point of origin," Andy said. "And it's doing it in ways that were previously only seen in insects. It's an airborne fungus."

"I thought you said it was a parasite," I said.

"It is," Andy said. "But it is also a fungus."

"How does *that* work?"

"It is breathed in by the host. Then it attaches inside the body of the host. It spreads to different areas of the body where it consumes soft tissue without doing any immediately life-threatening damage. This causes tissue to die, which causes infection. That's when people begin to get sick, but it's too late by then. When the host gets sick, the fungus prepares for reproduction. It focuses solely on the nervous system for that part. It releases these proteins into the host's brain. Those proteins control the host's brain, causing the host to succumb to, more or less, the will of the parasite."

"That sounds really gross," I said. "What does it do to people, turn them into zombies?"

"Kind of, minus the eating people part. When the parasite starts calling the shots, it controls the host like a remote-control car. It eventually makes the host climb to the highest point around—whether that's a tree, a basketball hoop, a billboard on the side of the highway, whatever. When the host can't climb any higher its muscles contract in a death grip around the object it was climbing and it sinks its teeth into it as well, regardless if it's wood or metal or something else. If the material is too hard, they'll usually break their teeth trying to bite into it. Then the host dies, and the muscles of the jaw and body remain tightly frozen in place, turning it into quite the spectacle."

"Whoa," I said.

"But that's not all," he continued. "A long, thin spore—kind of like what grows out of a potato if it sits around too long, ya know what I mean?"

Working hard to follow along, I missed the question.

"Hello?" he asked.

"Huh? Oh, yeah. Uh-huh, yeah. I know what you mean," I said.

"Well imagine the potato was your head. The spore grows out of the brain stem, *just* below the base of the skull where it connects to the spinal cord."

My building anxiety showed as my shoulder blades began constricting, crushing the base of my neck like a vice.

"These spores," he continued, "well, I've seen them grow from around a foot, up to maybe two—two and a half feet long. When they reach their full size, they harden and...kind of...blow up. This sends new spores everywhere. As they fall, they spread and travel in the wind until a new host is found and the cycle repeats."

"Is there anything you can do? Medicine or surgery or something?" I asked.

Elizabeth shook her head and said, "No, unfortunately there's little that we can do once someone is infected."

"What do you mean, 'little you can do'?" I asked. They looked at each other like I had spoken in some peculiar, unknown, made-up language. "Are you saying there's something you could have done, and you didn't?"

"No," Andy said.

"Then what? *What?*"

He said nothing, just looked at the ground. I looked at the others—they were all looking up, down, and around, looking at everything but me. I didn't like it. It felt too much like the moment before my parents told me my grandpa died.

"Well, it spread so fast, by the time the powers-that-be figured out what it was, and how it worked, whole cities were wiped out.

"Wait," I said, thinking out loud. "So, everyone who got it just died?"

"Yes," Andy said.

"There's nothing anyone could've done about it?"

"Pretty much," Andy said. He pointed a finger and we all started walking.

"What happened to the people that got this mutant parasite thing, then?" I asked.

"Do you really want to know?"

Maybe I don't really want *to know. But I need to. If my family got this thing...*

I nodded.

"Alright. When someone was found to be contaminated, they were euthanized, and the body disposed of. But containment was too difficult. Eventually, groups were recruited to live underground until a full-scale invasion—which meant a fresh start for humanity—was prepared."

"That's what's happening now?" I asked. "*Euthanizing?* You just *kill* them?"

Andy nodded.

"How bad *is it* where you...at your point of origin?" I asked.

"Terrible," Katie said.

Elizabeth said, "We have protective suits that enable us to go outside of our compound, but it's done rarely and only by scientific teams with armed protection. Most of our society is dead. There are a few hundred people at our compound. I can't imagine that many people are alive outside."

"But there are *some*?" I asked.

They looked at each other, not saying a word.

"Are there?"

"Look," Andy said, "if you have any more questions, we'll have to talk about it later."

I wanted to ask about the invasion. How could anyone morally accept what they were doing, which was the equivalent of pushing someone's head underwater to keep afloat? But I saved it. What would be the point? To single-handedly convince them to knock it off?

Yeah, right.

"We're currently avoiding the ongoing conflict and its fallout by traveling through the forest on foot." Andy said. He looked at the others —the switchers. "ETA: a little over an hour from right now—two tops. Alright, I think that's everything." He grabbed his backpack and put it on.

"One more thing, actually," Patricia said. "Kurt?"

"Yeah."

"Don't be annoying by talking on the hike. Like, at all."

Great—sounds like fun.

CHAPTER
TEN

TUNING EVERYTHING OUT, I listened to the wind in the trees and the occasional skittering of chipmunks and squirrels. We walked without talking, eyes straight ahead, in complete silence, for what seemed a very long time. We walked over downed trees and branches. A few times we came upon brush that might as well have been tangled up razor wire—completely impenetrable. It was so thick I couldn't even see through it, like a prickly, dark fog. So, when we had something in our way that we couldn't get over or through, we went around. Going out of your way is annoying, but then there were also hills. Not slight inclines either. I'm talking about hills you couldn't even try to ride a bike up. So, we had to dig in, grab hold of smaller trees, roots, embedded rocks, and hope that we didn't fall and break a leg.

All the while, we stayed in a very dense part of the forest where slivers of light rarely made it all the way to the cool, damp forest floor. The sounds of the birds hung in the air like a zoo. It was important to Andy and Patricia to stay under the cover of the trees. Near the halfway point, we opted to walk through a creek rather than walk over a conveniently laid out tree that bridged the shores perfectly because it was "too exposed." Everyone had to take their socks and shoes off for the crossing. Once we got to the other side, I quickly put my socks and shoes on while everyone else dried their feet. I realized too late—after my damp socks began rubbing my skin raw—that I should have taken more care drying my feet like the others did.

I could feel whole chunks of skin rubbing loose, breaking open, and causing sores that felt like hot iron rods piercing through my feet. I tried to push through it as best I could—not wanting to be the first to break the silence, especially by complaining. I began walking on my heels, but even those were getting hot and stingy. Luckily it wasn't long at all before I heard the sound of running water, which was where we took our only rest before reaching the rendezvous point.

When we heard the water, Patricia said, "Let's break for a few minutes before we head north."

"No, let's keep going," Andy said. "I don't want to be the last ones there, Patricia. If you're early, you're on time; if you're on time—"

"You're late," they said in unison.

"Yeah, yeah. *We*," she gestured to herself and the other girls, "are stopping. And *we*," she said, wagging a finger between herself and Andy, "have orders to arrive together. You leave us, you go against your orders."

Andy was momentarily at a loss for words. An entire range of emotions flashed through his face at once. He looked everywhere except at Patricia. "Fine. It's unprofessional and, quite frankly, shows weakness, but I'm not going to leave any man, or *you guys*," he said, mocking her gesture, "behind."

"Whatever you have to tell yourself," she said as she walked away.

When Patricia started walking away, I turned and walked as quickly as I could—without trying to look too eager to get off my feet—for maybe thirty seconds before the river came into view through the trees. It was a good-sized river. Not huge, but not a tiny little creek, either. I'd say it was roughly twenty yards across and moving steadily. No one would confuse it for raging rapids, but if a mediocre swimmer tried to swim straight across, they would probably land on the other side at least the length of a basketball court down river from where they started. Everyone on the outer lining of the semicircle sat down. I did the same and took my shoes off.

"Your feet okay?" Elizabeth asked.

"Sore. A few blisters," I said.

"One second..." she said. She went over to Evan and took the backpack he was carrying. He didn't seem to care.

"Let's get this on," she said waving a roll of duct tape as she walked my way.

I watched her rip off some small pieces and wrap them gently around each of my toes, around the front pad of my feet, and along my heel. It was snug but not too tight.

"Won't it come off?" I asked.

"Shouldn't. If it does, just put more on, dummy," she said.

I looked at her, a bit stunned.

She smiled.

My mouth slowly broke out in a smile. And, if I'm being honest, it felt really, *really* good. It was the first time I felt genuinely good since this whole thing started. Elizabeth stood and gave me a parting smile. It almost felt like she was flirting with me, but I remembered that she was actually an adult, even if she looked like a cute girl my age.

If she is flirting with me, that's pretty gross.

"Hey," I called to her. She turned. "Are you a doctor or something?"

"Or something. Let me know if that doesn't do the job and we'll take another look at it when we stop for good. Shouldn't be too much longer."

Patricia stood up and faced the group. Andy anticipated what she was getting up to do and beat her to the punch. "Break time's over, folks," he said. "Let's keep moving."

143

CHAPTER

ELEVEN

WHILE I WAS TYING my shoes, the group—moving together like a synchronized swim team—got to their feet and started following the river north. I finished tying the last knot and ran to catch up. My feet felt amazing! A little sore, like a tender bruise, but nowhere near the eye-watering pain I felt before. The rest of the walk felt like it couldn't have been more than thirty to forty-five minutes before we got to the rendezvous point, at a split in the big river.

We were the only ones there, which Patricia seemed happy about, without saying so. Dylan looked mad, for some reason, but didn't say anything either.

I was curious who we were meeting but thought asking might be too much. Instead, I asked, "So *this* is the rendezvous point?"

"Not quite," Elizabeth said.

"We're close," Dylan said. "Why are we stopping, anyway?"

"We're not," Andy said. "C'mon, you guys."

"We're obviously early," Patricia said. "Let's hang back until the others get here."

"We should keep going, though," Dylan said. "Right, Andy?"

"We *should*, but she gets an idea stuck in her head..."

Dylan looked at Patricia, who shrugged with an *aw-shucks* smile.

Dylan huffed and walked away, while the girls took off their packs and plopped down. Me, the other guys, and Andy's switcher did the same. I took my shoes off and rubbed my feet. I had a few blisters where the tape didn't cover. One, on the arch of my foot, looked comically like a dead fish—both in shape and, thanks to the wet socks, in color. After a short break, people started getting back up one by one. Some of the switchers started gathering sticks for a fire, laying them together in a small teepee. I guess the rendezvous point was also going to be a camp. Evan and Katie were collecting water into milk cartons they had flattened and stored in his backpack.

I looked up at the tree we were camped under. Its branches reached out about halfway across the river. Our makeshift camp was between the river and the tree, safely under the cover of the tree's dense canopy. Looking down at the top layer of the tree's roots, I noticed that they were large and stuck out of the ground the way the veins on the backs of my future-hands did.

And that thought made me think about switching.

Thinking about switching gave me the chills.

As I thought about the world they described outside the base, I let my backpack slide off my shoulders and fall to the ground with a *thud*.

"*Hey* man," Dylan complained. "Quit throwing stuff around."

He stood angrily and started walking towards me.

My chest tightened. I felt a little dizzy. I knelt by my bag.

Things began to blur. The blurring swirled around like a tilt-a-whirl —until all the blurred movements became one—and faded to white— from the edges of my vision—at first—but continuing to bleed—the pace steadily increasing towards center—until the whole of my vision was awash in whiteness.

I sat that way until the white started to dim, darker and darker, into complete and total darkness. My eyelids fluttered in hopes of clearing my vision at least a little bit. Slowly the picture started to come back. But it was fuzzy, complete but out of focus. I was having trouble opening my eyes all the way—like stepping outside on a sunny day and catching the brunt of the sunlight on your face. I was back in the lab.

"No," I said.

"It's alright, Mr. Stephens," a voice from the surgical-masked mob said. "Try to remain calm."

"No!" I yelled, pressing against my restraints.

I closed my eyes and concentrated on the place in the woods, by the big tree next to the river. I concentrated on it so fervently that my muscles—from the combined physical *and* mental effort—tightened and shook against the restraints.

The crew in the surgical attire mumbled nervously amongst themselves. The ones who weren't already standing or watching me were now doing both. One grabbed something off a tray and ran it up to me, taking hold of my arm below the elbow. They called for something with their hand open upward to receive it. Someone else quickly handed them a needle, but before they stuck me with it the lights went out.

CHAPTER

TWELVE

I WAS LYING on the dirt. I rolled to my side. My elbow screamed; some skin tore off in my fall.

I was still in the woods, under the big tree. Everyone was gathered around me.

"Kurt!" Elizabeth yelled.

She ran at me and knelt over me.

I thought she was attacking me at first, so I yelled, "*Agh!*" and scooted away from her.

The look of concern melted into a glowering stare.

"What just happened?" she asked.

"I think they tried to switch me. I felt like I was, I dunno, fading away. I saw the lab for a second, but I tried to fight it. Then I was back here."

"No," Andy said. "It doesn't happen that way."

"Well," I said arrogantly. "I guess it d—"

CHAPTER
THIRTEEN

"—oes," I said, but in a deeper voice.

I was back in the lab, sedated, and barely able to stay awake.

"We got him," a voice said, but it sounded weird. It reminded me of the radio when the bass is turned all the way up and the treble all the way down. The same as listening to people talking on the other side of a door or wall.

Oh boy—I was back and full of more drugs.

"What happened?" someone asked.

"I don't know. We had him, but then he was gone."

"*Gone?*"

"Well...switched back."

"Who switched him back?"

"No one."

An argument broke out, but I couldn't keep up with it. Everything looked, sounded, and felt out of place. The urge to sleep went from strong to overwhelming.

Whatever happens is gonna happen.

I passed out.

CHAPTER

FOURTEEN

I SLEPT A DEEP, undisturbed sleep. The medication they gave me was so strong I didn't even dream. Barely conscious one moment, blinking my eyes awake the next. I must have been out a long time, too; I didn't even feel the drugs anymore, and they had given me plenty.

Things looked the same as I remembered them, which wasn't a surprise—styling options are limited with concrete floors, walls, and ceilings. I guess you could use mirrors to open the space up. That's what my mom did in our basement. And I must admit, it did feel a lot bigger. But that was years ago. With the parasites—and God knows what else —I had a feeling the house, mirrors or no mirrors, probably didn't look too good. Might not even be there.

All that got me thinking: my parents weren't that old twenty or so years ago. I wondered where they were now—*if* they were still alive. Then I forgot about myself; I had my friends (and *maybe* family) to think about. *Some*where.

The curtain slid back. It was the same nurse from earlier. "How are we feeling today, Mr. Stephens?" she asked.

"Is there a way to contact people outside this base?" I asked.

"No offense, but who do you think you're looking for?"

"My family."

"I see. Well, you have some big plans in the works. I'd wait until later and ask someone from your patrol about all that. I'm just trying to make sure you're ready to go."

Patrol? Big plans?

The confusion on my face must have prompted her to say, "Don't worry. I know that's easier said than done, but trust me, we're good at what we do, and you'll be safe. If you think you might have family out there, your patrol commander is the one to talk to about finding them."

"Now, are you feeling alright? Headaches, cramps, nausea, or anything else ailing you currently?"

"No," I rubbed my temples to make sure. *Hey, I'm not strapped down!*

"Happy not to be in restraints?" she asked.

"I guess. More surprised, really."

"That's fair. After we spoke with the original owner of this body," she patted my shoulder, "we realized that you were drastically underprepared for your first switch. And all of them, actually. That was a mistake on our end. We're trying to build up a little more trust."

I thought about that for a moment.

"Are the parasites real?" I asked.

"Unfortunately, yes."

"Are you guys part of a takeover of my world?"

"That one's a little trickier. I'd ask your patrol leader. They'll probably tell you before you go, anyway."

"Where am I going? And who am I going with?" I asked.

"Us," a voice from behind the curtain answered.

I leaned to look beyond the nurse and saw the older versions of Andy and Dylan walking towards me.

"No way!" I said.

"Yeah, dude," Dylan said. "They're finally letting us out of this giant grave."

"*Grave?*" I said.

"That's what Dylan calls it," Andy said. "Because it's underground."

"*And* because it's spooky, and depressing as hell," Dylan added. "No offense," he told the nurse.

"Hmm," she said, not thrilled by his comment. "Well, I don't completely disagree with you..."

"Where are we going?" I asked.

"Don't worry, we'll get to that after we eat." This voice came from behind Andy and Dylan. A man was leaning his shoulder against the end of the open wall of my cement cubicle. He looked vaguely familiar.

"Who's that?" I asked, leaning again to get a better view.

"Lieutenant Berder," the nurse said. "The patrol commander you'll be joining."

"Patrol?" I asked. "What do you mean I'll be on his patrol?"

"*Joining*," she corrected. She pointed back and forth at Andy and Dylan with the clicky end of her pen. "These gentlemen's switchers are already *on* the patrol. You'll be...*accompanying* Lieutenant Berder's patrol."

"Wait," I said. "This guy is *Birdie*?"

He laughed, reveling at the old moniker. "It's been a long time—years—since anyone called me that." He continued laughing, soundlessly, wading through the ensuing silence. The silence was beginning to curdle into an uncomfortable state, then Lieutenant Berder stood tall and erased the easy-going expression. "Alright, listen up," he said. "There are some clothes over there."

Great, more black fatigues...

"As soon as you're up to it, get dressed. I'll head over to the cafeteria and get us a table. Can you guys show Kurt where it is?" Andy nodded; Dylan stared blankly. "Great, thanks. See ya soon." Big smile. Exit stage right.

The guys and I stood there. I listened briefly to the sound of a clock ticking somewhere nearby. Then I asked, "This patrol...are we going somewhere?"

Dylan theatrically opened his eyes and nodded slowly. Andy backhanded him in the chest.

"Where?" I asked.

"Who cares," Dylan scoffed. "So long as it's not *here*. I can't stand these people and this place is the shithole to end all shitholes."

Andy wrinkled his eyebrows at Dylan. Then he looked back at me, shrugging. *Dylan's still Dylan.* Some comfort to be had in that, I suppose.

"We're going somewhere to meet up with another group of switchers," Andy said.

"For some dumb reason they think we can help them," Dylan added.

"Probably not *us*, Dylan," Andy said, really hitting each syllable in probably.

"Our switchers?" I asked.

Andy nodded. "Makes more sense than us. Right?"

I thought about it, shrugged, and went over to the pushcart in the corner. It wasn't far from my weird hospital chair-bed. Someone had nicely laid out the black fatigues on it. I was glad to be able to move; the drugs had completely worn off. But, due to sleeping so long and not being used to this new body—longer arms and legs, stronger muscles, aches, and pains that, I guess, come with age—I was still a little slow and needed to move cautiously.

"Do you need any help?" the nurse asked.

I told her I didn't. She began giving me parting instructions. I wasn't really paying attention, but I made eye contact and nodded—a neat little trick I picked up to avoid confrontation with long-winded middle school teachers. She finished her spiel and took off.

"Are the girls from back home coming with us? Or Evan?" They shrugged. The questions kept mounting up, swirling in my brain, making me feel a little lightheaded. "What about Birdie? What's up with him?"

"You mean the guy from here?" Andy said. "He's...kind of in charge around here."

I looked to Dylan for confirmation. He looked like he couldn't believe it either but nodded.

"What about us? Did anyone say what our deal is in the future?" I asked. This question had been scratching away at my mind since the first time I took stock of this strange place. This was my first real opportunity to ask about it.

"We're kind of badass from what I've heard. Special ops type stuff," Dylan said.

"Yeah," Andy said. "They didn't get specific. Back at our point of origin, that's what they call—"

"Yeah, yeah," I said. "I know what that means—point of origin, PO."

"Oh, yeah. Okay. Well, yeah, back at our PO, our switchers are on some kind of special mission."

"Doing what?"

"Not sure. I get the impression it's pretty big. Did you see anything, I guess, out of the ordinary?"

I told the guys what I saw, which was definitely out of the ordinary, but it wasn't much, really. Not for what they were *hoping* to hear. They looked excited when I started, but as I went on, disappointment slowly washed over their faces. But then, in my recap, something caught Andy's attention.

"Wait—you switched on your own?" Dylan asked.

"*Yeah...?*"

"How?" he asked. But he didn't even give me time to answer. "Wait —can you do it again?"

"I don't know, but, if I'm being honest..." I sighed. "I don't really want to."

Dylan looked at me as if to say how could I *not* want to get out of here.

"Y'know, when I keep coming back unannounced like that," I said. "It really seems to upset those guys. And especially now that they're some kind of special ops guys, I'm not trying to piss them off."

Dylan looked like he was about to say, *Oh, they don't like it? Well, they can go f—*

"Hey," Andy said. "We gotta go meet up with Lt. Berder. Finish getting dressed. Oh," he added as an afterthought, "and don't call him Birdie, either. He's not a fan."

I had stopped getting dressed at some point during our conversation. I refocused, sat down and finished pulling the black pants over my legs, tied my black boots, stood back up and put on the black under-shirt, then put on the black button-up, working the black buttons into place as we walked out of the infirmary. Did I mention all the clothes were black?

CHAPTER

FIFTEEN

WE WALKED down a short hall before we came to an unassuming door. Dylan walked in first, opening the door just enough for himself to enter, letting it quickly shut itself in our faces.

"That guy..." Andy said.

I shrugged back—*whaddya gonna do?*

Andy opened the door into a large room, about the size of an elementary school gymnasium, full of round tables meant to seat roughly ten people each. The room was longer than it was wide. The serving line was at the far end of the room. We made our way through. About halfway in, we saw the old Birdie (not *our* old Birdie, but the one from the switchers' PO) sitting at a table by himself in the corner closest to the serving line. He stood and waved us down.

"Gentlemen. Please, get something to eat and come join me," he said.

We walked to the line and got our food and drinks. It was pretty basic: mashed potatoes that tasted like the powder you simply add water to, along with a fruit medley and green beans that still had the vague taste of the can they came out of.

"I know the food here isn't exactly gourmet," Birdie laughed, "but it'll keep ya going."

Dylan and Andy picked at theirs. I devoured mine. With everything that had gone on the last few days, this body had hardly been fed.

"Hope you don't mind talking and eating; we don't have a lot of time here," Birdie said. We all muttered something in the affirmative. He gave a single nod and continued: "We're going to meet the girls. They're not at this base, but they're safe. They'll be waiting for us."

"Well, then where are we now?" I asked.

"We're a safe but not too distant...well, uh, *distance*...from where we need to go," Birdie said.

"What are you talking about, Birdie?"

He pursed his lips and straightened up in his seat. "Listen, around here it's Lieutenant Berder. I don't care how you feel about me or having to address me in a formal manner. If you don't listen, you'll die out here. That's just the truth.

"I'm *Lieutenant...Berder*; Birdie is back at your PO, and that place isn't much better than here. Be thankful you're in *this* position, and don't screw anything up, for *his* sake, while you're here. If you don't listen to us, some or all of you will end up getting stuck in the wrong place or killed. Whether it's your PO or not, that's where you're stuck. And once you're stuck, all assistance ends. No more help from this base or its allies. You *or* your switcher dies, you're cut off. Best of luck..."

We all slumped deeply into our plastic cafeteria chairs.

"*Guys*," he said. We looked up. I tried my best to look him in the eye. "This is a big deal. But honestly, it's nothing you can't handle. It's important that you listen and take orders. Taking orders is going to be the hardest part. But if you can do it, you'll have someone watching you every step of the way. Just listen. If someone says, 'Go throw a rock at that guy with the automatic rifle,' *obviously* don't do that. But if it's a reasonable task, doing it right—*and* right away—is probably going to be the difference between life or death. For you, your switcher—maybe both."

We looked around the table at each other. Dylan and I looked at Andy. He nodded a few times and shrugged. I looked at Dylan. We nodded, not *quite* sure at first, but soon more decisive about it.

We all nodded in understanding.

Then something occurred to me. A question. One I wasn't sure I wanted the answer to. But it burned inside my mind. I blurted it out. "What about our families?"

His head and eyes dropped towards the ground at his side. He raised his head, and in a very thoughtful voice, said, "I understand this is not an easy situation. Every answer just creates more questions. What is this base? Who are all the people *at* this base? What's happening in *my* PO while I'm *here?* Can I go back? Can I stay here? What *is* here? And on, and on. Who, what, why, how, rinse, repeat, and over again."

"*What?*" Dylan said.

"The point is: we are, for myriad reasons, in the business of keeping you guys alive. This is a confusing and complex situation. We'll have more time to talk about it while we're walking. Now, *none* of this conversation leaves this table. Understand?" We nodded. "If things go as planned at the rendezvous point, then all your worries are basically over. Trust me." He sat back upright again, returning his voice to normal level. "Now. We have some stuff to do around here. Well, not in *here,*" he looked around the facility and made a spinning gesture with his finger, "but outside."

"Wait, wait, no, no, no," I said. "We can't...we can't go outside. The parasites—"

"Keep your voice down," Birdie smiled and nodded for the benefit of the people around us who turned to see what the commotion was all about. "We have the ability to go outside safely; we have *extremely* dependable safety gear. Plus, we'll have a few folks from here going with us. At least for a *little* while. But don't worry about those guys. Just leave them alone. Don't even look at them. They've got better things to think about than, *Why's this guy staring at me?* And don't. Tell. *Any*body. What we talked about. Don't want to clean up any more messes."

Messes? Is he talking about me?

"Dude. Birdie. *Lieutenant.*" I said, my mouth trying to keep up with my thoughts. "I have to know if my family is still alive."

He was quiet for a second. Appeared to be deep in thought. Finally, he sighed and said, "I don't know. Honestly. And as much as it sucks to say this, but, since I have no idea..." He paused for the right words. But instead, this came out: "It's probably better for your mental health right now to assume and accept that, at least in *this* PO, they aren't...alive."

My chest felt like it was going to implode.

CHAPTER
SIXTEEN

SWITCHER-BIRDIE DIDN'T TELL us anything else beyond giving us a brief mission overview. In short, we were going to be joining some other switchers from *this* PO on a five-day, round-trip hike. Something to do with an "important communication relay." Our path would mostly be old state park trails, which crisscrossed the state through forests and a huge, protected nature reserve, skirting several towns both large and small. But above all else: *talk to no one about any of this.*

Andy, Dylan, and I followed Birdie (ahem, *Lieutenant Berder*) from the cafeteria to an elevator. The inside looked like any other elevator— brushed steel wall and ceiling, hard rubber floor with little raised circles evenly spread in rows and columns from wall to wall. It was my first time in an elevator—in my switcher's body, I mean. As I was looking it over, I noticed the guys were all looking at me. Andy was stifling a grin. Dylan was trying not to laugh, air rushing in and out of his nose in short, hard clusters. Lieutenant Berder grinned at me and hit the button.

"*What?*" I said. But they just stared back at me with twitchy, stifled grins.

The elevator jumped into high gear insanely fast, and my knees buckled. My back fell against the wall of the elevator. A half-step farther from that wall, I would have fallen right on my butt. Maybe even onto my back. As it was, I had my back literally against the wall, legs bent close to a ninety-degree angle. Probably looked like I was sitting on an invisible chair. Everyone giggled. Well, Dylan brayed like a donkey—the other two giggled. I stood up, but it was difficult from that position while we were still in motion. When I gave the final push to come to a full stand, the elevator abruptly stopped, no slowdown whatsoever. My right foot came off the floor and I had to do a controlled fall onto my left foot and knee, and my hands. Then they all lost it, even the lieutenant.

We came to a stop and got out of the elevator. Immediately upon stepping out, we found ourselves near a fenced window with a retractable roll-down metal door hanging out slightly above it. This was right next to a steel door with a spray-painted stencil job that read *SUPPLY ROOM*. Five black-clad switchers were adjusting backpacks, checking their gear, and, mostly, hanging around waiting for us, I guess. Lieutenant Berder and the other men barely acknowledged each other. The switchers ignored us. There was someone behind the caged window, a man who looked to be, at most, a year or two removed from high school. He had the same black uniform as most everybody here. But he opted not to wear the long sleeve shirt—that was thrown haphazardly over the back of the black office chair he was slumped in. Instead, he was sporting an untucked and slightly wrinkled black t-shirt, like the ones we were wearing, only his looked, as my mom puts it, "a little more lived in." The man's demeanor suggested he was absolutely *not* thrilled about his lot in life.

Hey! Finally, someone around here I can relate to.

Lieutenant Berder told him we needed four extended-leave travel packs. He told the man to put some extra odds and ends in, in place of the usual this and that. I didn't understand any of it and didn't really care.

From his chair, the man in the cage looked back and forth at the four men standing in front of him. For a moment I thought he might not do anything but stare at us.

"Why do they need all of that?" the disheveled supply guy asked.

"*Sir...*" the lieutenant said.

"Huh?"

"Why do they need all of that—*sir*," he corrected.

"Oh. Yeah. Sir."

"These guys are from the other PO. They're going to carry extra supplies to make themselves useful."

Then the man—who obviously didn't give two shits in the first place—gave a disparaging nod before using his hands on his knees to push himself up. He grabbed a clipboard and wrote quickly before pushing it through the opening to our side of the counter.

"Sign for em here. I'll bring em out in a sec." The tone of his voice wasn't far off from Pooh's friend Eeyore. The lieutenant's eyes narrowed at him. "*Sir*," the man added mid-turn as he sauntered off into the belly of the supply room.

Lieutenant Berder signed for them on a lime-green, hardcover logbook with lined pages.

Only he didn't actually sign for them.

He pretended to. Then, while the younger guy wasn't looking, Berder checked to make sure the other switchers weren't paying attention. He then cleanly and carefully ripped the page from the logbook, shut it, and pushed it back through the opening on the desk. I looked at him and opened my mouth to ask what he was doing, but we met eyes, and the severe look in his shut me down in an instant.

A few moments later, the man came out the door backwards, using his backside to push the door open, pulling a flatbed cart with four hiking packs on it. The *big* Birdie grabbed one and threw it on over his shoulders. We all followed in kind. The man—who, thinking about it now, probably felt like a full-grown adult in front of us—started helping Lieutenant Berder adjust and fit the pack properly. It didn't take but half a minute.

"Want help with yours?" he asked me.

"Sure."

He did a long nasally sigh, then he walked behind me. I felt him pulling at straps and cords as it sent my body swaying this way and that. Once mine fit nice and snug, he did the same for the others.

Before we left, the man, now back in the cage, started to grab the logbook off his desk. Lieutenant Berder said, "Hey. Stand up real quick." The man sighed again and stood up, forgetting—at least temporarily— about the book.

"Sir?" he said, not trying to hide his *Dude, WHAT?!* attitude.

Lieutenant Berder took a minute to look him over. "How about a little more care, concerning your appearance."

The man put his arms out and gave himself a quick once over. He didn't say anything in response, but going off the look on his face, I imagined him saying, "Yeah, I'll get right on that—*sir.*" He grabbed his over-shirt and pulled it on over his head. He had taken it off completely buttoned, save for a few at the top. Then he sat back down and resumed his languid existence, annoyed enough that he didn't think about the logbook this time. The lieutenant gave him a disapproving look, but it was met with indifference. The lieutenant shook his head and told everyone to follow him down the hallway.

As we walked, I kept thinking about the guy behind the cage, him and all the other people at the base who were too young to switch to my point of origin with everyone else. Something was weighing on the guys' minds, too, because their faces looked equally troubled as our patrol walked down a dead-end hallway where two armed guards stood by a seriously heavy-duty door. These guys were also dressed in black but, unlike the rest of the herd, they were also wearing full combat gear —black gloves, elbow and knee pads, bulletproof vests, and black helmets with tinted face shields. If not for the little bit of skin showing between their black turtlenecks and helmets, I might have guessed they were robots. Some seriously scary-ass looking robots at that.

"Are they keeping us in, or something else out?" I whispered to the guys.

"Which would be worse?" Dylan whispered back through gritted teeth.

When we reached the end of the hall, Lieutenant Berder spoke to the guards. "Communications patrol going out. Berder in command."

The guard to my left looked us over while the one to my right didn't so much as turn his head. "Destination and expected time of return?" the guard asked rather routinely as though he had said this hundreds, if not thousands of times. It struck me that his voice sounded like that of someone who wasn't tall enough to ride the time travel ride.

What are they going to do with all these people? Do *they* know what's in store for them? How are they not freaking out right now?

"Classified," said Lieutenant Berder.

The guards looked at each other.

"Sorry, sir?"

Lieutenant Berder calmly and slowly repeated himself: "*Classified.*"

"Sir, I have to keep tight records, which includes time out, expected time of return, and actual time of return."

"I understand that," Lieutenant Berder said, "but all aspects of this mission are classified. I'm sure you understand."

"Yes, sir, but you don't have clearance to come and go without documentation."

"Excuse me?" Lieutenant Berder said. His tone sounded almost playful, but I knew that tone. My father used the same tone, and said the exact same thing, when he heard me say something unflattering about him under my breath, almost daring me to say it again. Both guards turned into bobbleheads, looking at us, each other, and us in an amusing cycle. I imagined them stuttering silently under their faceplates, trying to form words but scared of using the wrong ones.

"Excuse me?" he repeated. His voice at that moment sounded like he was channeling my father's voice, the one he used when he expected me to do something, not right now, but five seconds ago. "You do understand what's going on right now. Right? Okay, good. Now—look at the people you see here. Then, after you let us through, *forget* you saw them. Simple as that. Thanks."

The guard didn't speak right away. Must've been shaken by the speech. He craned his head and looked at us. Then quickly back at Lieutenant Berder.

"Sir, I uh..."

"'Uh?' Is that all you can come up with? 'Uh'?"

"No, sir. I mean...y-yes. Well—no." He cleared his throat and straightened back into guard posture. "Of course, sir. Good luck, gentlemen."

"Very good," the lieutenant said, still sounding authoritatively annoyed. "Forget your records, forget us, we'll see you when we see you."

The guard on my left looked at the guard on my right.

The other guard spoke: "Sorry about that, sir. Go ahead." He nodded to the embarrassed guard, who opened the super heavy-duty door with the turn of a key and push of a button.

As the door opened, they each put their backs to the walls on each side of the door. The door opened to a large freight elevator.

The lieutenant and the other switchers calmly and confidently strode into the elevator. I and the guys followed, trying to hide the slightly stunned looks on our faces. Once the elevator doors closed, Lieutenant Berder said, "Can you believe that guy?"

The other switchers chuckled.

The elevator continued for a few seconds before coming to a stop. The doors opened and overloaded my eyes with thick, bright sunlight. It took a few seconds, but my eyes began to adjust. I looked out at the silhouettes, watching them become blobs of varying colors, then becoming sharply clear as a vast, thick forest.

CHAPTER
SEVENTEEN

I TOOK in my surroundings like I was on an alien planet. It was the first natural atmosphere I had seen since I switched. I half expected to see the charred remnants of a nuclear holocaust or something to that effect. If anything, it was remarkable that everything—as far as forests were concerned—looked rather *un*-remarkable. It was exactly as it looked in my time. The switchers got out ahead of us, weapons drawn, except for Lieutenant Berder, who stayed behind with us. Once I processed the basic geography, I started looking for any kind of observable evidence of the parasitic fungus. But it was just forest, for all I could tell.

We all stepped out after a momentary hesitation. Lieutenant Berder smiled at us—though he looked grave and serious—and motioned us to follow him out. The forest was as dense as any I had ever seen. Where there were openings, downed branches and thick patches of wide ferns made for a difficult path. Lieutenant Berder started talking to the other switchers about mission related stuff.

At that point, I started looking around and kind of spaced out, I guess. I didn't realize Lieutenant Berder was standing almost right in front of me until he said, "Got it?"

He said something. Obviously. And I completely wasn't listening.

My brain flooded with anxiety. *Just look confidently forward, avoid eye contact—don't look nervous!*

Luckily Andy recapped: "Hike to the rendezvous point. Meet up with the others from our PO. Two, *maybe* three days from here. Let you guys do your thing. We go home and," the next part sounded like a question, "everything's Okay?"

The lieutenant's head bobbed in agreement. "Good. Now keep that to yourselves." He started walking and motioned us to start falling in behind the switchers. I started walking, not sure if it would be safer with some distance between us and them, or if we should stay close in case something terrible happened. I wondered what nightmarish things might lurk just beyond the line of my visibility, which wasn't very far. There were just so many trees. *Everywhere.*

"Why are you taking *us*?" I asked. "Why not more people from this point of origin who are, I dunno, better trained?"

"By bringing you, I am bringing exactly the people I need," the lieutenant said. "Sort of..."

"You mean we'll be switching whenever you need them." Andy said bitterly.

"Possibly, yes."

"*Possibly?*" Dylan asked.

"Fine—*certainly*," the lieutenant said. "I'm not sure when, or how many times, but you will have to switch. At *least* twice: once as we approach the...at the rendezvous point. And, if things go well, again at the end of the line." Then he turned to me. "And no more funny business during the switching. You might get yourself killed if you try to interfere again."

"Okay," I said. "I won't. Why do we need Evan? And what's the deal with future us? Like, what's their role in all this?"

"It's not that we *need*...Listen, don't worry about Evan. Alright? He's not *that* smart. I mean, he's definitely smart, but he's not even the smartest person in your little group. Not by a *long* shot."

"Seriously?"

"Seriously. As for you guys: Dylan, your switcher works with weapons and explosives. Andy's is, well, I guess, field ops."

"Dude, I'm more awesome than you," Dylan mocked Andy.

"How? Field ops means I could kill you in a fight."

"Bring it," Dylan said. "I. Would. Blow. You. Up. Oooh, sorry about blowing you up into a million pieces, awesome fighter guy."

"Yeah right—"

"Settle down," Berder said. "Man. You guys sound so stupid right now. Just...knock it off. Alright? Anyway, Kurt over there—"

I interrupted him silently, shaking my head and waving my hand for him to stop. Hearing about our switchers—even though I asked—was making me uncomfortable. It felt...*unnatural.*

"Oh. That's fine. Let's all take some time to be quiet for a little bit. Might as well enjoy it *now*. Just remember. Listen to what I say, and when I tell you to do something—do it *immediately*. It's gonna be fine."

We looked at each other a bit confused. But none of us spoke. Not for a while. But I'm not sure any of us took the opportunity to *enjoy* the quiet, either.

We walked. Maybe an hour or two. Could have been more than that. I last checked my watch when we had been gone about forty-five minutes. I kind of went into a trance at some point after that (*Left, right. Left, right. One, two, three, four; one, two, three, four...*). Eventually the quiet, as well as my trance, was broken when one of the switchers up ahead said, "*What was that?*"

Everyone stopped and crouched. I did the same.

CHAPTER
EIGHTEEN

"Alright," Berder said, his head spinning about. It reminded me of the way my mom would look around in the parking lot when she couldn't remember where she parked. The other members of his team, the armed ones, were on guard, readying themselves for something.

"What's going on, Birdie?" I asked. I didn't mean to call him that, it just happened. But he didn't correct me. Didn't even look mad. He was looking at his watch, nodding his head. Staying crouched, Lieutenant Berder ambled over to Dylan. He took a knee and grabbed Dylan by the shoulders.

Dylan looked at him with disgust. "Dude, what are you do——"

Dylan passed out for a heartbeat, going limp in the lieutenant's arms for a second, then jerked a little and came to with his arms out for balance.

"What just happened?" I asked.

"Shh," Berder scolded.

I remembered what he had said about shutting up and doing what I'm told. I shh'd.

"Your Dylan's fine," Berder said. Switcher Dylan nodded to confirm it. "I need my Dylan for this part. You guys just need to be able to run."

Run?

"Sir," one of the switchers up ahead called. "Stay down, keep quiet. and stay put. We're gonna check something out."

Berder nodded and gave a thumbs up. Then he turned back to Dylan. "You ready?"

"Just...*one* second," Dylan said, going for his backpack. He went into one of the pockets and pulled out something. At first, I thought maybe it was a switching device. "Ready," he said. A little smile was creeping up on his mouth.

"Alright," Lieutenant Berder said. "On the count of three, we're gonna run in the opposite direction. One."

"Opposite direction of what?" Andy asked.

"Two."

"Opposite direction of this," Dylan said, as Lieutenant Berder was saying, "Three." Dylan pushed a button, and I felt the heat of the explosion as the sound rippled through my eardrums.

We didn't have to be told—when Lieutenant Berder ran from the explosion, we all did. We kept up with his pace, almost overtaking him, but holding back because we didn't know what was happening, or where to go, or...anything. Then another series of other explosions went off: *boom, boom, boom, BOOM!* The explosions were getting closer to us. I kept running and running.

I didn't know which direction we were running, but I was pretty sure it wasn't back towards the base. It hardly seemed the time to ask, especially since he already told us to shut up with the questions. We ran well over a mile. It didn't feel great, but my body seemed up to it. Eventually Lieutenant Berder stopped without warning. He put his hands on his knees and took a minute to catch his breath. Andy stood tall, hands on top of his head. Dylan sat down and used his pack to get into a reclined position—his back at roughly a forty-five-degree angle to the ground.

Lieutenant Berder walked over to Dylan. "Stay right there. Ready?"

Dylan gave him a thumbs up without looking at him. Then his arm fell. As soon as it hit the ground, he flopped a little, then coughed and wheezed. Our Dylan clearly was not expecting the sensation of spent lungs.

"Hey. What's the deal here? I mean, how is any of this even possible?"

Lieutenant Berder sighed, "That's not an easy answer." Then asked, "Have you ever heard of the many-worlds theory?"

"The *what*?" Andy asked.

"It's a theory—"

"Buh-dir." Dylan mocked, then coughed some more.

"—that basically states," he thought for a moment, choosing to ignore Dylan. "Hmm. Okay, say someone asks you to try out for the football team. You do and you make the team, then go on to play in high school. Well, the many-worlds theory states that alternate time-lines are created at the point you made that decision: one where you play football, and another where you don't. Then every time there's a situation with multiple possible outcomes, you choose one, and other worlds are created where alternate versions of you live out the other outcomes."

"Uh, I don't get it," I said.

He picked up a stick and drew a picture in the dirt.

"That looks like a March Madness tournament bracket," Andy said.

"Yeah, it does. Anyway, that straight line at the left is our common bond—your PO and ours. When Andy went into the basement of that house, follow the line that goes up at the fork. If he hadn't, you follow the line that goes down. At that point, you have split your timeline and created another world where the other choice you could have made takes you down a different path. At every split, *you* follow one line, and another world is created where an alternate you does the opposite. So even though the DNA in you and the people you switched with is the same, the odds that you make all the same decisions as the person whose skin you're in is very unlikely."

"Then how can you switch with us if we're not you?" Andy asked.

"Because we travel back on our own timeline. You *were* us at one point. Or we were you. Either way—doesn't matter."

"That doesn't make any sense," Dylan said. "How does that make us any less real?" Dylan asked.

"It doesn't..." he said.

"Oh, cut the crap," Dylan said. "You guys went back in time and murdered people for—wait, why did you have to kill all those people?"

"That. Wasn't. *Us*. It was *some* of the people at that base. But not everyone is a part of it. Some people are...working towards a different outcome."

"What do you mean?" I asked.

"Our group, the ones that you grow up to be a part of, is holding out to find a different way. One that doesn't upend *every*thing. The guys we ditched—not onboard. Simply put, what remains of civilization are basically two groups: People who have the means and the opportunity to switch, and people who either don't have the means and opportunity, or people—like us—who *do* have the means but choose to use it differently."

"What about the people on our side?" Andy asked. "From *our* PO? Don't they count?"

"If we're right, no. Not really."

We stopped walking and formed a circle around him. He might be a lieutenant in the hope for humanity's army, but he was an army of one and there were three of us. We started to tighten the circle slowly. It felt like back at the lake; we were ready to take him down the same as we did Evan.

"Now hear me out," he said. He spoke calmly, looked cool. But his hands were up, palms out, in a defensive gesture. "What I'm saying is, it...it makes you more of a reflection of the past. We'd be able to help you move back to a pre-invasion time and you could live your lives like nothing happened. But—like I've been saying—we gotta hurry up and get to the rendezvous point."

His face tried to sell a, *See, everything works out fine in the end, fellas*, type of look. I wasn't buying it. We looked at each other and I read it on their faces too, Dylan and Andy's minds weren't put at ease by this answer either.

"Would we be switching with these people?" Andy asked.

"No. Well..." he looked up, eyes moving side to side. "Maybe. I'm not one-hundred percent sure."

"No," I said. "We can't do that. That makes us as bad as you." I didn't mean it the way it sounded, but I stood by it once it was out.

"Alright, listen. I'm sure this has been hard. But anyone who died would be restored, none the wiser, if we're right *and* we can get to the right people in time."

"Yeah, but you'll still have little kids all messed up from seeing what happened, man," Dylan said. "People were killing each other for, like, no reason. When the bombs came, everyone tried to leave at once in every direction. Wherever seemed safe. Or to wherever someone they cared about was. My mom left to get my sister and didn't come back before I left. I don't know what happened to them. They could be dead for all I know." His chin was starting to tremble. "We go and find out they *are* dead, then I see them next week and everything's supposed to be fine?"

"It's not ideal, but it works for everyone."

"No, it doesn't!" I said. "If we end up having to switch with some version of ourselves, then other people will be thrown into this bullshit."

"One more time," Lieutenant Berder emphasized. "We *think* it can work where no one switches, and that's the best available option at this point."

I looked at the guys. They looked at me and each other. None of us were convinced.

"You guys," Lieutenant Berder sighed. "I get it. I didn't say it was the best possible scenario; you've gotta play the cards you're dealt, and we got a terrible hand. I'm not trying to make excuses, just telling you what's what." He turned and kept going. We stood and looked at each other. Without a word, as if by telepathy, we all broke at the same time and half walked, half jogged back into formation with the lieutenant at the lead.

CHAPTER
NINETEEN

WE HAD BEEN WALKING for about an hour—in complete, awkward silence —when the lieutenant abruptly stopped, dropped his pack off his shoulders and scuffled through the clips to open the top. Just under the hood was a mask. It was a little bigger than a painter's mask, but not quite as big as the gas masks from the movies. It also had a round little snout sticking straight out of the front of it. He looked it over and threw it on over his head. And (surprise, surprise) it was black.

"Quick, you guys, get yours on, too," Lieutenant Berder said as his fidgety hands wrangled his mask over his face.

Andy was the first of us to see what Lieutenant Berder saw. He gasped. Dylan saw it next and mumbled some incoherent profanity. I followed their eyes. They were looking at a dead pine—a really, *really* dead pine. Its bark looked like burnt meat. The branches were mostly broken off, leaving shards and nubs of wood stabbing out. The remnants of the once tall and mighty tree resembled a crusty, used pipe cleaner. But the tree wasn't what caught their attention. I was worried I knew what had, and I didn't want to see it.

"Quit staring and get those masks on!" the lieutenant ordered.

I looked at them again. They were looking up, towards the top of the tree. I hadn't noticed, in part intentionally, if I'm being honest, but also because the tree extended very high into the air. It looked to be the tallest object within view, and the object of their attention was at the tree's highest point, beyond where it should've been able to climb. But there it was: a man in jeans and a tattered blue t-shirt had climbed almost all the way to the withered tip of the tree. He was hugging the tree tight to his body in a crushing embrace. His lips were snarled back revealing his teeth sunk into a branch about as thick as my ankle. The man's head was turned at a funny angle, the way one might peer carefully out from behind the side of a good hiding spot. Just as described, a rod of sorts had ruptured out of the base of his skull, about as long as my forearm. The comparison of what grows out of an old potato was a good one, only, instead of a potato, this dug its way out from under the back of that poor bastard's head. It stuck straight up in the air like a white beacon, and it had a silvery sheen to it. Most troubling of all was the look on the dead man's face. It was disturbingly vacant. Not the face of a dead man, but that of someone absently taking a bite of a sandwich while casually adrift in a current of meaningless thought.

I didn't even know I had done it, but my pack was on the ground, and I had taken a knee, fumbling with the mask all while still fixated on the uncaring symbol of humanity's termination.

"If that guy's in the tree, does that mean people are close?" Andy asked.

"Not necessarily," the lieutenant replied. "Could have been part of a wandering group. My guess—more likely we're near a dump."

"A what?" I asked.

"This type of fungus—before it mutated, or whatever—was originally used by farmers to keep bugs off their crops. When a bug became infected by it, the healthy bugs took the affected members of their colony and dumped them somewhere away from their habitat. That way they wouldn't infect the rest. People took a page from nature's playbook. They'd kill infected people—not in cold blood, but for the sake of survival—and...well, dump them."

"So, there are dumps with lots of infected people brewing more fungus inside them?" Dylan asked.

"Yes and no. The fungus only spreads when it stays alive long

173

enough to spike out the back of someone's head like that poor sucker up there. If the host dies before that thing grows out the back of the head, the fungus dies and won't spread."

We stood and stared—speechless, thoughtless.

"Wait," Andy said. "People just killed and dumped anyone who had it?" His anger was replaced with pure shock and horror.

"Unfortunately, yes. Now I suggest we keep moving before that rod explodes and sends spores all over the place. These masks will prevent it from getting into our respiratory systems causing us to wind up like that guy, but I'd rather not bathe in the stuff if I don't have to."

We walked away, but I couldn't stop staring at the man in the tree, at least until I tripped on something sticking up from under the leaves. Then I focused intently on the walk ahead of us. And did my best to think about *anything* besides what I'd just seen.

CHAPTER

TWENTY

UNLIKE BEFORE, the new silence, after seeing our first victim, was woven together with fear and surrender. Behind Lieutenant Berder, the three of us walked with our heads on a swivel, looking for more people. For a dump site. But the rest of the day was uneventful. We headed south and walked until the sun started to dim as it lowered towards the horizon and descended below the tree line.

"Who's ready to call it a day?" asked the lieutenant.

"We're going to stay out here?" I asked.

"Well, yeah. Where did you think we would sleep?"

"Not out here, where we're exposed," said Andy.

"We'll be fine. Trust me."

"How are we supposed to trust that we'll be safe? What if we get exposed to spores in the night?" Dylan asked.

"Fair question," Lieutenant Berder said. "Affected people aren't hostile, and we have tents with an airlock seal and air filter. They are extremely lightweight, and we each have four of them in our packs. We can double up in the tents. Four tents per person times four people is sixteen tents. We can use each tent one time, and at two people per tent, that's two tents per day. At two tents per day, with sixteen tents, we have shelter for—"

"Dude, this sucks enough—don't make me do math," Dylan said.

We laughed humorlessly, hoping it might help alleviate the stress and desperation of the situation.

"Eight. Eight days," Andy said, while I was still bobbling the numbers around in my head.

"Right. And that is more than enough with four—five or six, max—days of travel," the lieutenant said. "Now, let's get set up. Darkness comes early in the woods; you won't be able to see your hand in front of your face in a few minutes' time."

He was right. I had never seen light turn to complete and utter darkness so fast.

Andy obviously didn't want to share with the lieutenant, and quickly asked me if I wanted to be tent-mates. Andy and I made quick work of setting up one of the tents from his bag. We hurried inside with our gear and tried our best to get comfortable on the rough, uneven ground.

That night brought next to no sleep. Every time I managed to doze off, it felt like only a handful of miserable minutes before my arm went numb under my body, or my lower back would get sore, or my neck started to ache. Uncomfortable as it was, I was grateful for what little sleep I got between wondering what the next day would bring and whether I'd live through it.

CHAPTER

TWENTY-ONE

I WAS MOSTLY awake already when the first dull bits of sunlight started poking through the dark canvas of the windowless tent. Andy and I slept with our backs to each other. I don't think either of us wanted to see the grown faces of ourselves. Besides the jarring effect it had, it was just a reminder of our lives being erased from the board, the board being destroyed, and us left to clean up the mess before the mess killed us. And a reminder of who did this to us (ourselves, in a weird way) as well as the disappointment, anger, and bitter disbelief that came with that knowledge.

Trying to put it out of my mind for a little while longer, I turned my face to whisper over to Andy. "You awake?"

For a moment there was nothing. I started to roll back away from him. Then he answered, "Yeah."

"Did you sleep at all?"

"Not much."

"Me neither."

"Yeah."

We've got to be north of Lansing. We've been heading south, I think. The switchers went north. Who were they going to meet at the rendezvous point?

"We've been heading south, right?" I asked.

"Um...which way does the sun set?"

"West. I remember watching the sunrise once on Lake Huron. That's how I remember."

"Oh, uh...okay then. Yeah, I guess we've been going south. Why?"

"When I was with the switchers in our PO, we were in the woods going north. We were going to a 'rendezvous point.'"

"Okay..."

"I think we're heading to the same spot."

"Why? What would be the purpose of doing that?"

"I don't know. Maybe it's part of what Birdie was talking about—"

"Don't call him Birdie."

"Oh...sorry."

He rubbed his eyes as he half groaned, half yawned, "It's alright."

"So anyway, the *lieutenant* said they're trying to rework the device to make it so they can send us back to before everything happened, no switching. I dunno, I could be wrong, but it makes as much sense as anything else we've been through so far."

"I don't think anything would surprise me anymore."

"Right?"

"Did you see Birdie when you switched back?"

I nodded.

"How did he look?" With a kid's voice he would've sounded scared and weak, but with an adult voice, he sounded more like a worried parent.

"He looked alright. Worried about why he wasn't switching like the rest of us."

"Why? What did they tell him about it?"

"They told him he wasn't in the future. Kind of left it at that. I figured he died or something. It was weird—for all of us."

"Who told him that?"

"Andy."

"What?"

"No, I mean the other Andy."

"Oh."

His anger momentarily outweighed by disappointment, probably at not having someone he could get at face-to-face. Or that it was him—even if it wasn't *really* him.

"But he wasn't giving up," I said. "He was sticking it out alright, you know, considering…"

"That's good. He's tougher than you'd expect. Ya know?"

"I didn't know you were cousins. I always thought you were just being nice to him." I laughed a little. "Were you guys pretty close?"

"Yeah. Why?"

"I dunno. I mean, I guess you didn't say a lot to him."

"He didn't say much to me, either—did he?"

"Well, no. Not really."

"Well, there ya go, he was just quiet. That's all. But yeah, besides being cousins, we were close. *Are*," he said a little too emphatically. "We *are* close." Andy's whisper downshifted to a deeper and more intense tone. "Hey, how did you do that thing before—where you switched on your own?"

I don't know how I did it—I just did it.

I didn't know how to answer. Luckily, I didn't have to. At that moment Dylan shouted, "You guys awake?"

"Yeah!" Andy yelled back. They hollered back and forth a few times. Shortly after, we were all outside.

"Alright, gentlemen," the lieutenant said. "We are going to hike the better part of the day alongside a river. We'll stop and make camp along the same river probably late afternoon—"

"Until we hit the *rendezvous point?*" I asked.

"That's right," he said, studying my face intently. "Very good."

"Then we'll switch?" I asked.

"Yes," he said, causing a riot.

"Whoa, whoa, whoa," Dylan yelled.

Andy simultaneously said, "Wait, no; you can't just spring it on us like that!" and so on…

"Okay, *enough!*" the lieutenant shouted. They stopped talking, but the anger was still on our faces. "I already said that would happen. Don't act surprised, like I somehow caught you off guard with this little tidbit. It's for your own good, believe me. When we're moving through unclaimed territory, you're safer leaving these bodies in the care of trained professionals."

"They're already at the rendezvous point," I said. "Will they be okay?"

"I figured as much," Berder said. "Yeah, they should be fine."

"*Should* be?" Andy protested.

"I have all the confidence in them," Berder said. "But not knowing for certain is all the more reason why we need to switch you guys—to maintain contact and find out for sure."

"Hey, why don't *you* switch?" Andy asked.

"Well think about it—someone had to stay behind, make sure you guys got out of the compound without getting yourselves killed. Like in any science experiment, you need a control and a variable. *I*," he paused, "am the control."

"Why didn't the other Andy just tell Birdie that? Why did he have to make it sound like there was no one for him to switch *with* in the future?"

"Unfortunately, Andy—not you, but the Andy from my PO—has been...shaken up. This whole thing has wreaked havoc on all of us. Some of us bend, some break. Some hang somewhere in the middle, like Andy. I apologize for whatever he might have said—or *not* said. He's a good guy, but he's seen and been through more than most, and for what he's gone through, I think he's handled it about as well as anyone can be expected to."

"Is that why Patricia is there, to keep him in check?" I asked.

"More or less. Listen, we don't have time for this right now."

"Or *ever*," Dylan sighed.

"Less talking, more walking," the lieutenant said. "The more air you breathe, the quicker you wear out the filter in your masks. And now that we've seen one, there's bound to be more. We are officially heading into territory that we don't have a claim on. That means we don't know what we might be walking into. From here on out, watch your ass."

We walked the rest of the day without hardly a word, except to spot out more people in trees. The first few hours, we saw four—an old man, two young children (a boy and a girl hugging the same branch, eternally locked together), and a woman in her thirties or forties. After that, we started seeing them every ten to fifteen minutes or so. Each time, the look became more disheartening. Dylan asked if I thought they looked like they were frozen while eating corn on the cob. I giggled automatically but stopped myself and gave him a disapproving look. Then it was back to business hiking, hiking, and more hiking.

Until we came to the river.

CHAPTER
TWENTY-TWO

THE LIEUTENANT MAINTAINED A FIFTEEN-FOOT LEAD. When he stopped, we stopped. It was unspoken from the get-go—or at least from the time we saw the man in the t-shirt embracing the dead pine—that he would lead from the front, we would stay out of the way, doing our best not to get killed. We were within a few hours of the rendezvous point. The woods still didn't look much different from when I was a kid. No different at all, actually. This feeling of sameness calmed me like a mild dose of the drugs from the lab. As soon as I felt it and tried to hold it, swim in it, it began to change and ultimately slipped away. The lieutenant walked over a small ridge and abruptly stopped dead at its peak.

What is he looking at?

As we stood behind the lieutenant, waiting for *something* to happen, I looked around and took in the forest. I noticed for the first time the sound of flowing water.

That's what he's staring at.

It didn't seem strange at first, the stopping to scope things out, but he kept standing there. Staring. Not moving an inch.

Maybe he just hasn't seen water in a long time.

I started walking up to the lieutenant. Even if that was it, that he really hadn't seen water in a long time, he couldn't drink it, couldn't swim in it, so what was the big—

Bodies.

Lots of bodies.

Floating aimlessly downriver, bobbing up and down and bumping clumsily into one another, a few washed up on the shoreline, torsos face down in the muddy banks, legs moving with disturbing grace in the swirls and eddies that licked the water's edge. From the corner of my vision, a few bodies looked as though they were moving on their own. It must've been a trick of the eye caused by the moving water. There were several bodies that looked fresh, skin colors mostly that of living people, but many were bluish, and quite a few were disgustingly bloated beyond recognition, like they were wearing scary, oversized rubber masks.

"What the hell is this?" Dylan asked in one hurried breath.

"I...I don't know," the lieutenant responded absently.

"There's gotta be a buttload of people around somewhere for all these bodies to be piling up like this. Am I right?" Dylan asked no one in particular.

He was on to something. No one said so, but no one took it up for debate either.

"Were they dumped?"

"Seems like it," the lieutenant answered with some uncertainty. "There shouldn't be hardly a person alive in the unclaimed territories. But this..."

We all looked on silently as the bodies below floated carelessly in the midday sun.

TWENTY-THREE

We stood there watching the bodies flow past us for what seemed a long time—though it may have been only a few seconds—until I didn't even see them in front of me anymore. I leaned up against a tree with my backpack on. It felt good to have the weight temporarily off my shoulders. But then the contents of the bag pushed into my back kind of funny, so I stood up straight again. Suddenly everything had a translucent quality to it, all the colors and shapes dissolved into a formless, bright brownish-yellow glow, a singularity. I remember feeling this way at the hole before everyone switched. I felt this way, too, when I forced myself back from switching.

Maybe this anti-awareness—this tuned-out-but-not-turned-off feeling —means that there is some kind of channel open that I could switch if I wanted to. Then again, maybe it means a channel is open and someone could be about to switch with me—whether I wanted to or not—at any second.

I wanted to go home, I wanted it so bad I could see it—the rendezvous point. The last place I stood on *my* legs, in *my* time. I could smell the sweet summery air that blew across corpse-less water, free of the stingy smells of bombs or wet, rotting flesh. I could see their faces, Dylan, Andy, Birdie...and Evan...and the girls. And they're all looking at me, but in a strange way. I can see them like they were just out in front of me on the other side of old glass, with little bubbles eternally trapped, little ripples frozen in time where the glass wasn't completely smoothed. Then, as a camera coming into focus, everything lost its ethereal luster for a more lifelike view. From feeling like I was floating, it suddenly felt as if my midsection quadrupled in weight—my legs buckled but didn't give out entirely.

I had switched.

Hey, I'm getting better at this; I didn't even fall down this time!

I didn't even mean to do it.

Maybe they *did it...*

Judging by the looks I was getting—which were in an even tug of war between stunned and pissed off—they didn't see this one coming.

"What in *thee* hell are you doing here, man?" Dylan said.

I guess they weren't excited to see me.

This should be fun.

CHAPTER
TWENTY-FOUR

PATRICIA BEGAN TO SAY, "Oh, what the—" but spun violently away from me for the last part. I don't know *for sure* what she said—all I heard was a visceral, incoherent grunt—but I'm certain I got the gist of it.

Andy, loving her reaction, smiled and shook his head. He walked towards me, arms folded, a used car salesman's easy grin. As he moved, he looked at me, the ground—taking his long, slow strides—then me again.

"Seriously, now," he said, coming to a stop, shifting his weight. "Thought we made it clear last time. Did we not?" He spoke loudly and slowly: "You don't belong here. So, please—why *are* you here?" His smile waned but didn't altogether disappear. Except in his eyes. It was gone there. Everything was. Those empty eyes put ice in my stomach.

"I didn't do it on purpose," I said, backpedaling to counter the angry mob lurching towards me.

"Well, *that's* bullshit," Dylan said, closing in like a zombie.

"Oh, you don't know," Elizabeth said, prompting the two of them to start at it with their *Don't you tell me...* and *Get off my case...* rants. This drew everyone's attention away enough that they stopped closing in on me. I exhaled and let my muscles go limp while they argued about getting to the rendezvous point on time, if at all, with the "constant setbacks" (meaning my little interruptions) and everyone trying to be in charge of everyone else.

Things must've really taken a detour into the unpleasant while I was gone.

"Knock it off, Dylan," Patricia shouted. She took one step towards the ongoing feud before Andy stole her attention with his own venomous comment.

"Why don't you tell your girl over there to knock it off, *Patricia?*" which prompted the two of *them* to start going at it with their *You know what...* and *Let me tell you something...* tirades.

Katie was standing behind everyone on the other side of the pack from me. Evan and Birdie were directly between her and me. She walked up and whispered something to Birdie. He nodded. Katie walked up to Patricia and grabbed her by the arm. She didn't pull on Patricia's arm, didn't have to—Patricia stopped and looked at her. Katie gave her a sideways nod, signaling that she wanted to talk away from the group. Patricia dropped the argument and walked away while Andy was mid-sentence. As his verbal assault came to an abrupt, clumsy end, he yelled, "Hey! Hey, come on! You can't just walk away like that..."

Everyone else stopped yelling, one by one. All eyes focused on Katie and Patricia's sidebar. Katie's mouth moved rapidly as she whispered into Patricia's ear. Patricia, meanwhile, nodded with solemn under-standing. With her final nod, she mouthed what looked like *Okay, thanks.*

Patricia took a few steps forward and looked at me. "How far are *you guys* from the rendezvous point?"

It took me a second to realize what she meant by *you guys.* "We're there."

"Is everyone else there?" she asked, pointing around at everyone.

"No, I don't know where you girls are," I said.

"But you're with Evan and," pointing around at the male switchers, "all the other guys?"

"No..."

Patricia didn't flinch. Just stood there, reading my face. Everyone else's shoulders, however, shrunk noticeably at the news. Except Andy's.

"None of that matters anyway," he said.

"Wait," I said. "Why doesn't it matter?"

"It just doesn't," he huffed.

I wanted to reach out and slap him in the face for that answer, but I thought better of it. Perhaps a different tact.

"Oh, never mind," I said dismissively. "Lieutenant Berder said Patricia was the one to ask if I had any questions, anyway. I'll just stick to talking to her."

When I looked at Patricia, she looked away. Her forehead scrunched together while her eyes roamed the distance. Like she was thinking, or possibly trying to remember something.

His eyes narrowed, but he didn't take the bait. Not all at once, anyway. When he looked at Patricia, her eyes didn't come up to meet his. He looked back at me. I could see his jaw tighten and shoulders hunch, ever so slightly.

Birdie studied me with both hope and despair in his eyes. I could see the wheels turning in his head: *Is he telling the truth? Is he lying? Either way, why would he say it now?* He remained silent, emoting very little, while his thoughts and emotions swirled in his head. I shot a quick wink to relax him. He leaned his head forward slightly, his face tightened with a bemused look.

"You know what. Maybe I'll just switch back and—"

"Whoa, whoa, *whoa!*" Dylan said, putting his hand out at me like a crossing guard. He looked at Birdie and said, "You got that thing turned off, right?"

Birdie was watching me like a deer surveying growing beams of light on a dark road. Dylan repeatedly snapped his fingers at Birdie. "Hello? Anybody in there?"

Birdie looked at him. Nodded.

Dylan shook his head at Birdie. Then turned to me. "Alright. Now. How about you show me that trick."

"It's not a trick, really. I just...kind of...come under this trance... where I ignore everything around me—"

"Like you do in school," Birdie said. God it was good to hear his voice—it felt like being home again. Okay, not like being home, but a sliver of that feeling. But, like all blissful moments when you stop to notice them, they become a memory.

"You *huh*?" I said.

Now everyone was giving Birdie a look like he'd just farted at a funeral. He either didn't notice or didn't care. No—he just didn't care, God bless him and his social ineptitude. Birdie was speaking to me only; the rest be damned.

"You're always looking out the window or just staring into nothing, that blank stare of yours," he said, giggling and shaking his head. "Remember the time in Mr. Simmons class when he said your name, like, at least five times and you were looking right at him, but you were completely gone? It was great; he didn't know whether to call you an ambulance or kick your chair out from under you."

"Oh...yeah," I said, returning a giggle. There I was giggling after I had just seen a river of corpses in this timeshare-body while some jerk version of me from the future wanted to...

Wait, what does *he want?*

"Great," Dylan said. "Turns out all we need is to have ADD like janky brains over there—"

"Stop it." Patricia said. But it was how she said it: barely above a whisper, not with anger but something deeper.

Dylan stopped, alright. He looked like he was deciding whether to choose fight or flight, not taking his eyes off Patricia even to blink.

"He's going to switch and I'm going to watch him do it," she said. "Alone."

CHAPTER

TWENTY-FIVE

THERE WAS NO ARGUMENT, no discussion. It was simply understood: me and her and that's it. Everyone walked away. The circle of switchers expanded unevenly, eventually breaking apart.

Patricia and I sat across from one another, our legs crossed "Indian style." We were close enough to set a Ouija Board on our knees. She looked at me, all business, and said, "I want the truth, how—"

"First *I* want the truth. The sooner I get it, the less you'll have to worry about me popping in unexpected," I said plainly. "Deal?" I offered my hand. She looked at me, clearly annoyed, mulling over the offer. Then she looked at my hand. I wondered what was going through her head—then decided I probably didn't want to know. I was getting tired of holding my hand out. Since that gesture was getting me nowhere, I withdrew to put it back down at my side. Before my hand cleared the space between us, she reached out with startling speed, grabbed it, and shook.

"Quickly then," she said with a slight roll of her eyes. "Ask only what you need to know, I'll answer the best I can. Then you keep up your end and stop slowing down the operation. Got it?"

I nodded. After some careful consideration—didn't want to waste time with dumb questions—I asked, "What side are you on: the switcher invasion or finding another way to survive?"

"You really don't know?" she asked

"I know what I've been told, but I don't know what's the truth."

"That's subjective anyway," she sighed.

"Thanks. Super helpful..."

She narrowed her eyes, but they weren't angry. "Berder told you to talk to me about what was going on?"

I looked down. "No," I admitted. "I just said that to get a rise out of Andy's switcher."

She rested her chin on a fist, covering her mouth with the edge of her index finger. Just staring me in the eyes, until, finally, she said, "Well it worked. *Too* well, maybe."

"What do you mean?"

"Nothing. Listen. Don't try to stir the pot—you're working with forces you don't understand. As far as *we* go," she looked around at the other switchers, who were watching from a distance with clear interest, "Berder might be the only one you can trust. I won't try to convince you who's who. You'll put it together."

"Just be honest with me," I said. "This one time. Are you with the people who invaded my PO?"

"I'm with the people who are going to do what's *right*. Not what's right for the right people; just what's right."

"Where are you in the future? Because I'm pretty sure you weren't at the base with us."

"I'm not. Me and the other girls *were* there, but we left a little before the alarm went off."

"So, *you* set off the...wait. Then who was it in the lab with us that was dying?"

"That was orchestrated to distract you."

"What? Distract me from what? And why?"

She sighed. "I guess to keep you on your toes so you wouldn't get in the way."

"So that's why one of the girls was yelling when everyone started switching? I thought one of you got hurt or something."

"Wasn't a girl," she laughed through her nose. "That was your boy Birdie."

"What happened to him?"

"He just got scared when everyone switched, and apparently, when he gets scared, he screams like an infant."

We laughed together for a second. I looked at her, but she looked away and stopped laughing. I composed myself and asked, "Wait. So, everyone's okay?"

She nodded calmly. Took in a deep breath. Let it out. Looked back at me. "Look, we gotta wrap this up."

"Okay, uh..." I said, trying to get my brain going. "Oh!" I said, just a little too loudly. "When are we going to switch again? We're near the rendezvous point and the river was filled with dead people. Lieutenant Berder couldn't understand how so many freshly dead could be out in the unclaimed territories and I'm not looking forward to going back to that—which is kinda why I'm here in the first place."

"The river was...was full of...of *what*?"

I didn't want to say it again, so I nodded with pleading desperation.

"Okay," she said more to herself than me. "Okay. Wait here. Don't... don't go anywhere. Good? Don't move. Don't switch either. We...we need to...just wait here."

She got up and started walking quickly towards Andy. The wide circle closed in until everyone was back standing under the big tree that sheltered camp, Andy meeting Patricia just under the far edge of it. I sat unmoving between the base of the tree and the river.

The bodies...

There was not much deliberation—only a handful of excited gestures accompanying the short exchanges between members of the switchers. Then they all converged on me, Evan and Birdie following submissively, but also obviously intrigued by what they had heard.

"Alright, Kurt," Andy said, striding towards me from the broken huddle. "We're gonna keep you here. The lieutenant and the commander can hash out a plan. If they want you to switch back, they can do it from their end." She looked at her watch. I did the same. The second hand was still stuck in place. "They haven't switched you yet, so they're probably still working things through."

"Oh. Yeah, that's fine with me, I guess." That might have been the most understated thing I had ever said. I could still see them.

The bodies.

Floating in the water.

Hey, no staring off, especially at the water. I don't want to think about that place. If I'm lucky, I won't have to go back. Pleeeeease let me be lucky.

"Your stuff's over there," Patricia said. "Get comfortable." Her face was vacuous; it caught me off guard. She usually projected confidence mixed with hostility. Her game must be totally off.

"For what?" I asked no one in particular.

"Not much—from the sound of it. We're playing the waiting game," Katie said.

"Whoa, did you just talk to me?"

She smiled weakly.

"Sorry. It's just that I haven't actually heard you say anything since... well, since I met you." But I might as well have thought it in my head; she walked away before I was able to get the complete sentence out. Except for Dylan, all the switchers had settled back under the tree with their gear.

As the others dissipated, Dylan stood there looking at me.

"*What?*" I asked.

"Listen, man. It's nothing personal. They just don't like you." I looked at him uncomprehendingly as he laughed at his *joke*(?).

CHAPTER
TWENTY-SIX

I SAT DOWN AND RELAXED. I took a few seconds to appreciate where I was —*my* time and place. Then my mind started racing. I figured sleep was the best thing. Just shut it all down for a little bit. There was a blanket made of some rough, woven material. It was somewhere between gym class rope and yarn. But it made a somewhat clean place to lie down, and I did just that. The branches of the large tree moved up and down, back and forth; the breeze sent the wide leaves flittering like schools of fish.

Everything was as good as it could possibly be, given the situation.

I took one more sweeping, panoramic view of the forest, the clear river reflecting the glowing orange sun hanging above the treetops. Then my eyes, sweeping slowly to the left, picked up Andy talking to Dylan. The side of his face—the one mending from the shot *my* Andy took—was showing and I thought, somewhat strangely, that his bruise complimented the color of encroaching nightfall in the far end of the sky. My eyes swiveled slowly, and I saw Patricia sitting down, absorbed by some far off thought and absently playing with the ends of her hair. A second later I saw Katie pacing, a little way from Patricia, back and forth, arms folded. Still turning, I saw Evan and Birdie sitting with their backs together, talking and moving their hands through the grass. They were a little closer to me than the girls were.

Elizabeth was the last person I saw before I brought my head back to center. She was sleeping or trying to. I steadied my head, lifting my body here and there to get comfortable, wriggling like a worm on a hook. Then I closed my eyes and concentrated on how soothing the breeze felt, running over the skin on my face and arms, rolling in and over me like ocean waves, in strong, sustained bursts.

That's when all the switchers fell to the ground. I rolled onto my side and started to get up. I heard Birdie and Evan and swung my head in time to see them hauling ass into the woods. I started after them.

"Kurt?" Andy asked, sounding like he just woke up.

I slowed to a hop step, said, "Tell everyone to stay here," and took off running.

"But Kurt—"

I didn't hear what he said next; I had already shifted into high gear, heading into the pathless forest after Birdie and Evan.

CHAPTER
TWENTY-SEVEN

THE HILLSIDE WAS LITTERED with thick roots that seemed to reach up and grab at my toes. Birdie was in pretty good shape from all the bike riding, so he didn't seem too put out by the running. If anything, he was pacing himself to keep near Evan, who, I've got to say, looked and sounded less like a young, vibrant human and more like a wounded buffalo. This was almost funny to me, except running in my original body again—after having just switched from using the older one for a few days—I could feel the difference in my bones, joints, and muscles. Not that I grew up to become a ridiculously talented athlete or anything, but my adult body had more natural strength and had clearly been through more physical conditioning. I mean, we hiked with packs for hours on end in our adult bodies. At the end of the day, I was itching to take some over the counter pain pills. Other than that, I was fine. Running at top end for thirty seconds in my younger body—on feet that were sore after hiking with a lot less on my back—and the gears in my chest were grinding, rasping, and emitting a metallic-tasting sludge. Had I not closed a considerable distance on the pair, and rather quickly, I probably would've pulled up and wheezed myself into a coma right then and there.

Those tree roots that nipped at my toes moments ago seemed to feed on my spent energy; the harder I tried to jump over them, to lift my legs a little higher, launch off my toes a little stronger—the roots seemed to get taller. One scored a direct hit on the front edge of my big toe. The nail felt like it shattered to pieces. The bone felt as if it exploded. This time I had to pull up. I jumped a few useless, miserable steps on my good foot. The runners were gaining back some ground, while I did a few more hop steps, before I put my foot down under the full weight of my body, forcing the pain out.

I was relieved to find that I was able to withstand the pain. Almost proud, really. I continued the hunt. The breath from my flambéed lungs sounded like a ship's sail shaking fiercely, but ineffectually, in the breeze. I found myself wishing that I *couldn't* physically go on, that my injuries would have prevented me from going any further. But I was closing in on them and would be able to grab one of them. But which one?

Shoot—they're not both gonna stop if I jump just one of them. Birdie'd be the easier of the two to drag back, but if Evan is in this with Birdie, he might beat me up while I've got Birdie. On the other hand, if I knock Evan down, Birdie will probably stop. But, whether I take Evan down or not, am I setting myself up to get beat up?

I was within reach of both of them, thinking about my strategy: *Am I close enough to launch for a tackle? Do I go for Birdie's shoulders and pull him down off balance, or do I go for Evan's feet? He's probably too big for me to go high, so—*

Evan planted his feet like a hockey player coming to a quick stop and put his trailing shoulder down for impact. Before I could react, he dropped me with a squarely placed shoulder to the chest. My body stopped, its contents shifting mid-flight. My arms and legs flung out in a joint-cracking whiplash. He hovered over me.

"What are you doing?" Evan spat through gritted teeth. Sounded like the hit knocked the air out of him a little. Or maybe he was just kinda fat and out of breath.

"What are *you* doing?" I groaned. I laid my head back, coughing a few times while rolling side to side on the ground in a rocking motion. After a few breaths my lightheadedness subsided. Then I stood.

"*Me?*" he said, looking around as he got to his feet. He leaned in and lowered his voice. "I'm *trying* to get *away* from those guys. You should, too. I'm not saying follow me but get somewhere away from where *they* can get you."

"I don't know what you mean."

"I know what they're saying—about trying to help us somehow. But I'm not sure what their game really is. I have yet to see them act in a way that leads me to believe their goals are as mutually beneficial as they say. Can't trust em." He stopped and looked around some more. "Let's go before another window opens and they come for us."

"Wait, everyone switched. They're not switchers right now."

"Sure, but it's a matter of time before they come back. I'm sure they're planning something now, if it's not already being undertaken."

I shook my head.

"You really think they're good guys?" Evan asked.

"I don't know. Maybe some of them. I mean, Andy could've killed you with a rock by the lake, but he didn't," I argued.

"Alright," he said as if it all made sense. "He could've kidnapped me AND killed me, but he only kidnapped me. You're right. Good guy."

"What are you talking about? How did he kidnap you? You didn't have to be at our spot."

"Remember when he was holding the rock over me? He told me—under fear of death— to meet up with him and the girls later to figure out that device and everything. Then he forced me to come to your spot, saying he would call the police on Mike and me for messing up his face if I didn't. Then he reminded me of all the trouble I'd be in if I wasn't there when he got back. Then the bombings started. I wasn't going anywhere after that. Then you showed up, and the bombings started again."

"But you could've left when all hell broke loose. Why didn't you?"

Evan thought for a moment. "He said, 'Good, you're here. I'm going to Kurt's house to check in. You stay here. Stuff is going to get intense around here, but this place is safe. Stay here, live; leave, die.' So—between that and the other trouble I could've got it—I stayed. Then he took off, and the girls showed up. Dylan and Birdie showed up almost right when the first bombings started, and, like I said, I wasn't trying to go anywhere after that. Then you guys showed up. Fast forward: here we are."

"Okay." My attention shot back to Birdie. "Hey, Birdie said he turned something off before he ran away. What was he talking about?"

"The device."

"What device?" I asked.

"If it has another name, I don't know it. That's what *they* call it—*the device.*"

"What does it do?" I asked.

"Hold on," he said. "I want some information, too. When you switched—did you see the parasites? The ones they were talking about?"

"With the thing that grows out of your head?"

He nodded.

"Yeah. I saw it. And I saw how they handle it."

"What do you mean?"

"I saw...bodies. They...they were piled up...piled up in the water."

"Why?"

"They toss their dead in the water to float them downriver, I guess. And they piled up in that particular spot."

"Whoa," he whispered.

He had only a moment to consider this before the mechanical thrum of jets—that devastatingly familiar sound—flooded in from some corner of the sky.

CHAPTER
TWENTY-EIGHT

THE BOMBING STARTED SOUTH of us, maybe a few dozen city blocks away. The noise was not deafening, more like a concert—you could sort of yell over it if you had to. The ground shook with each hit. From the hillside I could just see over the trees growing down by the river. The bombs were making a straight line for the position of our camp, spitting flames and plumes of smoke.

"GUYS!" I screamed so loud that my voice misfired and became an airy screech. I cleared my throat and yelled again. Right as I did so a small cluster of bombs exploded, one after another, after another, after another, after another, after another. I screamed through it and through the brief ensuing quiet and stillness that followed.

"Shut up!" Evan ran up and grabbed me by the shoulders. "What are you doing? If they're bombing over there, they think that's where we are. Let's *let* them think that."

I wasn't following. "What?"

Then another cluster of explosions went off. This time we both fell to the ground, covering ourselves like helpless children hiding under the sheets from some imagined horror.

"They're targeting us," Evan said. "Why else would they have bombed right where we *were*?"

"I don't—"

"Listen," Evan said. "I've heard enough from these guys to know they aren't fully on board with everything that's going on around us, but they are definitely associated with them."

"Evan, I have no clue what you're—"

"Birdie and I figured out how to work that machine they use for switching. Birdie waited for the clocks to get stuck, switched them, then shut that damned thing off."

I said, "I still don't—"

"We gotta get outta here before they come through on foot."

I was getting frustrated.

"Wait," I said.

"Why?" he asked warily.

"What about everyone else? We can't all scramble into the forest."

"Fine—where are they?"

"They're..." I looked around, back and forth, searching for them. *They've got to be close. Unless...unless they didn't get out of there.*

I told him to wait there...

Oh, my God...

With my hands cupped at the edges of my mouth, I yelled, *"GUYS!"* No sooner had I gotten the G-sound out, than Evan punched me in the shoulder so hard my neck cracked.

"Ow!" I said, massaging my shoulder. "What the hell, man?"

"I. Just. Told. You. The same people that dropped those bombs are probably on the ground out here somewhere. So maybe it would be nice if you used your *indoor* voice..."

He was right—but I didn't have to like it.

Then I heard footsteps. Rustling through the leaves and pine needles. On the other side of some tall, thick brush. I looked at Evan to see what he was going to do, but he ran to hide immediately at the sound. I watched him. It was like it happened in slow motion. He tried to get one foot on top of a fallen dead tree to do the ol one-foot-on-and-jump, but he slipped and fell. Kind of forward, kind of sideways, arms out at hilarious angles, spinning around in meaningless little circles. Then bigger circles. Then he was on the ground and out of view. I'm not

201

sure *how* someone would have to fall to make the sound of crunching potato chips, but he did it.

My feet were stuck in place. As the noise drew closer, my mind just... sort of...stopped. I closed my eyes and balled my fists. I opened one eye just enough to see the brush shake a little, then they were upon me. Fortunately, it was just Andy and Dylan.

"Oh, thank God," I exhaled. As the imagined burden of my friends' deaths lifted from me, I laughed at the amazing-as-shit way Evan slipped off that log. Then I realized how white-knuckle tight my hands had clenched, and I released my fists. The knuckles in my fingers protested in pain as I worked my fingers open and closed a few times.

Dylan, wheezing from his trip uphill, asked, "Why'd you...take off like...that?"

"And where," Andy asked, hardly out of breath, "is everyone else?"

We all looked around expectantly, hoping they might magically appear out of nothing. Hey, stranger things have happened.

"We're over here," Elizabeth said.

The girls were coming up the hill at a different angle. I figured they must've scattered like cockroaches when the bombs initially fell, trying to find a place to run to that *wasn't* exploding into the sky. I took roll in my head, accounting for Evan, who was still hiding behind the log—possibly injured—and everyone was here, except Birdie.

Where did that sneaky little guy get off to?

"Are you all okay?" I asked.

Patricia and Elizabeth both looked immediately to Katie, awaiting her response. "Yeah. I'm fine. Could be better. But yeah."

"Are you sure?" Andy asked. He took a step towards her, then stopped. She did look worse off than the rest of us. She wasn't wounded or anything, but her face was sour and hard-set.

"She almost got hit by a tree," Elizabeth said.

"It's nothing," Katie said.

"It's not *nothing*," Patricia said. "A bomb landed right next to us—"

"No, it didn't," Dylan interjected. "You wouldn't be here if it landed right next to you."

"Close then. Whatever." She spoke at him without looking at him. "It took out a tree. It fell towards me and Elizabeth. Katie pushed us out of the way at the last second."

"Seriously," Katie said. "It's nothing."

"She *did* get hit by a smaller branch," Elizabeth said. "It'll probably leave a bruise."

"I said it's *nothing*," Katie said. "Can we just drop it? Please?"

Taking that cue, I switched my attention back to Evan, still hiding behind that log he had slipped off. At least I hoped so. I can't lose him *and* Birdie—they're the only two who know anything.

"Evan," I said.

Nothing.

"Hey. Evan. C'mon dude."

For a moment my heart seized. Those two were our link. *And* they have—and know how to use—that stupid device.

Then, like a groundhog, he slowly peeked the tippy top of his head above the log.

Dylan whistled and patted his knees. "Come on, boy. Who's a good boy? Come on." Then up an octave. "*Come on.*"

Evan stood quickly. He looked at Dylan with considerable disdain. Then he cast a mistrustful look at the rest of us. "Why? Why would you blow my cover like that?"

"Because—it's just *them*. No switchers. Right guys?"

They all agreed. A few yesses, a few nods. Everyone looked scared and confused.

"Still..." Evan said. He got over it. At least enough to come join us.

"Where's Birdie?" Andy asked.

"Over here." The voice came from behind us.

We all whipped around. He had either been hiding behind us this whole time, or he just walked up on us. I wasn't sure and it didn't seem to matter. As he walked towards us, I could see the faces of the group getting ready with their questions. I had a few ready to roll myself. Before anyone could ask anything, Andy hugged Birdie so fiercely he practically tackled him.

When Andy was done, he took a step back, still holding Birdie by the shoulders. Contrary to Andy's smiling face, Birdie's was serious. Gravely serious.

He dropped to one knee and took off his backpack in one movement, leaving Andy momentarily standing with his arms out like a zombie. He pulled something out of the pack. It was a little silvery metallic object. He held it up for everyone to see.

He said, "This...is the device. It's what they use to switch you guys." He held it out for us to gawk at. He saw our discomfort and said, "Don't worry. It's off now."

Andy reached out to touch it, but Birdie gently pulled it back and put it away in his backpack. He looked at Andy, but Andy didn't seem to take it personally. Just kept his eyes on it until it was out of sight.

Evan added, "When it's on, it can be used anytime."

"Well..." Birdie said, "so long as the watches are frozen in that weird way."

"Right, but when it's off, you can't be switched," Evan clarified.

"What if there's another device?" Katie asked. "I assume that's not the only one around."

"What?" Evan said. It was a question but—with his look and tone—it sounded more like a dismissive statement.

"Other people are switching. Is it all because of *that* one device?" she said.

Evan and Birdie looked at each other in stunned silence. Evan's face was tinted with anger; Birdie's with the genuine shock of being caught totally off guard.

Finally, Evan said, "All the more reason to make sure we stay away from the other switchers. Every little group like ours could have one. Let's get outta here."

Patricia said, "Yeah. I'm going to assume that anyone else out here either has a gun and/or a device. *I* don't want them to use either on me."

The girls looked at each other and nodded. The guys kind of looked around at everyone with their lower lips out and eyebrows up. That, apparently, was code for *Let's Go*. And on that note, we walked. The guys talked about baseball and the girls talked about, I don't know—girl stuff. We headed towards home until nightfall. Then we walked some more.

CHAPTER
TWENTY-NINE

IT WAS GETTING NOTICEABLY DARKER by the minute. In what remained of the light, I had to struggle to make out the silhouettes of my group members. The lines of their faces were blurred and indistinct. Chirps and chitters from the trees rose and fell among the summer evening sounds. The ground underfoot was level, especially compared to the terrain we had started on. Still, there were rocks, roots, and other natural imperfections to deal with.

In the growing darkness, Dylan, while following along in the middle of the pack, tripped, lost his balance, and fell to his hands, landing awkwardly on his hip. He broke the longstanding silence with an almost artful display of creatively interwoven swear words—which was his way of saying he would be fine, just give him a minute.

Dylan composed himself. "Can we be done walking in this...stupid forest...with all its stupid...dumb...crappy...*crap?!*"

Then an odd thing happened. No one jumped to have the last word. It was nice being away from the switchers who *all* wanted to be in charge, but this moment called for a leader. For *someone* (and preferably not Dylan) to take the lead. Any other day Andy would be my first choice, but he hadn't been the same since everything went down, and he didn't look particularly up to it now. Patricia—I didn't know enough about her. Not the kid version, anyway. The kid version may have been better...

All the same, I didn't want to give control to her based on the way her switcher handled things. Thanks, but no.

So, I threw in my hat and said, "Sounds okay, I think. Everybody good with that?"

The group unanimously consented and immediately dropped their gear where they stood and took to the ground.

Now, say something to really drive home that you're that boss.

Looking towards Evan and Birdie—the only people in the group I was pretty sure hadn't switched at all—I asked, "How long did it take us to hike out to the rendezvous point from home?"

Birdie thought it over a second. "About four."

"*Four...*" I dragged out.

"Days," Evan added.

"Oh," Birdie said. "Yeah. Days. Four *days*."

"Okay," I said. "Then it shouldn't take any more than that to get home from here, right?"

Everyone stared at the ground in silence.

"What? We're going home, right?"

"I don't know if that's a good idea," Birdie said.

"This whole thing is too confusing," Andy said.

"Seriously," Patricia agreed.

"You think that's confusing?" Evan started. "Ask yourself this one: Why did they bomb us at the river?"

"I don't know," Elizabeth said. "Same reason they bombed all around Lansing."

"No," Katie said. "Before we were in a huge group of people, important places—water, electricity, things like that. We're miles from anything out here. This is different."

"What's going on then?" Elizabeth asked.

"They're targeting *us*," Dylan pointed around the group.

"No not *us*," Birdie said. "Our *switchers*. They didn't know I was gonna switch you guys back. Somebody was going after *our* switchers."

"That makes even less sense," Andy said. "They bomb us, then start going after their own?" He sounded like all this caused him actual, physical pain.

Birdie sat quietly for a moment. Then he looked at me and said, "I actually have a theory on that."

CHAPTER
THIRTY

"Is it just going to confuse us more?" Dylan asked.

"*Some more than others,*" Birdie whispered under his breath.

Luckily it seemed to go right over Dylan's head, so it didn't stoke his rage. That or Dylan had matured some and was handling the situation calmly and rationally, controlling his temper. Probably the first one.

Everyone scooched up in front of Birdie like children at story time. Some of us laid back using backpacks as backrests and pillows. After a brief settling-in period, Birdie got started. The poor guy looked a bit nervous—not used to having a group's attention willfully on him. But he worked through it.

"The switchers...they're not so great. Their strategy *here* is basically to do enough damage—ya know, kill a lotta non-switchers and create chaos amongst the survivors—to break any resistance before it can start. You saw that with the bombs and shootings."

"Wait," I said. "The shootings weren't *all* the switchers. Mr. Miller is ancient, and he was sitting in his lawn chair shooting reckless drivers from his driveway. He can't have a switcher over there; his switcher would have to be over a hundred years old."

"All the more reason, if he *does* somehow have a switcher, for him to be on their side. Then he gets an extra twenty-some years to live," Patricia said.

"I'm sure some of the people from our PO got into the action on their own," Evan said. "But most of the shots came from the switchers. Or they were people defending themselves *from* the switchers. Either way, more of the shooting was done by, or in response to the switchers."

Everyone let that sink in a moment—our quaint little subdivision's a *battlefield* now.

Birdie continued. "But *our* switchers aren't part of what's happening." This spawned a collective sardonic stare from the group. "Okay, they're part of it, but they're not fully on board. Yes, they're switchers. But they seem like they're up to something else. Something different from the rest."

The group looked at him questioningly, but without the anger and all-out doubt as before.

"Instead of helping with the main attack," he said, "they were coming out here to meet with others. At the rendezvous point. But the bombs flushed them—*us*—out of there."

"Hold up," I said. "How do you know they were supposed to meet someone at the rendezvous point?"

Katie laughed while she answered, "Because that's what *rendezvous* means." She didn't sound like she was trying to be rude, but, if I'm being honest, I had a strong urge to tell her to shut up. I *didn't*, but I *wanted* to.

"That's right," Evan said with a grin. "So, *the* switchers"—saying it *thee*—"found out your switchers weren't on board and that they were gonna meet up with more rebel switchers…"

"And *the* switchers were going to kill them," Andy finished.

"Right," Evan said.

"*Rebel scum*," Birdie mumbled. We all ignored it, as usual. But I was glad to have Birdie around to ignore again, strange as that sounds.

"How would the switchers know what was going on?" Patricia asked.

I looked at Andy. In part because he knew—he was there while I was running my mouth back at the lab. He saw me spill everything without a second thought. I didn't want him to tell on me. But I also looked at him to apologize. Or at least *look* apologetic without actually revealing to the rest of the group what we both knew.

Andy looked away, refusing to meet my eyes with his own. That moment was like a kick in the gut. It physically stung my brain a little. But he said nothing. Knowing he was keeping my secret—and not happily by the look of him—somehow seemed worse than him saying it. Like I had wronged him by burdening him with this knowledge. Which I had, I suppose.

Elizabeth broke the short silence, saying, "What's it matter *how* they know? Can't be put back in the bottle now."

The girls agreed. The guys just kind of shrugged with indifference.

Andy looked back up, still looking like he swallowed a mouthful of vinegar. "So, what now, then?" he asked no one in particular.

"Whaddya mean?" Birdie asked.

I had come to appreciate Birdie a lot more recently, but the guy always had a tendency to bounce in and out of a conversation, forcing us to explain what was obvious to the rest of us.

"Like—what do we do now?" Andy said slowly. It was weird; it wasn't like him to get so obviously annoyed with Birdie. Or anyone, really. "Where are we gonna go? Where will we sleep? Where will we eat when we run out of pantry snacks, which is going to be soon, ya know. And what's our long-term plan—run away from the switchers for the rest of our lives?" He calmed himself and asked again like it was his first time saying it: "What do we do now?"

Again, no one wanted the full responsibility of the group's actions on them—particularly the *consequences* of those actions. I was ready to call it a day and suggest we sleep on it, circle back around to it in the morning.

I prepped myself to speak up, but as I went to clear my throat, Birdie said, "Let's switch one of them back here. You know, in a careful, controlled way."

He may as well have suggested mass suicide by the way everyone spazzed out about it. There was a barrage of name-calling, insults, and statements of disbelief and anger at how stupid an idea this was to the collective group. Birdie's head dropped in shame as the outrage continued to pour out.

But his idea didn't seem all that bad to me. We could do it like the way TV cops interrogate bad guys.

"Hey, hey, hey," I said. "It's risky, but it has the potential to do a lot of good for us. What's the range on that little switching doohickey? Like, how close do you have to be for it to work?"

Birdie and Evan looked imploringly at the other to answer. Neither did.

Great—they can work it a little, but they don't know anything about it.

"Whatever," I said. "Doesn't matter. Evan isn't part of this from the sound of it. Me and him can go off a ways and wait for the clocks to stick. Then *bam*—switch me, interrogate my switcher, and swap me back ASAP."

"I don't think that's a good idea," Katie said.

"Why? I mean, yeah, the switchers won't like it, but they aren't in a position to hurt me or anything. Not until they're ready for the last switch, anyway."

"I don't know..." she said. "They're probably over there trying to figure out what happened—"

"If they haven't already," Evan said.

"Yeah," she agreed. "So, when one of us switches, they'll just sit back and wait for the next pathway, or whatever, to open..." She crossed her arms. "I don't know—I just don't see it working in our favor."

Andy said, "And we don't know, man. Maybe they *are* ready for their last switch. How would we know?"

Couldn't argue that. Didn't want to, now. They convinced me. At that point I was hoping it would just pass over like one of Birdie's weird mumbly jokes.

"It's not entirely a bad idea," Patricia said, chewing a thumbnail with her arms crossed. "We just need more information before we can do it." She dropped her arms and looked around the group. "Let's hold onto that idea. We might need to use it later."

(*Dammit...*)

"In the meantime," she continued, "maybe we *should* start heading home. Not to our actual homes—probably not much point in that—but to that area. If the switchers are setting up headquarters near down town, home's the best place to go. We can look for a resistance group there, maybe finally get a handle on...all this."

"How are we gonna find a group like that?" Dylan asked. "Walk around yelling, 'Anyone around here in a resistance group? A bunch of kids wanna join the resistance!'"

"Resistance is *futile*," Birdie said. Then, in response to the disapproving stares from the group, "Sorry."

Birdie's awkwardness used to be weird and annoying. But I saw something in it that I hadn't before. By throwing out absurd non sequiturs, he wasn't being socially inept. Not entirely, anyway. It was almost like magic. By the time everyone got past Birdie's strategic interruption, they'd forgotten—or at least moved beyond—the unfinished argument. Not the smoothest way to change the flavor of the conversation, but he made it work.

Finally, after some quiet deliberation, everyone—one by one— agreed to the plan. We settled in for the night, doing our best to get at least *some* rest.

Then...we would be heading home.

CHAPTER
THIRTY-ONE

THE NIGHT AIR in the forest was still and heavy. Tired as I was, I couldn't seem to coax myself to sleep. It took focus to keep my eyes closed. Whenever I lost concentration—*WHAM!*—they would pop back open like pull-down shades. But I remained still.

No one talked. Hardly moved either. No one got up at any time. We all just lay there. Tired. Achy. Nervous.

Mostly nervous, I suppose.

Every so often there'd be a noise in the brush. Or twigs cracking. A few times I swear I could hear something *breathing*. But I told myself it was one of the others, if not just my imagination, and did my best to ignore it.

Through it all, I lay there. Tricking myself into believing it was all going to be alright.

Just be still. Don't make a sound. Don't open your eyes. Eventually it'll be morning.

Just be here, right now. Appreciate the safety of this very moment, however fleeting it *might* be. Just breathe—*in...out...in...out...*

CHAPTER
THIRTY-TWO

I'M SURE EVERYONE—JUST as I had—spent the last hour staring through the trees, waiting to see dark purples and oranges spread up from the horizon, casting a sleepy, pale light. Everyone conveniently pretended to "wake up" at almost the exact same time. Like dominoes in reverse, one person craned up, then another, and another, and ta-da! *Rise and shine, campers!*

We were all up, but no one bothered with the usual, *Good morning! How'd ya sleep last night?* Forget the pleasantries. It was just a handful of tired eyes deeply set into hard, resigned faces. Everyone was up and on their feet quickly. They stretched, readjusted their packs, rubbed the knots out of their necks and shoulders.

"I gotta pee before we get moving," Dylan said. He walked off. The rest of the guys grunted at each other and followed suit.

"Ew," Elizabeth said, genuinely disgusted.

But when we got back, the girls packs were piled neatly together while they were all off in the opposite direction, probably doing the same thing. When they got back, just a few short moments after us, Dylan mockingly said, "Number one or number two?"

They shook their heads, making faces as if they had caught him picking his nose and chowing down on it, but otherwise said nothing.

Birdie quickly jumped in with, "That means number two!"

While we struggled to hold in our laughs, the girls said something to each other, grabbed their bags, and the three of them headed off side-by-side-by-side, leaving us to trail behind them. We scrambled, but quickly caught up and headed onward, towards (or at least in the general direction of) home.

CHAPTER
THIRTY-THREE

I WAS PLEASANTLY surprised at how rested I felt, considering I hadn't slept. We walked peacefully, even making a little bit of chitchat along the way. It went on like that for the better part of the morning.

"So, what's it like over there—where *they* came from?" Evan asked me.

"Uh, not that different really. You know, except for the whole parasite thing."

"Hmm," Evan said. He looked at the ground, scrutinizing his thoughts.

"What?"

"I was expecting you to say something different."

"Like what?"

"I don't know what I was expecting exactly, I guess. I thought maybe there'd be some barren, post-apocalyptic wasteland or something."

"It *could* be like that," Dylan said. "Ya know, in certain areas. We were out in the middle of nowhere. It could've been way worse, in like, city areas."

"Yeah, for sure," Birdie said. "Downtown got hit left and right!"

"Guys," Patricia said, but went ignored under our voices.

217

"Totally," I said. "*Some* of the planes swung out our way, but they *all* took turns on—"

"*GUYS!*" she screamed.

We stopped, looked at her. She said nothing. I was confused for a second, but I heard sniffling. It was Katie.

"Both of her parents work downtown," Elizabeth said. She put her arm around Katie. Katie turned and wept into Elizabeth's shoulder. She did it almost soundlessly. I could hear her long, hiccupy inhale followed by short heaves of exhaled breath. It came in a series of waves, each one harder to listen to than the one before it.

We all offered clumsy, eyes-down apologies. They went ignored.

Dylan—never one for emotion, unless, of course, you count anger—was the first to excuse himself.

"I'm gonna leave my stuff here while I," he thought hard for a moment, "uh—I'll be right back."

At least he didn't say, *I gotta take a dump*, or something worse.

"We'll go with you," Andy said. All of us, even Evan, set our bags down in a pile and followed in his direction.

I turned to the girls, all huddled together, and said, "We're gonna leave our stuff here, so..."

They didn't appear to be paying any attention to us, and I wasn't about to interrupt them. I dropped my bag and ran to catch up to the guys, who were speed walking to catch up with Dylan.

Dylan stopped and spread his feet out. Without any verbal direction given, we simultaneously fanned out, backs facing into a large semicircle, and assumed peeing position. It was kind of impressive, like we had been practicing it or something.

Dylan finished first. I heard him start to walk further away from the girls and our stuff, but I thought little of it. I looked over at him to see what he was up to. He was squinting his eyes a little, looking out into the forest. A few seconds passed. Then Dylan—his voice full of shock and surprise—yelled, "*YOU GUYS!*"

CHAPTER
THIRTY-FOUR

AFRAID WE WERE in some new kind of trouble, my head snapped around to find the cause of the noise. But I quickly noticed Dylan wasn't hurt or running or taking cover or anything.

"You almost made me piss myself," Andy groaned. "What's the BFD?"

Dylan looked at him, jaw hanging open, and simply pointed as a little smile edged up on the corner of his mouth.

"*What,* dude?" Birdie said.

That was when the girls arrived at the scene. They appeared quietly and quickly, probably just as perplexed as I was by the sudden shriek. The worry on their faces disappeared immediately once they saw Dylan pointing at the road like a toddler pointing at the cookie jar.

"Geez," Elizabeth scolded. "We thought something terrible happened..."

"Well, it didn't, so...chill out," Dylan said. "But look." Now Dylan was pointing but emphasizing it by making little jabs at the air with his pointer finger.

Up a slight incline I could make out a small sign. A black and white state highway marker.

"It's 127. We follow that, it'll take us straight to Lansing," Dylan said.

"Yeah, but we *just* talked about how that's the last place we wanna be right now," Patricia said.

"Well, we don't have to go all the way into town. We should see signs telling us when we're getting close—"

"If we even *need* signs," Birdie mumbled to no one. Patricia looked like she wanted to be mad that he would again bring up the state of things downtown, but she bit her lip. He made a good point, and she knew it.

Dylan finished his thought, "—and we can veer off before we get too close. We know we're east of Lansing, so when we start to get kinda close, we start heading southeast. That way we can avoid...whatever."

We all knew US-127. It led into downtown and was the only north-south highway that cut directly through the city. I think it even went all the way to the Mackinac Bridge.

If it's still there.

Dylan walked up the slight hill and stood on the dirt shoulder, taking in the road like it was the first time he had seen such a wonder of modern engineering. Following cautiously behind him, I felt the exact opposite. Where we stood, the highway looked as though it had been neglected for years—potholes, faded paint, grass and weeds sprouting through the web of cracks that spread over the surface like varicose veins.

The girls followed close behind us, more reluctant than us in their half-speed movements. We understood without speaking that there were positives and negatives involved in this. Would there be other people on the roads? Would they be friendly? How would we know? Would we be safer in the woods? Would we be able to find our way back without the road?

Us guys made a quick stop for our bags. Then, without argument or discussion, everyone began the southbound walk on the gravelly shoulder.

CHAPTER
THIRTY-FIVE

THERE WERE STILL TREES EVERYWHERE, but there was an unnatural clearing where the road sat frozen like a dried river of magma. Trees hung forebodingly over the dirt shoulder we traversed, as if they were threatening to swallow us and the road whole. The sun was approaching the middle of the sky and my shirt was beginning to dampen with sweat, my upper lip tasting of bitter salt. The heat by itself was far from unbearable, but the Michigan humidity was, at best, a pain in the ass.

I was still going over the possible consequences in my mind when we started walking. I kept turning things over and over again in my mind. Thinking about what would happen to me. To us. And also wondering if my parents were still alive, and what happened to everyone from school. All my neighbors. Everyone everywhere. All thoughts, regardless of how they started or who they included, ended in a pretty dark place.

"Kurt," Andy said, breaking up my sad, self-indulgent reverie. He sounded like he'd said it a few times before I heard him. "Don't tell me your brain's broken, buddy."

I had either slowed considerably or stopped moving altogether; the whole group had gotten almost fifty feet ahead of me. Without registering what my eyes were seeing, I had been looking down at the heavily cracked line near the edge of the pavement. "No. I was...I just... I'm coming," I said. I picked up a jog and they turned and kept moving.

We walked a long way before we saw much of anything. We eventually came upon a car. It was a gray Volkswagen with a hatchback.

"Guys!" Dylan barked with glee. Rather than finish his thought, he just ran to the car.

"Hey," Andy shouted after him. "Be careful, man!"

We stopped and watched him approach the car. He got behind it in the car's blind spot. He crept up and looked cautiously through the back window. Then he stood upright and smiled at us.

"It's empty," he hollered. He reached for the driver's door handle, pulled it. His mouth opened wide as he slowly opened the door, then peeked in. "Keys are in it, you guys!"

Dylan hopped in. As we closed on the car, we heard the mechanical groans and whines of an engine that won't turn over.

"Of *course* it's out of gas," Patricia said. She stomped passed the car without pausing for a nanosecond. I stopped at the car and put a hand on Dylan's shoulder. He was slumped over with his eyes closed, head on the wheel. I looked in. Whoever left the car there didn't leave much behind except some spare change, a few mixtapes, and some mints with the Lions Club logo on it. Ignoring the change, we each enjoyed a mint and kept moving.

There were other cars every so often, but they were either also out of gas or had no keys. Dylan wanted to give hotwiring one a try, but none of us wanted to waste time doing that. Dylan, while not afraid to steal things occasionally, wasn't mechanically inclined and we were even less inclined to sit by while he got all pissed off trying to figure it out.

After a couple hours hiking along US-127, we finally saw something that lifted our spirits: a roadside used car dealership. There was a painted orange sign, faded and chipped, that said *Big Tom's Luxury Used Cars*. There was a poorly painted picture of a fat man's head, receding hair combed back, with a cigar hanging from his cartoonishly big smile. I've gotta say, the selection—a few dozen cars in all—was anything but luxury. Hell, only one or two, *may*be three of them were visibly free of both dings *and* rust, and even those looked like they had rolled off the production line about the same time I was born. From the look of it, we would be lucky to find one that was fully functional. Not how I envisioned getting my first car. Oh well.

We cautiously walked up to the small building. It was as out in the open as we had been since *it* began, and none of us had to verbalize our discomfort with being so vulnerable. The building looked like it may at one time have been a walk-up ice cream shop or something. Nothing more than a small, light blue, square building with a flat roof angled slightly to the back. The windows, which dominated the storefront, wrapping halfway around the sides, started at the waist-high brick ledge and went all the way up to the roof. There were white and yellow painted letters on the windows indicating the unbelievable deals that were once to be found here, as well as the name of the proprietor and the phone number. One phrase in particular caught my attention:

Act fast—what you see today will be gone tomorrow!!!!!

When the dealer—who I pictured as the fat man from the sign with greasy hair, a cheap suit, a predator's instinct—put those words up, he must have had no idea how true they were.

We all huddled together under the small overhang of the storefront, looking pleadingly at one another for someone to open the door, afraid it may be booby-trapped or some such nonsense. Patricia sighed angrily —her catchphrase—and pulled the steel handle. *Clink, clink, clink.* No go.

"Great…" she said. She put her hands on her hips and turned 180 degrees on her heels.

I started to open my mouth mid-brainstorm for another way to get in when one of the side windows broke violently without warning. The guys ducked—Birdie went belly first completely to the ground. The girls huddled together with their heads down, grabbing on to one another.

I looked to see if anyone had been hurt by whatever force had destroyed the window. *Andy's okay; Birdie's on the ground, but fine; the girls are good; Evan is still here; I'm okay. Where's Dylan?!*

"You're welcome," Dylan said with a sly grin.

"What the hell, dude?" I said.

Dylan said nothing, just raised his eyebrows up and down a few times, still with that shit-eating smirk. He climbed through the window in a careless way that I thought for sure would end with him slicing something open on a jagged, hanging piece of glass. But, as he seems to do, he made it through without much of a problem.

He walked up to the glass door and stood there with a conflicted look on his face that said *Should I or shouldn't I let them in? Hmm...*

"Come on, man. Open up," I said.

He mouthed, *What? WHAT?!* He pointed back and forth between us, mouthing again, *I can't hear you.* He cupped his ear and got close to the door. Patricia smacked at the glass with an open palm. Dylan wasn't expecting it and flinched so bad he almost lost his balance.

We all started laughing. Except Patricia and Dylan. They looked like two wild animals about to fight to the death. Then we heard an engine going full bore down the road. It was coming from the direction we were heading. There was a hill farther south. The car was on the other side of it. We couldn't see it, but we could hear it approaching.

Fast.

We looked from the sound back to Dylan, who was now staring stupidly in the direction of the increasingly loud humming.

"Dude, open the door!" Andy said, shaking the door handle.

"Al*right*, geez," he said. He put his hands to where the inside of the lock was but wasn't doing anything to switch open the latch.

"Come on!" Elizabeth said. Usually calm in all situations, she banged desperately on the door with one fist and one open hand.

"I'm *trying*," Dylan said. "There's no thingy to turn. I need a key or something."

"Quick, everyone through the window," Andy said.

We scurried around the side and started frantically crawling through. Andy grabbed Birdie off the ground and pushed him towards the gaping window. He went clumsily through.

"Here," Evan said, offering a hand to the girls.

Andy flanked the other side of the window and similarly put a hand out. Elizabeth went first, slipping slightly on the narrow frame. She sucked in air and grabbed her calf when she landed inside.

The car engine was a muted scream now, followed by another engine, faint but growing fast.

Patricia went next. Then me. Evan told Andy to go, but he grabbed Evan by the back of the neck, practically throwing him through the window like a WWF wrestler throwing their opponent over the top rope. I fixed my eyes on the crest of the hill, hoping that Andy would make it through before the car, now sounding not so distant, came over the top of the hill. Andy took a few steps back, warning us to move out of the way. He got a sprinter's start and jumped the belly-high wall with ease at almost exactly the same moment the first car came over the hill.

We all grabbed at each other in a motion to push one another down and out of view. Within seconds, the next car came over the hill with such speed the back end wobbled side to side, threatening to go into the ditch before righting itself.

We got into position along the back wall, covered by shadows, where we could see the action unfold through the still-locked glass door. The car giving chase caught up to the lead car almost even to the driveway of the dealership and hit the back end, sending the first car into a screechy, slow spin as it came to a stop.

The second car came to a rolling stop next to the spun-out car.

We took turns looking at each other, waiting for someone to say something. Then someone got out of the lead car.

CHAPTER
THIRTY-SIX

WE ALL DUCKED out of view before we could see who was getting out. I took notice of the tile floor inside the tiny car dealership. It had a muddy hue to it, the sort of brown that looked more like a coffee stain than an intentionally produced color. I was face down on it arching my back to minimize the area my body touched. Yelling coming from out by the cars drew my attention away from the questionable sanitary conditions —I pressed the side of my face into the cold floor tiles.

Four people got out of the chasing car, which looked like a Honda, maybe Toyota. They surrounded the fleeing vehicle—a boxy-looking Chevy idling with three wheels on the dirt shoulder—with guns drawn.

"All of you! Out of the car, now!" They took turns yelling and pointing their guns, their bodies rigid. It felt like watching a live filming of *Cops*.

The driver of the spun-out car turned off the engine. Besides there being a driver (obviously), I could make out a front-seat passenger and at least one person in the backseat. They were frozen. The four gunmen stood strategically positioned at each corner of the car. They were still shouting when the one posted on the rear driver's side cautiously approached the backdoor, opened it, engaged the passenger in a head-lock and dragged him out through the back door. Within seconds the front passengers were out of the car. By the time I heard the door shut, the other gunmen had bound the three passengers' hands and put sacks over their heads.

"What're they doing?" Dylan asked.

"Taking those guys prisoner, looks like," Patricia said.

"*Duh...* But why?"

While we searched for an answer, the captives were sat down cross-legged on the side of the asphalt. The guy flanking the front passenger side pulled a walkie-talkie from his waist and spoke. Listened. Spoke again. Put it away.

"Maybe they're with us," Katie said.

"Whaddya mean, 'with us'?" Dylan barked.

"I mean our switchers. The people who got caught were probably part of the group that we were supposed to meet at the rendezvous point. The guys with the guns are probably the *main group* of switchers."

Everyone mulled that over. It made as much sense as anything I could come up with.

In short time, a white work van with no windows behind the cab—like you might see a plumber drive—pulled up. They put hoods over their captives' heads and loaded them into the back. One of the gunmen talked to the driver of the van for a moment in the same quick rhythm from the walkie talkie conversation. Finally, he nodded and started backpedaling away from the van. Then he stopped, and looked right at the little building we were in.

And pointed right at me.

I grimaced and closed my eyes, hoping I was wrong, that he hadn't seen me.

Us.

I kept my eyes pinched shut.

Go away, go away, go away, go away...

Then the icy pit in my stomach exploded as I heard two sets of vehicle tires crunching their way onto the dealership's gravel parking lot.

CHAPTER
THIRTY-SEVEN

I FORCED my eyes open to see where the cars were, but they weren't within the narrowly confined view of the glass door anymore.

Please, don't let them see the busted window, I prayed.

Andy tapped my shoulder and whispered, "Get up against that wall so they can't see us."

He directed all of us to the side with the intact glass, so (thank God) they must have gone to that side. One of the cars came to a rolling stop next to the building, close enough that the reflection of the sun off the car shone little scraps of light on the ceiling and opposite wall of the building. The engine growled at us for a few seconds before the driver killed it.

Elizabeth startled me by grabbing my hand. Her palm and fingers were warm and sweaty. And soft. A tingle, almost like an electric shock, started at the skin contact and waved through my body. But it didn't last long. The car door opened and shut. A single set of footsteps traced along through the dirt and rocks. Evan reached into Birdie's backpack and pulled out the device.

"What're you doing?" I whisper-yelled.

"We can switch him if he tries to come in."

"You can do that?"

"I can try." He held the device in his hand and looked at his watch. "If a window opens..."

I didn't think that was a great idea, but I didn't have a better one to swap out. The footsteps got louder.

Closer.

The mysterious person's shadow now crept along the floor, running from one end of the room to the other like a spilt drink. Now the shadow was defying gravity, moving up the far wall of the shop.

He put his hands on the glass, his face to his hands, like he was looking through binoculars. We were all bunched into the protective shadow of the wall, but the stranger's shadow was directly above me. All he had to do was look down.

Evan had the device in his hands, ready to tinker with it, but Birdie put a hand over it and shook his head emphatically, looking like a stubborn toddler absolutely refusing to eat broccoli.

Just then the other car honked its horn. Couldn't have been more than twenty feet away. "Al-*right*," the voice complained.

The footsteps shuffled through the parking lot again as the shadow disappeared. Another car door opened and closed, sending the light sparkles on the ceiling into a brief frenzy. Then they started up the engine, revved it once, and drove off.

I was still holding Elizabeth's hand. I looked at her. She looked back at me with something like a smile. Not quite a smile, but a smirk.

As I smiled back, I felt my cheeks go red.

THIRTY-EIGHT

No one moved for several seconds. Elizabeth took her hand away from mine when the tires screeched back onto the pavement. There was no other movement until the engines were a distant, fading sound in the wind. Andy was the first to get up and look out the window.

"They're gone," he said as he stood fully upright.

"What the hell was *that* about?" Dylan asked.

Patricia shook her head. "Before we go anywhere else, we've got to figure out what we're heading into."

"You're right," Andy said. "But how are we gonna do that?"

Don't say it. No no no no no...

"We could do like Kurt said before."

Shit.

"We could switch him out—get some answers from his switcher."

"That sounds kind of dangerous," Elizabeth said. "Are you sure it's a smart thing to do?"

"It was *his* idea," Katie said. "First we should ask if he still even *wants* to."

I looked at Elizabeth. She waited for my answer with a strained, anxious look the others didn't seem to have. I wanted to say no, but at the same time, I didn't want to look like a wuss. Must have been what my mom referred to as "the silly male ego" taking over, saying, *Don't look like a wiener in front of her, stupid!*

"Um...*yeah*," I mumbled, nodding weakly. "Sure."

"What's that, little fella?" Dylan said. "D'you say somethin?"

I tried to sound tough and cool. "Yeah, no, uh...I'm in." I nodded and scoffed. "Totally. Let's do it."

Elizabeth turned away.

Dammit...

Andy turned to Evan and Birdie and asked, "How are we gonna do this?"

Birdie instantly pursed his lips in a don't-ask-me kind of way.

Evan was quick to respond. "The device is pretty simple to operate. My biggest concern is that if anyone besides me uses it, they could end up getting switched. As far as we know, I'm the only one that doesn't have a switcher waiting on the other side, right?" A mix of nods—some easy, some begrudging. "Right, so Kurt and I will have to get away from the rest of the group in order to keep you all out of range of the device."

"How far do we have to be to get out of range of it?" Elizabeth asked.

Evan looked at Birdie. Birdie jumped a little when he realized the spotlight was on him. "Oh, uh, you have to be pretty close—like, within fifty yards or so. Maybe closer."

"Okay, then we should probably be at least two-hundred yards away," Katie said. "Just to be safe."

"Yeah, but then what?" Elizabeth asked. "Evan one-on-one with a switcher—any of us one-on-one with one of them—is dangerous. Right?"

Dylan stuck his chest out. "I'll come too. In case you need help."

"Then *you'd* be at risk," Patricia said. "Or you'd be putting Evan at risk. Or Kurt. Or Both. No good."

Dylan took a long, slow inhale, getting his mouth ready to shoot off. But, to my surprise, he kept quiet. She was right.

"Can you turn it off after the switch?" Elizabeth asked. "Then we can get in close, question him, and skedaddle before you turn that thing back on and get *our* Kurt back."

Birdie and Evan shrugged at each other. "I guess so," Birdie said. It seemed weird—Birdie and Evan were acting all buddy-buddy. Not in an overly friendly way, but more like an old married couple.

"Cool, let's do that then," Andy said. "But we have to restrain him somehow. For our safety."

"What?" I asked. "No. What? What do you mean?"

Dylan said, "My dad taught me this knot—you tie a guy's thumbs together behind his back, then you tie the other end to his big toes, and the more he struggles, the tighter it gets."

No one moved or spoke right away. They stared at Dylan, silently, for ten seconds or so before I started to wonder: Are they actually considering this? I better just tell them I'm not—

"That's a ridiculous thing," Patricia said, her face contorting in a pained look. "What you just said," she sighed and shook the sour expression off her face, "was just so...man, it was just *so unbelievably*—"

Birdie sidestepped conventional manners and cut her off absent-mindedly, raising his hand and saying, "Oooh, oooh, oooh," like he was back in class, trying to answer the question before the teacher finished asking the question.

"*Dude...*" Andy said. He wasn't mad so much, maybe a little embarrassed *for* his cousin's lack of social awareness.

"Oh," Birdie said, looking slightly confused. "Uh...I saw an old cop car towards the back of the lot. If it's still rigged like a cop car, it should have a barricade between the front and back, the back doors should only open from the outside, and all that jazz."

"Well, if our only other choice is that ridiculous thing Dylan said," Patricia said, "then I'm for Birdie's idea."

"Yeah, sorry, man," I said. "But I'm not feeling the thing with the thumbs and the toes..."

"*Whatever*," Dylan mumbled.

Everyone—except Dylan, who, with his arms crossed and his back turned, abstained from voting—agreed.

CHAPTER
THIRTY-NINE

Evan took it upon himself to go check out the cop car.

Having forgotten about our trials getting into the building, Evan pulled hard on the door handle and his hand shot backwards as it slipped off the handle.

"*Durrr...*" Dylan said.

No one—besides him—laughed.

Evan ignored him, grabbed an office chair, and set it in front of the broken window to use as a step ladder. Evan perched in the window frame for a second, then hopped to the ground, landing as loudly as you can without hurting yourself.

Evan was back fast, before any of us had time to say anything to each other, his eyes bright and wide. "It's got the barricade still!" Evan said. "But it's locked. Someone toss me the keys!"

We all stood, but Dylan yelled, "I got it," shouldering his way through the rest of us to the key box on the back wall. While he rummaged through the box, Patricia folded her arms and watched with amused curiosity. Roughly four seconds into his search, Dylan said: "None of the keys are labeled. How the hell is anyone supposed to find anything? *Ugh.* So *stupid.*"

Katie walked over silently and looked over his shoulder. Then she turned to Evan and asked, "What kind of car is it?"

"Uh..." Evan thought about it a second. "Crown Victoria. *Ford!*"

From near the center of the room, she looked at the box again, taking her time to look at all the keys.

"*See*?!" Dylan said, throwing his arms up in the air, then let them go limp and they slapped the sides of his legs.

She said, "Excuse me," while she slipped past Dylan and proceeded to grab all the keys with the Ford logo. There weren't too many. She cradled them in her hands and walked them to the window, transferring them carefully into Evan's hands. "Here," she said. "Hopefully one of these works."

He took the pile of keys, gave them a little shake to settle them in his hands, and walked off.

Patricia still had her arms folded. But now she was looking at Dylan, biting back a smile. Poorly biting it back. It looked worse than if she had just outright laughed at him.

Evan, again, came back super-fast. "Got it on the third try!" he said. "Are you ready, Kurt?"

(*Nope.*) "Yup."

"All right, let's go," Evan said.

My heart tightened.

CHAPTER

FORTY

EVAN SAID SOMETHING, but my ear was buzzing like a hard-struck gong. He looked at me, nodded towards the door, started walking. Autopilot kicked in again. My head felt like it was filling with foam. I couldn't think. My thoughts were stuck in drying cement. We moved briskly but calmly towards the old cruiser. It was blue, no decals or lights on top. The searchlight on the side was still connected, but probably didn't work. Maybe it did. Who knew? And who really *gives* a shit?

Evan opened the door, said something. I got in. Scooched towards the middle. The divider was still up.

"Kurt?" Evan said.

"Huh?"

"You didn't hear any of that, huh?"

"Sorry."

"Nah man, I get it. All I said was: I'm going to wait until they're in the tree line on the other side of the road. Then, whenever the watches stick again, we'll get started. K?"

I nodded. He nodded back.

He looked over the shoulder of the driver's seat, one hand on the wheel, the other on the passenger seat headrest. The device, meanwhile, sat on the dash, just ahead of the steering wheel. Evan turned forward in his seat and took a few breaths, then grabbed the device and set it in his lap. We waited and kept our eyes on our watches. I got bored and kept an eye on how long we were waiting. Shortly after my watch hit the seventeen-minute mark, the second hand started clicking in place.

Evan looked at me through the rearview mirror. "Ready?"

I took a deep breath. Nodded. Let it out slowly. Closed my eyes.

"Here we go," he said.

And I was off.

CHAPTER
FORTY-ONE

I CAME TO, back in Switcherland, with a short but violent spasm. You know those dreams where you fall from some ridiculously tall peak, but then, at the last, impossibly close moment—*whammo*—instantly awake, alert, but not sure where you are, what just happened, or if you're still dreaming? It was like that. And it was weird every time. *Bleh.*

Prior to my surprise visit, I had been standing—or my switcher had been. You know what that woke-up-falling sensation feels like when you're lying or sitting up in bed. Imagine having that but you're upright and flat footed. It's not exactly *easy* to stick the landing on that. But this time I had a little experience. Without lifting a foot off the ground, I braced my knees for the jolty spasm, and I caught myself. I hadn't, however, accounted for the instability of the ground.

It wasn't slippery; my feet held to the surface fine. It was more like trying to stand up on a swing. My feet didn't move uncontrollably. They were firmly fixed to the ground, in theory, but swung around in chaotic swirls under my knees. Like waking up standing on a skateboard, but instead of only moving side-to-side, this thing I was trying to stand on moved every which way. I looked around for something solid to grab onto, but only saw green fluttering leaves swishing in the wind. It turned the sunshine into a strangely disorienting, yet hypnotic strobe light.

As I got my body in sync with my feet, I realized why it felt like I was standing on a swing. Hung from its four corners, up in a tree, I was standing on a large platform. Then, remembering how much I hate heights, I thought, *AAAAGGGGGHHHHH!!!!!*

I felt the same clumsy desperation as when I almost fell off my bike down into the hole. But I wasn't on a bike, didn't have any forward momentum, so I dropped straight and hard onto my stomach, knocking the wind out of me, causing a mild gag-like reflex.

The surface of this thing was wood and felt like the back deck at my house. It was a platform, roughly an eight-foot, maybe ten-foot square. There were rudimentary, but solid-looking safety rails around the edges. Ropes led up into the tree from each corner of the platform. It was basically a tree house that was suspended from the tree rather than built directly into it. There were small but surprisingly complex systems of ropes, pulleys, and knots of different shapes, sizes, and (I assume) purposes.

The pack I carried out from the switcher base was up there, unopened and lying on its side. Same clothes. No aches or pains (or new ones, anyway). I hadn't been drugged that I was aware of. I didn't appear to be being held against my will. *So far, not too bad. But...where am I?* Still laying on my stomach, I looked through the slats towards the ground below. Maybe it was my overall negative feelings about heights, but I swear I must've been close to 100 feet above the ground.

"Hey, boss!" someone on the ground yelled. "Got one comin in hot over here!"

Until they started to scatter, I hadn't noticed the dozen or so people down there. Within seconds of my announcement, they were all out of sight.

I managed to get on my hands and knees. The dangling platform jiggled in a very off-putting way against every movement, big or small, I made.

What is this place?

Then, on the ground below me, I noticed a stocky, bearded man walking in my general direction. He never took his eyes off me.

He came to a stop below my platform and said, "We need to talk."

CHAPTER
FORTY-TWO

I SAID NOTHING, hoping that somehow he might be addressing somebody, *anybody* other than me. I focused on the green, leafy trees all around. I couldn't tell what kind they were, only that they had thick green leaves that, when the wind stopped, were almost able to mute the brightness of the sun completely. I couldn't see through my tree's umbrella-like canopy to see how many—if any—of these platforms there were.

I had a few things to consider. Who is this guy and what does he want? Should I consider these people friendly until proven hostile, or vice versa? What should I be prepared for? What should I do? My thoughts raced on and on.

I took a breath and forced my brain to stay in one lane. *Okay. Think...*

For starters: This dude must be in charge—why else would he show up after someone yelled, "boss"?

"I'm coming up there," the bearded man said. His voice was calm but assertive, like a teacher or a principal.

Better to assume they are not on my side. Why would they be? Okay, then. Should I try to escape?

"Just relax, alright? Nothing to worry about. I think we both have some questions *and* some answers for each other." He bent down around a mess of ropes. "Be right there."

Relax? Nothing to worry about? That sounds like something a farmer would tell a sheep right before slitting its throat...

Down below, the man had grabbed a rope and began fidgeting with it. Hunched as he was, and up almost directly above him as I was, I couldn't tell what he was doing, which did nothing to inspire confidence. I tried to breathe slower, relax. The bearded man stood upright and walked to where the rope was tethered. Before I could make sense of what he was doing, he was coming up towards the platform, shooting up on the rope like Kevin Costner in that forest scene from *Robin Hood: Prince of Thieves.*

Fat chance of escaping now.

As the man got closer, I noticed his beard was scruffy, but not altogether unkempt. Perhaps he had the whole professor look going at one time. But after a while of hiding out in the woods, it was turning into a straight-up hobo beard.

As he neared the end of his ascent, I saw ropes, weights, extra pulleys, and some odds and ends on the ground in the space between the tree trunk and the platform. My mind started to go blank, and an odd thought popped in—this place is kind of like a crappier version of where the Ewoks lived. Birdie would probably love it.

The man was nearing the edge of my platform. In his last second or two before joining me, I scolded myself for having such stupid—and possibly last—thoughts at such a huge moment like this. He was more or less even with me but had yet to step from the rope to the platform. He just hung there looking at me.

"I'm stepping on," he said. "No sudden moves, huh?"

I nodded. He nodded back.

He took his eyes off me, but only for a split second, to get solid footing on the platform. He took a few carefully measured steps from the edge and delicately sat cross-legged opposite me.

I hadn't yet moved from my hands and knees, sitting like a dog does. He said, "You might try sitting..."

Unsure about the wobbly platform, I slowly, and I'm sure clumsily, went from hands and knees onto my butt, to the crabwalk position, and eventually to the same legs crossed, upright position.

He waited patiently until I was settled, then said, "We've been wondering when you'd show up again."

CHAPTER
FORTY-THREE

"What do you mean?" I asked

"You have a habit of...random switching," he said. "I thought we fixed that..."

I didn't know how to respond so I looked down—listening to the rising and falling cycle of leaves purring in the wind. I got lost in the sound, until he spoke again.

"Stay with me, Kurt. Let's try to do this quickly."

"I don't understand," I said.

"We don't have a lot of time, so we'll start with the easy stuff and move along. First, every one of our guys, your switchers, are safe on this end. Is everyone in the group from your PO alright?"

"Yeah. I think so."

"You *think*?"

"Well...they've got my switcher penned up in the back of a cop car so he can't kill anyone or whatever. He wouldn't do that anyway, would he?"

He laughed. "No, I seriously doubt it. If anything, *you're* the one who should be afraid of him. It's you who keeps pissing him off." He smiled and chuckled inaudibly. "But it wouldn't really work to his advantage to kill himself, would it."

I assumed the question was rhetorical, so I started a new line of questioning. "What's really going on with this whole invasion? None of it makes sense."

"You already know about the parasite?" he asked.

I nodded. "Seen it."

"Well, there ya go," he said, as if that explained everything. Case closed.

"Hold up. That doesn't justify murder—whether it's killing people in my PO or switching them here to die."

"Agreed."

Didn't see that coming. I expected some kind of explanation. My face shrunk into its center.

"That wasn't *my* idea," he said. "It wasn't any of our ideas," he said, spreading his arms, as if there were people around. "We're the *good* guys."

"That's what they said, too. I've yet to see proof of it from either of you."

"Fair enough," he said. He put his hand to his chin and stroked his beard. "The guys you met, the switchers, are probably a little rough around the edges—"

"Or total dicks," I said.

His face set into a dark scowl, but quickly softened. He looked down, then laughed a little. The platform shook with his laughter, enough so that my hands went down to keep me from, I don't know...whatever. It was at first scary, but then—once my heart stopped slamming—embarrassing. He noticed and was polite enough to stop causing the platform to swing. But when I looked at his face, something wasn't right. He was still smiling. It was the smile of someone who'd been watching TV for too long and had a dumb permagrin stained on their face.

"Yes," he said. "Alright, yeah. I see where you're coming from. But, having seen where *we're* coming from—at least some of it—can't you maybe cut them, and us, some slack? You had a rude awakening to all of this, I know that. But it's been hell over here, too. And the fighting, like what you saw at the attack on the rendezvous point—it's been going on for a while."

"Wait, was that *your* people who attacked the rendezvous point?" I asked.

"No. Long story short, the people behind the big attacks with the air support and good weapons—they're the...people in power, as it were. Folks who had the most pull right up until everything went sour. Then there's, well, everybody else. The folks in power either invented or found the technology that allows the switching. As you might imagine, that became the only power that mattered—being the gatekeepers to alternate safe dimensions, if you will.

"After the parasite thing started, the people in power started recruiting and training for the invasion that started everything back at your PO. They needed the manpower to help them basically transition themselves *and* their power and authority back to your PO. But they ran into some difficulties."

"What do you mean?" I asked.

"As you can imagine, the rest of the world didn't like the idea of being stuck in a nightmare ravaged by this parasite, while a few got a chance to escape. Especially being stuck there with a bunch of scared, helpless people from a different time and space altogether."

"But," I asked, "if you guys beat them, what would stop you from using the technology to do what they're already doing? They say 'power corrupts,' so who knows *what* effect that kind of power might have if it were to change hands?"

"It's a valid point." All traces of his creepy smile vanished immediately. "But consider the situation as is. It's no good for *anyone*. Ultimately what they want is to kill everyone from my PO who wasn't one of their pawns—probably some that were, too. But ultimately, they couldn't stop us from infiltrating their groups, recruiting more of our own into the fold and all that. Eventually they figured out what was happening and changed direction slightly: trying to find the moles, trying to track our movements, trying to take us out at our meeting points. But, lucky for us, they didn't do a very good job. We know that someone from your little group has a switcher who is covertly aligned with The Alliance."

"Hmm. Wait, is that what the whole 'suspicion confirmed' thing was about?"

"Yep."

"Who is it?"

"If you haven't already figured it out, I probably shouldn't say. My turn—why haven't we been able to switch with anyone from your group?"

"We turned off the device."

"Yeah, but—" he started to say, but opted instead to ask, "why?"

Might as well be honest. "We needed to talk to my switcher. *And* we don't want to be here," I said.

He nodded as though my answer contained some deep, mystical truth that he could uncover if he thought about it hard enough.

"Where is your group now?" his eyebrows went up crazy-high.

"I...don't want to say." *This is too much like the questions at the lab, but this time I ain't sayin nothin.*

"Why?"

"Because *telling* someone you're trustworthy doesn't make you so."

"Fair enough," he said, looking at me like a boxer waiting for the bell to start the fight.

Silence passed between us for a long moment. The wind rose and fell a few more times. I checked my watch to see if I could maybe try to switch again. His face twitched slightly. *He's on to me. Quick—change the subject!*

"I, uh, saw some of the, uh, the people you're talking about. They chased some of your people down in a car. We saw them get hooded, zip-tied, and thrown into the back of a van. Didn't look like anyone was hurt. What are they doing to the people they catch?"

"I don't know," he said, staring off into nothing. "Hold them. Try to get information from them." He looked down. "There's no need to, but they *might* kill them. I just don't know for sure."

"How are you going to stop them?"

He looked at me as if he didn't know if *I* could be trusted. Then, as he was about to say something, someone did a kind of whisper-yell from the ground: "Boss! They're coming up on the village!"

"Looks like you're about to find out," he said.

CHAPTER
FORTY-FOUR

WE BOTH LOOKED DOWN. He stood and told me to do the same. He helped me get to my feet, then walked to the edge of the platform and handed me one of the ropes hanging from a pulley.

"Grab a solid hold and jump off," he said. "It has weights on the other end. You'll go down quick, but not too fast. It's safe. But we must go. *Now.*"

He didn't wait for me to go, or even to respond. As soon as I grabbed the rope from him, he jumped, holding a different rope. He went down so fast I wondered if he was going to hurt himself on the landing.

Immediately upon hitting the ground, he whisper-yelled up to me with soul piercing urgency. "Come *on!*"

As crazy as these tree people might be, I don't know anything about the people coming at us. Except that they most likely want to kill us. Forget *that.*

I moved quickly up to the edge of the platform.

I believe I have mentioned my disdain for heights. Bearing this in mind as I mentally prepared myself for the plunge, I made a strong conscious effort not to let myself scream as I fell. The trip down couldn't have been more than five seconds.

When I hit solid ground again, it felt foreign to me, like stepping on the dock after spending a few hours on a boat—the ground felt like it was moving when it wasn't. So, I had *that* going for me.

"You alright?" the bearded man asked.

I forced myself to let go of the rope, then said, "Yeah. All good."

"Glad to hear it." He started off. "C'mon—walk and talk."

I stood there as the bearded man walked away, roughly a dozen other tree folks gathering around him with bags. And guns.

BAM!

There was a huge explosion a hundred yards or so away. The wind was sucked towards it at first, then eased away, returning to its normal state.

"What the hell was *that*?" I asked in a panic.

Before anyone could answer, all the people I'd seen scattering for cover earlier had come out of hiding to reassemble in our vicinity. A few other people descended from similar platforms with big hiking-style backpacks. When they reached the bottom, they unshouldered their packs and started passing out guns of different sizes to the random...*tree people* that swarmed them.

"Hey! What was that?" I asked again, this time turning to the bearded man and grabbing him by the arms.

"We set up these fake little villages—camps, really—and boobytrap the hell out of em," he said, smiling. "Kind of like a perimeter defense. It's going to cut their numbers and disorient them, but some of them are going to come rampaging through here any time."

"W-what?"

Someone hollered to the bearded man again: "We gotta go, boss."

The man looked at me, registering the look on my face. "Hey, don't worry. It'll be fine, so long as you follow me right now. No questions. We'll send you back once we get through the gauntlet."

"The *what*?"

He didn't answer; he was too busy looking into the part of the forest we were going to be attacked from. Then he tapped me on the shoulder and said, "Let's do this." He jumped a few times, did a few high knees, then started running in the opposite direction from the popcorn sound of gunfire. I couldn't see anyone in the woods, but I could hear the trees in the uncomfortably close distance getting shot, the bullets making meaty thuds and splintering wood in every direction.

I turned to follow the bearded leader of the tree people. He was now about fifteen yards ahead of me, moving with a full head of steam. So, I ran like a crazy person to catch up.

"Hey!" I yelled.

"C'mon!" he yelled back.

The ground was covered with old leaves and twigs, making it difficult to change directions quickly when the bearded man and his small posse moved in aimless zigzags. Not totally aimless—they were incredibly well synchronized, like they had been through this route countless times. They took a hard right around an out-of-place pine tree. In the matter of seconds it took me to get to the pine, they had moved along far enough that I couldn't see them anymore. I stopped and listened, but the sound of them was hard to trace and quickly disappearing.

I knew they hooked a hard right, so I also took one and started, kind of, jogging in their general direction. *Which way did they go?* Panic was starting to set in. I was already sweaty, but I could feel a new sweat—a cold sweat—at my hairline. Even though I could breathe just fine, I had the same panicky feeling you get under water when you run out of air before you make it all the way to the surface. When your arms and legs stop paddling and start clawing like a wounded animal in the throes of death. Then my jog turned to a walk, which turned into a scared and confused stumble.

"*Psst!*"

There was no one in front of me. I snapped around and looked behind me. Didn't see anyone there either.

"*PSST!*"

It was from the direction the tree people had gone. I turned around again. Still couldn't see anyone.

"*Psst! Hey!*" someone said in a whispering yell. It was coming from—

"*Hey! Up here!*"

—*above* me.

I looked up. It was a woman in a pine tree. She was peeking her head and one of her shoulders out. She was difficult to see; she had tactical

249

face paint on. Or possibly mud. Either way, with her skin covered and the pines around her, she might as well have been invisible.

"*That way,*" she pointed, continuing to whisper-scream. "*Keep going all the way down until it turns into a gully. You'll catch up with em at the bottom. You don't have much time. Skedaddle!*"

I nodded and mouthed *Thank you.*

She shooed me away with gritted teeth and a few backhand sweeps. I began slowly backing away, still not sure if I could trust this stranger enough to turn my back on her. *Although...I guess she would've killed me already if she was—*

"*GO!*" she almost broke the whisper barrier. Then, with a constipated frown, she held up a ball. My head went to the side like a perplexed puppy. She rolled her eyes, pretended to throw the ball, then her hand bloomed open while she raised it slowly...

Oh shit! It's a grenade!

She opened her eyes as wide as windows and nodded her head in a mocking *nooooooooow*-I-get-it kind of way.

Her head continued bobbing up and down stupidly like that while I turned and ran like hell.

CHAPTER

FORTY-FIVE

A FEW HUNDRED feet into my sprint, I noticed two things. First, the forest abruptly switched from being solely leafy trees to exclusively pines. Second, the ground was getting steeper and angling to the right. I followed the ground until it leveled out, side-to-side that is. It was still very much downhill and getting irrefutably steeper. But now the ground was beginning to curl up on both sides into the beginning of the gully.

I couldn't see or hear anyone. The only thing I knew for sure was that someone angry was behind me and someone was going to further irritate them with a grenade.

What if there's hundreds of them? They definitely won't take mercy on me after they run the stupid gauntlet.

The further I went, the deeper the gully became until it felt like I was running down the hallway of a sinking ship.

Boom!

Then there was silence, quickly broken by a few seconds of intense gunfire.

Boom!

Boom!

BOOM! BOOM! BOOM!

"Hurry!" a voice yelled from above and slightly behind me. A male voice. "Go. Here they come!"

I looked up over my shoulder for a second. In that second, I saw a handful of people spread amongst the trees on both sides of the gully. But they were on the side of the tree that blinded them from the approaching traffic.

Gunshots echoed overhead from behind me.

I ran harder and faster than ever. The gunshots were cascading through the gauntlet from the top down. The sound of shots moved down the line of the gauntlet like the wave goes through the crowd at a stadium, but slower. Half, maybe quarter speed.

Up ahead of me was a series of downed trees bundled together to make a bridge over the gully. A head poked out above the tree bridge, then quickly back out of sight.

What the...?

At once, four faces popped up with guns jutting out in my direction. Moving full speed—and then some—I went into what I guess you could call a cannonball pose. I cradled my head, elbows meeting in front of my face, and pulled my knees into my chest. I hit the ground, my momentum carrying me through a few crooked somersaults, while an eruption of gunfire broke out just in front of me. The impact was no joke, but I didn't notice the pain. Not right away, that is. Thanks, adrenaline.

CHAPTER
FORTY-SIX

WHILE GUNFIRE EXPLODED in front of, behind, and above me, I rolled to a stop on my side, still bundled tight like a scared roly-poly. Pain broadcast out sharply from my ribs, just below the shoulder. It was sudden and hurt like hell.

I've been shot. This is how I die.

The gunfire stopped. Painful silence flooded my ears.

Two more shots went off. *Pfft. Pfft.* I flinched and the contraction of muscles spat a new wave of pain into my side. I felt for blood.

Nothing.

I looked at my side. No blood, no holes. Just a dirty shirt. On the back of my hand, I felt a half-buried rock. Must've landed on that. I could breathe without unbearable pain, so I probably didn't break anything—just a high-quality bruise from full-sprint cannonballing onto the rocky ground.

I lifted my head to look around. If I hadn't been shot, who had? About fifty yards behind me lay a few dozen people in the familiar black fatigues, most of them dead. A small handful moaned as the life drained out of them. Except for one guy. I saw him in the corner of my vision. He was the only one of the survivors not groaning and doing the worm-on-a-hook dance. No sooner had I focused on him when he, in one motion, rolled onto his side, whipping his backpack around in front of him. His hand dove into the pack, searching madly for the briefest moment. He pulled something out. Clutching it to his chest while the backpack strap hung uselessly from the crook of his elbow.

One of the tree people screamed, *"He's got a device!"*

As the wounded man set about opening the device, a torrent of bullets struck him until they were the only thing making him move. One in the base of his neck—a miffed shot, probably—and then another straight to the head. Lots of other shots followed. Quite a few missed completely, some hitting the dirt and corpses around him. For some reason my first thought was, *I hope he didn't want to have an open casket.* Which was immediately followed up with, *I need to find someplace private to throw up.*

CHAPTER

FORTY-SEVEN

I SLOWLY WALKED AWAY while the tree people closed in to deal with the dying switchers. I found a big tree just out of earshot, got out of sight as best I could, and threw up. There wasn't much to it, really. I dry heaved more than I actually puked.

As I wiped my face clean of sweat and vomit, I heard the bearded man behind me say, "You okay, kid?" It didn't immediately occur to me that I was the recipient of the question—the battle or slaughter or whatever it was still echoed crisply in my mind. "Hey," he said again. "You gonna make it?"

I stood up straight and looked at him. I tried to answer, but my mouth just hung open. My eyes were dry and unfocused. Hands uncontrollably shaky. He stepped right up in front of me. Moved his head side to side and snapped his fingers in front of my face. I knew what he was doing, and I wanted to respond, but it was like I was literally stuck inside my own head, looking through my eyes as if they were windows, unable to control my brain or body. *Maybe this is how the infected people feel.*

He grabbed my head, thumbs and pointers surrounding my ears on both sides, and turned my head this way and that like he was appraising the value of some strange never-before-seen object.

Then he slapped the shit out of me.

"Ow," I said, recoiling from him. Then a fresh wave of pain pulsed through my face. I clutched the side of my face and bowed over slightly, yelling, "*OW!*"

He smiled—again that dumb, fascinated smile—while putting his finger over his mouth to shush me. "C'mon," he said. "We gotta go get our stuff. The next group will be bigger, better armed, and seriously pissed off."

"Wait," I said.

He stopped and turned, gave me a well-let's-have-it-then stare.

Where to start? Well, I can't keep calling him the bearded man.

"What's your name?"

"Seriously?" His eyes squinted and his head cocked to the side.

I didn't know what to do, so I just stood there, waiting for his answer.

"I'm *Evan*."

"Wait..." I mumbled. "You're..."

A knowing half smile crept up one side of his mouth. He wiggled his eyebrows up and down a few times.

"Hold on..." I said.

"Can't," Evan said. "Walk with me. When you finish internalizing all of this, we'll talk more. Right now, gotta keep moving."

We walked with purpose back to the spot where I switched. I kept silent, partly due to the trauma of the whole gauntlet experience, partly because my mind was spinning like the wheel on *The Price Is Right* after learning that my safety lay in the hands of, grown up or not, Evan.

CHAPTER

FORTY-EIGHT

WHILE WE WALKED IN SILENCE, I thought, *Birdie isn't switching. Evan isn't switching. It almost seems like they're working together. Could that be right? They* do *seem to be getting along well back in our PO. Is that where all this started? Are we on an unavoidable loop? No—if we were, why would there be a resistance? There wouldn't be, dummy. But then why—*

"Hey!" Evan barked. He gave me a shove with his forearm.

I had been looking at my feet while my thoughts tornadoed around in my head, and walked right into Evan, who had stopped.

"Oh, uh—sorry."

"Just keep your head up. You could be walking into a lot worse if you're not paying attention." He turned away but kept talking. "This is our place. Or *was*, anyway. We have to get this stuff taken down"—pointing to all the hanging platforms—"and find a new spot."

"We have to carry it all?" I asked.

"No. We have a few vehicles nearby. We'll load up the big stuff, carry what makes sense to carry. First, though, you gotta get back where you belong. Your guys had enough time with *our* guy. Time's up."

"How'd you know we—"

"Because I'm smarter than you."

I was inclined to defend my honor, but I remembered that he was an actual genius. Or closer to being one than me.

"That's why Andy went off script to find *your* switcher," I said. "Because you're the smartest guy around. Right?"

"Smartest *guy*, sure."

"Huh?"

"Katie." He said it very matter of fact. No anger. No jealousy. Just... there it is.

"The quiet one?"

He nodded with an *mm-hmm*. "She's brilliant. As in...a whole other level of intelligence."

"But you went to college in 8th grade."

"Yeah—*about* that. I had two things working in my favor there: One, my dad was in the math department at Michigan State. Two, she turned down the opportunity first. *Then* I got it."

"Why'd she turn it down?"

"Sports. She wanted to play high school sports."

I didn't have to ask if she was any good; she looked stronger and more athletic than most boys our age. And I remember we did a school Olympics once and she came in third in the sprint. Not third for the girls. Third overall. Out of the entire school—girls and boys.

"When you have brains *and* athleticism like that, there's not much worry about how you're going to pay for college. She decided to take her time and enjoy being a kid."

Katie, huh? Interesting.

CHAPTER
FORTY-NINE

"HEY," I said. "Can I ask you something?"

"Shoot."

"Can I trust *anyone?*"

"It's like they say. If you have to ask..."

I twisted my mouth thinking of a better way to ask. "I mean—the people in black, from the base our switchers came from. They don't seem trustworthy."

"They're not."

"C'mon, man. Help me out here. Last thing I saw before we hatched this plan that brought me back here was a car chase. It ended with three people almost getting executed in the middle of the road. We're past the whole just-stay-out-of-our-way thing. We need to know what's going on so we can stay alive, whichever way this thing works out."

"Yeah, you mentioned that," he said dismissively. With more interest he said, "How'd you see a car chase, anyway? Didn't our guys take you out to the middle of nothing?"

"They *did*, but then planes came and bombed the piss out of the rendezvous spot. We had to move. Eventually we came across a road."

Evan looked down the bridge of his nose towards the ground. Then his eyes started doing little figure eights. "Change of plans," he said. "You're not going anywhere."

In less than a minute, trucks began rolling in from every corner of God knows where. Mostly small to midsized pickups. A couple had extended cabs. There was one huge one with exhaust pipes that came up over the cab like you'd see on a semi. It had four wheels in the back instead of two, which some folks call a "dually." Rounding out the fleet was a truck with a long flatbed. Must be for the platforms and whatnot.

Evan directed me to get in the passenger seat of a blue extended-cab pickup and wait for him, while he and the tree people loaded up their camp. They did this calmly, but at the same time, very quickly. It reminded me of the big ant colonies you see on the edge of the sidewalk in summertime—everyone moving in lines, stopping briefly to communicate this or that before hustling back into the groove of things.

Evan returned shortly after I was seated, while the tree people finished loading and tying everything down. He put our packs in the back. Some of his colleagues tossed a few random objects—tarps, ropes, and whatnot—in the remaining bed space while he climbed into the driver's seat.

"You want us to ride along, boss?" one of the tree people asked, looking back and forth between me and Evan.

"Nah," Evan said, closing the door. He stuck his elbow out the already open window and craned his neck to face his underling. "We'll be alright until we get to the next checkpoint. Just make sure everyone is ready to rock. Help whoever's dragging. We'll see all you over there."

"Alright, boss," the guy said. He gave the side of the truck a firm *pat-pat* and backed away with his arms folded. Evan turned the key in the ignition and the truck growled to life. He put it in gear and gave a short two-finger wave as we rolled forward.

CHAPTER

FIFTY

BEFORE LONG, we were on a two-track dirt trail. If you've never seen one before, it's like a bowling lane made of hard, uneven, grassy dirt, with deep-set tire track ruts for gutters. You ride with your tires in the gutters. Anyway, the bumpy tracks made our heads sway like bobble-head dolls. The truck glided over the bumps without effort, but the shocks didn't perform so gracefully. I asked Evan if his people made this trail themselves. "Nah," he said. "It's a seasonal road. Pretty common in northern Michigan." Beyond that it was a quiet ride.

As we came to the first spot where a real road intersected the seasonal one, he slowed the truck to a crawl, and began looking all around—left, right, ahead, behind. Even *up*. Then the truck came to a stop. Then he looked at me. At that point, my brain's security alarm went off.

Something's not right, something's not right, something's not right, something's not right.

The veins in my neck throbbed and my palms started sweating. The breaths coming and going through my nostrils sounded like someone messily shuffling paper around on a carpet.

Evan looked at me. "Easy, killer. We're just coming up to a road. I'm only doing this to be extra cautious. Don't freak out. Not until there's a reason to. Even then, don't. You panic, you don't think right. You don't think right, you get hurt. Got it?"

I nodded and closed my eyes, trying to get my breathing under control while I tried to discreetly wipe the sweat from my palms on my pant legs. With my shirtsleeve, I wiped the sweat from my face. Then I opened my eyes and tried to be cool. The shifter clunked into park and the truck did that little roll that cars do when you let off the brake.

He turned towards me, one hand behind my seat, the other wrist resting on the wheel, hand limply hanging in front of the speedometer.

"Alright kid. Let's have it all out now. Someone's gonna have questions when you go back to your PO. So, before we send you back, let's you and me have a serious Q and A."

Finally. I nodded.

"Why did you switch back here?" he asked.

"I was just supposed to come here long enough for my friends to get some answers from my switcher." I said. "Then they're switching me back."

"Well then this is fortuitous timing," he said with a genuine voice. But he also had an awful shit-eating grin.

Uh-oh. What's he know that I don't?

He reached into a pocket. My eyebrows went up and I stopped breathing, sure he was going to pull out a gun.

"Wha...wha...what are you doing?" I asked, scooching away until my back was up against the door.

"Hey now. *Relax.* I already said we're going to *help* you. *Geez,* kid." He shook his head and took another deep breath. Then he looked at me again and held out his hand that had fished something out of his pocket. "I assume you know what this is."

It was another switching device, nearly identical to the one the *other* Evan had. The whole situation was eerily similar to me and Evan, back in my PO, in that police cruiser, only this somehow felt like looking at a negative of the original picture. Goosebumps pricked up my arms and neck, and my stomach squirmed a bit.

"Yeah," I said. "It looks, I don't know, a little nicer than ours. Almost like we got the cheap knockoff of the brand name kind."

"Ha!" he said, smiling in a proud parent kind of way. "That's actually just about right."

"What do you mean?" I asked.

"Well, the ones we have are from the people you talked about, the ones that dress in black. Yours is a reverse-engineered copy of the original. Spare parts from here and there. Made parts when nothing else would work. It's not pretty, but it works. We got ours from people who defected from The Alliance. Then they helped us make some of our own."

"The Alliance?"

"I'll get there."

"How did the devices end up in my PO?"

"Andy and Patricia switched a few days ahead of the invasion and helped your Evan and Katie make it."

"They were able to make these in one night?"

"Hell no! Took working almost nonstop all weekend."

"That can't be right," I said. "Your switchers only showed up the night before."

"Wow. They *really* left you in the dark, huh?"

I exhaled violently and put my hands over my face.

"Think about it," Evan said. "What day of the week was it on the last day of school, when Andy got hit in the face?"

"Friday."

"And"—using air quotes—"*'the next day.'* Where were your parents? When the bombings started?"

"They were at...oh my God."

"That's *right*; it happened on a Monday. They switched you, too. Only, when you arrived here, they gave you drugs to forget you *were* here. But *your* body was hard at work in your PO that whole time, helping us get a head start on The Alliance."

He graciously remained silent while I took this new information in and accepted it.

"You keep saying 'The Alliance.' Now can you tell me who that is?"

"That cheerful bunch of all-black wearing assholes. The Alliance either invented or discovered—doesn't really matter at this point—the technology that became 'The Device.' It was just after the parasite became a thing. That, too, may or may not have been their doing. Another moot point. Once the parasite spread, people were freaking out. I mean, it was straight-up chaos. People were dying by the truckloads.

"Civilization as *you* know it basically fell apart. Some people were able to evacuate to Alliance bases, but you had to be important or know someone who was. The Alliance protected people, which in turn gave them authority over said people. Not a democratic authority, but more like a dictatorship."

"I can't believe people went for that," I said.

"Not everyone did. But some people were, I don't know, too weak mentally, physically, both. They weren't equipped to care for themselves. But it's not really a surprise, is it? Most people never had to go anywhere for food besides the grocery store, or a restaurant. Surviving the elements, hunting and gathering for food—forget it. So, people sought protection from The Alliance in exchange for loyalty. Anyway...at some point, people who weren't invited into the bases started launching attacks on the bases. But The Alliance was well armed and organized. What started as a battle quickly became a slaughter. From then on it was two opposing factions: The Alliance and everyone else. And everyone else retreated into the wilderness to escape the parasite plaguing the high-density population areas. Fortunately for us, northern Michigan is full of mostly empty space."

"Okay," I sighed. "Were you with The Alliance?"

"No. Andy, Berder, Patricia. They *were*, but they—and pardon the use of the word here—*switched* to our side."

That got me thinking. *That must be why they were so unhelpful—they needed to keep us ignorant until we were safely away from the Alliance base.*

"Alright, kid. Any other questions?"

"How have I been able to switch without a device?" This question had been plaguing me since the first time I did it. *Alright, I finally get some answers.* My fingers twitched with excitement. I bit my lower lip while grown-up Evan searched for the right way to explain this bit of magic.

"I don't know," he admitted.

The answer literally deflated me. I kind of melted into the seat. "What?" It was all I could think to say. So, I said it again. "*What?*"

His eyes narrowed but stayed on me. After some time turning it over in his mind, he said, "I'm not sure. Okay? I have a few theories, but..." He was quiet for a minute. "*Katie.* Katie might know. And in the meantime, I can also run it by Kurt after I switch you back."

I exhaled, long and dramatic-like, through my nose. It made a sound like a running faucet in another room, muted by closed doors and thin walls.

"Don't worry, kid," he said.

I looked at him sideways, jaw clenched.

He continued, "We're on our way to see her now."

He shifted the truck back in gear, looked around one more time, and began rolling the vehicle forward again.

CHAPTER

FIFTY-ONE

WE HAD A QUIET, uneventful drive. The landscape didn't change—leafy
trees here, pine trees there, hills, rocks, leafy plants of green and reddish
colors in the few open spaces. And tall grass on both sides—and the
middle—of the two-track road.

"Where are we headed, anyway?" I asked. Except it stuck in my
throat on the first attempted delivery. I cleared my throat and tried
again.

"I understand you've been jerked around a lot. But for your own
good, as well as a lot of other people's, I probably shouldn't tell you."

I looked back out the window. "Well, I can tell we're headed south.
Why *south*?" I asked. "I thought north was safe."

He looked at me for a moment, then back at the windshield.

"We're not in the *run-to-safety* business, as you may have noticed
from recent events."

"Right, but how can you fight The Alliance? They have planes and
probably way more ammo and stuff."

"Not like what they have in *your* PO."

"Right, but the name, the *Alliance*, kind of implies that there are
probably a lot of them."

"There are," he conceded. "And they're well organized. There are

266

also quite a few of us, and here—here we're on more of an even playing field. It's your PO where we have trouble. They have access to *everything* over there. But *here*," he said. "We're *this close*."

"What about the parasite? Is there any way to stop it?"

"No. It's not a disease you can vaccinate against, or an illness you can treat. That's why everyone is looking for a way to get away from it. We've become pretty good at avoiding it and taking measures to ensure our safety, like all the extra gear Berder had you guys bring. You don't need all that stuff—that's for us. They throw out those air filters on the tents and masks, but you can reuse them a few times if you're smart about it..." he trailed off, checking his watch. He brought the truck to a sharp, but controlled stop, pushing my chest into the seatbelt hard enough to lock it up.

"Alright, kid," Evan's voice sounded strained, verging on panic. "Hate to do this to ya like this, but the window's open."

"Wha-*huh*?"

"The switching window. Gotta send you back to your PO." Behind the steering wheel, he threw the shifter up into park and opened the device. "Listen. Your switcher is running point on this."

Running point? Like, in charge?

"Whatever he wants you guys to know," he jutted his lip out, shook his head, "I'm sure he told the folks at your PO."

"Yeah, but—"

"And don't worry about the"—air quotes—"*accidental switching*; it's probably not as random as you think. I mean, it's not magic. Just go with it until we get it figured out."

"Wait," I said. "What do you mean, not as—"

CHAPTER
FIFTY-TWO

THERE I WAS—BACK in my native body. Before I could process anything, I noticed something: air conditioning. *God,* I missed air conditioning. I also noticed that, although slumped kind of funny, I was buckled into a seatbelt. I looked up and saw a screen between me and the front seat. The police cruiser! I was still in the police cruiser, only now...it was *moving.* And I was buckled into the backseat on the driver's side so the first face I saw was that of the person riding shotgun. I was surprised to see Evan in that seat, looking over his shoulder at me.

"Everything alright?" he said, a little too casually for my liking.

I ignored the question because I couldn't believe what I saw. I asked my own question: *"Birdie's driving?!"*

"Yuppers," Birdie said, grinning at me through the rearview mirror. Then he pumped his fist at me, saying, "And if you don't keep it down back there, *so help me God...*"

"*Huh*?" I said, to which Birdie silently exhaled laughter and shook his head. *He's the funniest guy he knows. What a weirdo.* Rather than engage that stupid line of dialogue, I asked Evan to fill me in on what happened while I was gone, and what was going on now. Last I knew, we weren't sure *what* was going on, but now we were in a car, clearly going *somewhere*, and I was more than a little tired of being the one to figure everything out on the fly.

Evan started by telling me: "Well, you remember that whole 'Your suspicion has been confirmed' bit? Well, that was code. It meant that the rebel switchers' plan to meet up at the rendezvous point had been compromised."

I had to ask, "Compromised how?"

"Apparently," Birdie chimed in, "*someone* got a little bit too blabby back at the base." He stared dramatically at me through the rearview.

Ah damn. I was afraid of the answer, but I needed to know: "Did anyone...get hurt?"

Birdie held eyes on me for a moment. Then him and Evan shared a look of *who's gonna tell him*, which didn't inspire confidence. If anything, with a fresh stomach, it made me feel like I might throw up on the floor of the stupid old cop car.

"Doesn't sound like it," Evan said, breaking the awful silence. "At least, not any more than would've been hurt, anyway. According to your switcher, they were able to stop the information from getting out *just* long enough to escape the base—"

The contamination. It was a setup.

"—but then they had to drop back and punt. Backup plans went into action; everyone who was supposed to meet at the rendezvous point waited just out of harm's reach and countered the would-be attack."

"The gauntlet," I droned.

"The *what*?" Birdie asked.

"The counterattack. I was there. For *part* of it. Never mind..." Then I got upset. "You know, if they had just told us more about what was happening, this never would've—"

"No-no-no-no-no," Evan said in one breath. "Think about it. If you *had* known more, you would've been a serious liability."

"More so than you already were," Birdie said under his breath.

Don't get me wrong, I was glad Birdie wasn't dead or anything, but I was starting to remember why I found him so annoying in the first place.

269

"So, what are we doing now?" I asked. "And," looking around the car, "where's everyone else?"

"Right now, we're waiting for the next part," Birdie said. "And everyone else is in the other car."

I looked between the guys, out the front windshield. Nothing but tattered Michigan two-lane highway. Out the back window I saw a grayish black Honda Accord. I could make out Patricia in the driver's seat with Andy beside her. From this distance I couldn't tell who was who in the backseat, just that there were the appropriate number of obscured, shadowy faces in the back.

I turned back to facing forward and let everything sink in for a second. But these answers were no more answers than anything else I had heard since this whole damn thing began.

"Okay," I said with a sigh. "What is 'the next part'?"

Birdie and Evan looked at each other again, sharing a smile. Then they broke and looked out at the road ahead—still heavily forested highway, approximately halfway between nowhere and BFE.

Birdie said, "We go home."

"*Home?*" I said. "We can't go *home*. First of all, there's probably nothing left but ashes. Second of all, it's *waaaaaay* too dangerous. What are we gonna do if those bombers come back, throw rocks at em?"

"Worked for the Ewoks," Birdie shrugged.

"*Ohmygod*. Shut. Up. Birdie," I said.

"*No*," Evan said in an irritated high pitch voice. "You shut up. He's making a pretty apt comparison. The Empire—with all the tools in the galaxy at their disposal—famously fell thanks to a bunch of those little pygmy bear things that only had rudimentary weaponry. They didn't form in ranks and fight Civil War style, and neither will we. They fought smart and had home field advantage. That's how we're gonna do it, too." Evan waved his hands. "But we're getting ahead of ourselves. Here's what's really going down. All of it. You ready?"

I took a deep breath, exhaled slowly. "Yes."

CHAPTER
FIFTY-THREE

Evan started from the beginning and worked through to the present. According to my switcher, here's the whole story:

In the switchers' PO, that parasitic fungus mutated for reasons unknown and spread to humans. At first, it was treated like a disease—people were quarantined while researchers sought a cure, or at least a treatment. But the quarantine failed, and no real medical options seemed to exist for those who were infected. From that point on it was all about prevention. People who had access to places like the base me and the guys went to started taking cover with whoever else was deemed necessary to be there.

As one might imagine, this system led to fighting between the people in the bases and the people who were forced to live in *unclaimed territory*, which, as it turned out, 'unclaimed' is a term the switchers use that means land the switchers just didn't want. A lot of it is very much claimed indeed, and the term 'unclaimed territory' is just one more affront to the people who are making their own go of it.

Anyway, the bases were originally set up with various methods of inter-base communications systems, but those were all disrupted, or straight up destroyed by the Rebels. From that point, all communication was done the old-fashioned way: Go tell them yourself. Which is why

Lt. Berder told the other switchers we were leaving the base on a communications run.

Sometime shortly before communications were knocked out, the device, as it has come to be known, was either invented or discovered. All the outcasts living on their own got wind of it, thanks to people like our switchers who defected. They couldn't cozy up to the idea of indirectly murdering child versions of themselves, so they banded together with the outcasts who also didn't love this idea, or even the existence of such technology. From there, the newly organized rebels acquired a few devices from defectors, then used reverse technology to make even more. But the important part was finding out about the switching windows.

When he was done explaining, I had to ask, "I've heard some of this, and other parts—I guess I'm not sure what we're supposed to do with that info."

"Hang on," Birdie said. If his smile were any bigger, it would have broken loose from his face. "Tell him the *good* part."

"What's the *good* part?" I asked, skeptical that there could be anything good buried somewhere in all this.

"Well," Evan said, "assuming everything is above board, there might be a way to get back home."

"For *real*," Birdie practically sang.

"Get back for real—meaning..."

"*Meaning*, that if we play these switching windows right, we can use them to go home," Birdie's voice cracked right at the end. His mouth made a shocked **O**. I couldn't help but laugh. Birdie turned his attention back to driving the car, which had swerved mildly over the center lane several times. Normally I would have been more concerned about that, but, hey—traffic was light.

"*May*be we can go home. For real," Evan said. "Still don't trust anyone."

"Forget about that a second," I said. "How does any of what you're talking about work? Do we have to switch POs with someone else? I don't think I could—"

"No, no, no," Birdie jumped back in, turning to look at me. "That's the best part!"

"Whoa!" Evan yelled, grabbing the wheel to correct us off the dirt shoulder. Birdie's face went bright red, and his neck shortened, like a turtle with its head half tucked in. Apparently, all it took to get that kid to stop talking for a minute was a near-death experience. Noted.

Evan spoke, not taking his eyes off Birdie for the first few words. "Word is, if we can get my switcher and Katie's switcher together, they might be able to reroute us back to the beginning of the switching windows."

"What are *switching windows*?" I asked.

"When the device was first used, it started a chain reaction. Kind of like a series of echoes. Every time a window opens, time kind of pauses, which is why clocks stop in place like that."

"*Oh*...okay," I said. "Yeah, I know what you're talking about."

"Each successive window is like an echo of the original. And like an echo, it comes around fewer and farther in between, until, eventually, it stops. If we can get the switchers in the right spot at the right time—hell man, who really knows—we *might* be able to kind of smoosh our realities together."

"*Smoosh them together?*" I asked, the words tasted sour coming out of my mouth.

"That's a dramatic oversimplification. And it's not even a good one," Evan said.

It sounded like pure nonsense. Then again, it was as believable as anything else that had happened.

Birdie shrugged and kept driving.

"Whatever," I said. "What do we have to do?"

"Get back home and wait for the next part of their plan to go into effect."

"And were our switchers kind enough to tell us what the"—I made air quotes—"'*next part*' entails?"

Birdie and Evan looked at each other, this time without any smiles or knowing looks.

"*Greaaat...*" I sighed. "Why start now?"

"I mean," Birdie's voice was meek. "If one of us got caught or something..."

"Yeah?" I said. "Well, what if something happens over in Switcherland? If they all get themselves killed, then what happens to us?"

In a barely voice, Birdie said, "At least we wouldn't have to worry about the parasite..."

I scoffed.

But he wasn't totally wrong.

Hmmm...

I looked back at the car behind us. I thought about the guys, wondered how they were doing with all this. And, if I'm being honest, I found my mind drifting towards Elizabeth, too.

I put my head against the window. Looked out at the grass and wildflowers on the side of the road. Let my thoughts still themselves.

Until the surprisingly-not-defunct CB radio crackled to life.

CHAPTER
FIFTY-FOUR

EXCEPT FOR THE hum of the engine, we had been riding along for a while in welcomed silence. In something like a meditative state, I'd been mindlessly staring out the window right up until the radio's static crackled to life, pulling me back into the moment.

"Unit 19, HQ," said a voice, followed by another crackle of static. The sound quality of the radio was on par with a shitty drive-thru speaker. Evan reached out and turned up the radio to an *almost* uncomfortable level.

A slightly different voice quickly answered, *"Go for 19, over."*

"Where ya at, 19? Over."

"Copy, HQ. We're, uh..." Static, a few seconds of silence, more static, and, *"Yeah, HQ, we're on eastbound I-96, comin up on the Weberville exit. Over."*

"Copy that, 19. Anything to report out there? Over."

"That's a negative, HQ. Roads are clear. Haven't seen any stragglers. Over."

"Copy that, 19. Let us know if that changes. Copy? Over."

"Copy that, HQ. Will do. Over."

"HQ out."

The radio coughed up its final gag of static and went silent. Evan's hand reached for the dial, turned it down half a twist.

FIFTY-FIVE

Wanting to fill the silence, but asking no one in particular, "The radio in this thing still works, huh?"

"The dealer'd probably *just* picked this vehicle up. Mechanic didn't have time to finish gutting it out," Evan said with a shrug. "Not after stripping *all* the police the lights and decals and what have you."

"The *police* probably take that stuff off," Birdie said. "Don't you think?" He looked at each of us. No one responded.

"So, who was that on the radio?" I asked. "Good guys? Bad guys? Not sure?"

"Depends on your perspective, really," Birdie muttered, using his I'm-still-thinking-*as*-I'm-making-this-statement voice.

"Not helpful, dude," I said, scrunching my eyes closed.

"It was the Alliance," Evan said. "If I had to guess, they're probably broadcasting from the State Headquarters right off 496."

"Oh yeah!" Birdie said. "I love driving by there when they're doing tactical driving exercises."

"We only use the radio to listen in. Or occasionally, I *guess*, to spread misinformation."

"'We' spread misinformation? Who's the 'we' in that sentence?" I asked.

Evan turned and looked me in the eyes. His face looked confused, or maybe a little hurt. "The Rebels," he said. "*Duh.*"

"Oh, *duh*. Of course," I said. "Are we sure we wanna take sides in this? How do we know they're not just blowing smoke? You've made it pretty obvious that you don't trust everything they've said to you."

"Their story sounds as good to me as any I've heard."

"Right, but are they being honest, or telling you what you *want* to hear?"

"Doesn't matter," he said. Me and Birdie gave him matching confused, please-continue looks. "They're the ones who aren't trying to kill us in our PO *or* their PO. That's good enough for now. If everything else they're saying is true, that's just icing on the cake, man. They could've killed us if they wanted to. And they probably wouldn't give us switching devices to hold on to if they weren't a little trustworthy. But, I guess, who knows. I'm just weighing my options, and this seems the best."

I couldn't really argue. "Alright then," I said. "What were The Alliance guys talking about?"

Evan said: "They're patrolling the whole Lansing area. Looking for us."

"Well, not *us* us," Birdie added. "But Rebels in general."

Evan looked at Birdie the way someone looks at a mosquito they're about to swat.

"What are we doing, then?" I asked. "I mean, where exactly are we going? *And*...how are we supposed to avoid Unit...19, or...*whoever?*"

"We're going towards John's Rest Stop," Andy said.

"*What?* Why?" I asked.

"It's just outside of town," Evan said. "Not next to anything in particular, so it's a good place to ditch the cars. And, from there, home is straight through the woods," Evan said. "We can walk home, through the trees. If we stay just far enough from the main highways, shouldn't be hard to avoid detection."

"Will we make it home in time?"

"Oh yeah," Evan said. "Should take a *little* while, but we can get home before it gets dark, if we hike straight through."

With that in mind, I sat back, relaxed, and tried—while I still could—to savor the calm and quiet. And the air-conditioning.

CHAPTER
FIFTY-SIX

I DIDN'T FALL COMPLETELY asleep, but swayed back and forth between consciousness and, at best, *semi*-consciousness. But when the old cruiser came to a stop and shifted into park, I knew it was our final destination—so far as the car was concerned. We came to a stop (which began gently, then Birdie planted the brakes at the last second, giving us a small case of whiplash) under a bank of trees, on the dirt shoulder of the country, two-lane road. The road had been consistently tree-lined, not *always* in complete shade—there were patches of sunlight here and there—but well hidden by tree cover. We stopped short of coming to a boundary line, where the forest ends, and civilization begins. A short way up, the forest on the right side of the road abruptly ended to an open expanse of farmland, the circumference of which was circled with wire fence that once contained cows, or sheep, maybe. To the east, where we were headed, was untouched, thick forest.

Evan killed the engine, then he and Birdie got out of the car. I tried to but realized you can't open rear cop car doors from the inside. So, I banged on the driver's side window. Birdie stared blankly at me. Then he gave me a confused, why-don't-you-just-get-*out* kind of look. Behind me, the passenger's side rear door opened.

"Thanks," I said.

"No problem," Evan said.

"*Oh yeah...*" Birdie said. Then he looked me right in the eye and said, "You can't open it from the inside; it's a *police* car."

"*Mm-hmm*," I frustratingly agreed, getting to my feet, and closing the door.

"Hey guys," Andy said. Wasting no time, he addressed the whole group. "We ought to move the cars off the road before we start walking. Better not waste any time either; I think to get home before dark, we should've already left."

"Hold on," I said. "Sorry, still getting my head wrapped around everything. Can I just get a count of who's who? Like, who's from this PO and who's a switcher?"

Elizabeth said, "We're all from here. Originals, no switchers."

"Locals only, dude," Dylan said, trying a little too hard to sound like a badass.

"At least until the next window opens," Katie said. Everyone mumbled and grumbled in agreement.

"Do we know when that'll be?" I asked.

Everyone looked at Evan and Katie, who were looking at each other, both doing math in their heads.

"Tomorrow..." Evan said. "No later than midday."

"As early as...8 or 9," Katie said, staring into space. "No later than... yeah, 11. Noon at the *absolute* latest."

"How'd you know that?" I asked.

"They did it in their heads," Dylan said.

"Did what?"

"*Math*, genius."

"Yeah," I said. "But—"

"You wouldn't get it," Patricia said. She saw the look on my face and said, "I mean, *I* don't get it either. I'm just sayin..."

This Patricia speaks her mind, too, but she's a lot nicer—well, no. Not nicer; not as *mean*.

"Alright," Andy said, clapping his hands together once as if to say, *Good talk, everyone!* "John's Rest Stop is over there. I can *just* see it past that farm a ways. This is as good as it's gonna get. Let's move those cars and get going!"

We shuffled silently to the cars we arrived in, drove back a few hundred feet, and squeezed them into a tight group of fat pines.

We grabbed our backpacks out of the trunks—which were noticeably lighter than when we started—and collectively headed into the woods.

Next stop: Home.

CHAPTER

FIFTY-SEVEN

WE WALKED FOR A WHILE. Andy, Patricia, and Katie had maps and compasses. They passed them back and forth with everyone—one at a time as they asked about routes, times, and distances—except Dylan, who walked behind us the whole time, kicking rocks and sticks.

"Is tomorrow's switching window the last one?" I asked the group.

"No," Evan answered. "But it's the last normal one. After that, things get weird."

"Oh, *that's* when things get weird," Birdie said. "I was starting to wonder..."

"What's that mean—last *normal* one?" I asked.

"The windows have been coming at mathematically predictable intervals," Katie said. "But after tomorrow morning, after the last normal window closes, things kind of spin out of control. It's like...when you cut the head off a chicken, it still runs around for a little while. When the last window closes, the connection between our two POs spasms and flickers out, creating unpredictable, possibly unstable switching windows until, well, until the connection is finally severed."

"How will we know when it's over? For good?" I asked.

"Same way you know when a bag of popcorn is done," Birdie said. "When everything stops."

Birdie's Birdie-ism was at once annoying *and* apt. Kind of like Birdie.

"Okay..." I said. I had one last burning question I wanted to know before we got home. Well, I didn't necessarily *want* to know—more like I *needed* to. "What happens when the connection is gone for good? What happens here, and there?"

"Theoretically speaking?" Katie said.

I nodded.

"One of two things," She sighed. "A: The connection is gone. Wherever you are, you're staying. Things will be the way they are now, and we'll just have to deal with it. Or B: The time between the first window opening and the last one closing is literally eviscerated and everyone goes back to the moment just before the first window was opened. Before there was an established connection. In whichever PO you find yourself."

"Okay," I said. "Everyone in the new timeline...*disappears*?"

"Or gets cast off in a new timeline..."

"Wow. So, if it's B, would we still remember everything that happened?"

"I hope not," Dylan said.

"It would make sense if we didn't remember it," Evan said. "If the time disappears, so would anything attached to it, right?"

"Is consciousness connected to the fabric of space and time?" Elizabeth asked. "I mean, I know there's no answer to that, but that's at the heart of it. Am I wrong?"

Everyone shrugged in non-committance.

"Nah," I said. "You're not wrong."

She smiled at me.

Nice.

"So, if it were B, and you got stuck in the other PO," Dylan said, "you'd become that person—not just be in their body, but you'd actually think you were them?"

"But maybe not," Birdie said. "And it could just as well be A. I wouldn't bet on one or the other."

Katie squinted and twisted her lips again. She bit her cheek and said, "Yeah, I dunno..."

The ensuing silence was thick and oppressively heavy.

Birdie was the first to give, saying, "Hey, do you guys remember *Yikes!* pencils? The ones with the colored wood and goofy designs?"

"Yeah?"

"Yeah," Birdie said. Then he laughed a little, composed himself, and kept walking with his head down.

We all looked at each other with what-the-hell faces. Then Elizabeth started laughing. Then everyone else started laughing.

"Yeah," she said. "And *Umbro* shorts?"

And just like that, we were marching to the sound of light-hearted chitchat.

Say what you want about Birdie—every now and then he throws in a welcomed distraction at just the right time.

PART THREE

CHAPTER
ONE

WE WALKED FOR SOME TIME, talking about nothing in particular. After a while, once the sweat started beading on our foreheads, and our—or at least *my*—feet started to hurt, the conversation died. Except for the occasional, "Where are we on the map now?" or, "No, we're getting off course—we have to go *this* way," and, "*Ugh!* How much farther?" The only sounds were our feet dragging across the ground, our slightly strained breaths, and the rise and fall of the wind through the leaves above.

We crossed a small handful of tiny, empty roads. One small state highway, again, mostly empty. Abandoned cars were still on the pavement. I guess that road wasn't important enough to clear. Even though the coast looked clear, we took our time and made sure. Evan offered to cross first. He went across. We waited several minutes, then the girls all went together. A couple minutes later, me and Dylan went across. Andy and Birdie went last. We huddled in the trees and waited before continuing. No voices. No cars. Nothing.

All good.

Andy straightened up and said, "From here we shouldn't be more than an hour or so from home." He looked around one more time, took a few slow, careful steps, head constantly swiveling. A few steps in, he started walking normally. "C'mon," he said, waving us to follow, which we did.

I kept a close eye on my watch. I didn't say a word, only counted the minutes. *Six minutes—ten percent of the way there. Ten minutes—one-sixth of the way. Twelve minutes—one-fifth. Fifteen minutes—one quarter of the way there.* I played this little game until we hit the full sixty minutes. Then I started keeping track of how much over the hour we were. It took my mind off the pain in my legs and lower back. I just walked in time with the second hand—*one, two, three, four. One, two, three, four...*

An hour or so—as we discussed earlier when we left the cars—turned out to be an hour and twenty-three minutes. I looked through a small clearing, pointed, and said, "There's the water tower! We're home."

"*Almost...*" Evan mumbled. No one acknowledged it. Everyone was frozen in place, their eyes held on the tower. My thoughts had drowned in a powerful current of emotions. I wanted to go home, actually go in my house, see my mom and dad. Take a nap in my bed. Watch TV. Have everything be normal. It couldn't be. But I wanted it to be. But it couldn't be. But—

"How are we gonna do this?" Patricia asked, pulling my mind back to the shore. Then I got lost in how much softer her voice was compared to her switcher's voice. Her face was still stern and intense, but the anger of her switcher had drained away.

"Do what?" I responded.

"Where do we go first?" she asked. "Should we go back to our houses on our own? Go through them each one at a time as a group? Split up into smaller groups? Do we meet up somewhere?"

"I don't think we should split up," Katie said. Looking at her face I could tell she was deep in thought, too. Her mouth hung slightly open. She was looking directly ahead of her as if she were watching something happening twenty feet away. But there was nothing but the trees and the empty spaces between them.

We all agreed that we shouldn't split up, then put on our thinking hats for several seconds. No one was coming up with anything. I shrugged and suggested, "Why don't we stick together and walk through town a little bit? Figure out what's going on."

"That's not a bad idea," Andy said.

"No, it isn't," Elizabeth agreed.

We stood around, nodding in agreement. But nobody moved. Then we started looking at one another, eyebrows raised, waiting for someone to go so we could all follow.

"Well, come *on*, you guys. Geez," Birdie (of all people) said. He marched forward with the closest thing to a brave face he could muster. And I gotta say, it worked—we all started walking.

Walking *home*.

CHAPTER
TWO

WE DECIDED to use the same route that me and Andy's switcher used to leave town. Patricia told us her house was on the edge of town, and that trail went pretty much through her backyard. "We should try my house first, since it's on the way." Unable to think of a compelling reason to say no, we all agreed.

"Do you think I could take a shower and, maybe, borrow a set of clean clothes?" Elizabeth asked.

"Water might not be running," Evan said.

"Even if it is," Katie said, "I'm not sure anyone's been cleaning it."

"So?" Dylan asked. "You don't have to *drink* it."

"Think about it," Birdie said. "I mean, there's no magic filter under the toilet, dude."

Dylan twisted his lips and started walking faster, ahead of the group.

Elizabeth put her hand on my elbow. A shock ran through me, almost making me audibly gasp. She leaned towards me and whispered something like, "Did that *really* make him mad?" I had a difficult time focusing clearly on her words. It didn't matter, anyway—before I had a chance to respond, Patricia broke in and announced, "*We're here!*"

CHAPTER

THREE

THE GROUP VEERED off the trail in Patricia's wake, walking through some brush and wild growth. Not a far walk, but not an easy one either. In the time it took to wonder if there was a better way through, we were clear, looking at the back of her house. It was a two-story house with brownish-yellow siding on the back and sides. I recognized where we were. The house had a brick front with tall rectangular windows that rounded off at the top. I'd never seen it from the back. It had a glass sliding door just off-center from the small, simple deck. We stood, not budging to go forward, on the edge of where the yard met *actual* nature. I had the feeling we were telling ourselves that we were being cautious, looking for signs of trouble before exposing ourselves, but at the same time, it almost felt, I don't know...unnatural maybe—stepping back into civilization after everything we'd seen and been through. Even more troubling than that, was that there were no signs of *anyone*.

"Is it bad, or weird, or...*something* that no one's around?" Patricia's voice bordered on panic. It put her switcher's behavior into perspective. I wasn't thrilled with what we saw—or lack thereof—but I supposed I would've been more upset if it were my silent, empty house. I was starting to think it was a mistake to come back at all. But I didn't say that—what would be the point?

"I wouldn't worry until there's something to worry about," Birdie said. His nonchalance was intended to be calming and assuring, but it came out sounding more condescending than anything.

Patricia glared at him and opened her mouth to let him have it, but before she could, Dylan looked at him and said, "Thanks, *Mom*."

"No problem, little fella," Birdie said, tussling Dylan's hair. Dylan swatted Birdie's arm away with a hard backhand.

Andy stepped towards him, "Whoa..."

But it ended there—at least for Dylan.

Patricia was still visibly upset with Birdie. Sensing this, Andy said, "He didn't mean that the way it sounded."

Patricia *and* Birdie looked at him questioningly. I laughed. Then they were all looking at me.

(*Quick, change the subject!*)

"Maybe we should—if it's okay with you, Patricia—go inside. See if there's something to eat or drink. And," looking at Elizabeth, "like you said, maybe you can get something clean on. After that, we can go a little deeper into the neighborhood, look for all the people."

We went through the yard, up onto the deck, and to the slider.

"It's locked," Patricia said. She cupped her hands around her eyes and pressed her forehead to the glass. "Looks empty. Let's go around front?"

"Hold on..." Evan said. He grabbed the slider's handle in both hands, bent at the waist, butt out, and pulled once, twice, three times. Nothing. "I got this," he said. "I've seen Mike do it before." He wiped his hands on his shirt, grabbed the handle, and pulled again, grunting this time. It didn't go on the first yank, but the second time it bumped on its tracks and slid open with a soft purr.

Evan stepped aside and did the gentlemanly after-you-m'lady gesture. Patricia went in first, reaching for a bank of light switches on the wall by the doorway. She flicked them a few times.

Nothing.

Meanwhile, Elizabeth made her way to the sink, threw open the tap.

Nothing.

"Guess that solves the should-we-or-shouldn't-we on the whole shower debacle," Dylan said to no one.

Patricia made her way towards the garage door. As the door opened, her shoulders slumped and her chin dropped to her chest.

No cars in the garage.

Katie and Elizabeth went to console her. It was awkward for me, probably the other guys too, because we all walked towards the front door to give them space. I looked out the window. The neighborhood was in good shape—*this* part of it, anyway. But it looked odd too. Like a ghost town, or one of those fake neighborhoods—like I saw last summer at Universal Studios.

"Where to now?" I asked, still looking out the tall, narrow window by the front door.

"Your switcher was fairly vague about that," Evan said. "He didn't want us to know too much, so that no one is able to blab about—"

I turned to look at him and he abruptly stopped talking, mouth hanging open with the next word stuck in his throat.

"Sorry, Kurt. I...I wasn't..."

Birdie was quick to avert his eyes, looking at everything *except* me.

"I know what you meant, man," I said. "It's cool. And it makes sense, I guess."

Evan pursed his lips and nodded, looking down at his feet.

Dylan was looking at me throughout the entire exchange, but I couldn't read his face. The girls walked past us and up the stairs. After they disappeared into, I'm guessing, Patricia's room, Andy said, "I think Kurt's place is closest to here. We could swing by there and grab some clean clothes too."

"Pass," Dylan said.

"Why?" Birdie asked. "Because he doesn't have any *No Fear* shirts with food stains?"

Dylan looked Birdie up and down. Smiled, and said, "Whatever..." as he walked away.

The girls opened the door and came down with fresh clothes and brushed hair. I couldn't tell if they had put makeup on or if Elizabeth just looked like that naturally, but they all looked like new and improved versions of themselves. Compared to them, us guys looked like cavemen. Now I really wanted to go to my house, just so I could put on some deodorant, if nothing else.

Andy told the girls the plan about heading to my place. They were indifferent. Birdie finished by saying, "...and maybe we'll see some people on the way."

"Do we *want* to find people?" I asked. The question shot out of me without thinking. I wasn't trying to be a contrarian; I honestly wasn't sure of the answer. Sure there's power in numbers, but is that power going to be with or against us?

"Let's stay behind the houses?" Katie suggested. "Then we can keep an eye out for... what*ever*."

Everyone's eyes darted off in different directions. Some chewed their lips, some scrunched their foreheads. Then everyone, one or two at a time, began meeting eyes again. Everyone nodded and sized each other up. Patricia still looked a little weird, like something else was on her mind, which I understand. I was not looking forward to whatever we might find—or *not* find—at my place.

CHAPTER
FOUR

WE SLIPPED CAREFULLY BACK out into the backyard via the back slider. The guys went out first, the girls took to both sides of Patricia, kind of helping her along while she, I don't know—processed whatever it was that was still on her mind. Anyway, they slid the door back, very slow—too slow—into its place. With our backs against the house, the guys took turns running to the woods, Red Rover style. The girls ran together. It was uneventful and took entirely too long.

CHAPTER

FIVE

WE WALKED through the woods until we had to abandon them for another neighborhood. One of the older ones. The trees were mature, and the yards all had grass and flowers, though they had all become wild and overgrown. Moving carefully from tree to tree, we were trying to stay in the shadows of trees, houses, sheds. As we snuck along the sides of the houses, we also looked inside, not sure what to look *for*, but figuring we'd know it when we saw it.

But house after house offered nothing. No air, running water, signs of life—except a few penned-up hungry house pets. A few dogs barked at us through basement windows. They weren't normal hey-get-out-of-my-yard barks. They were more like I'll-rip-your-face-off-and-eat-it barks. I was scared of and felt bad for them.

But besides that—nothing. There was no one around. We moved in complete silence. I don't know if it felt weird because I had never been around when *no one* was around. Mr. Miller never went anywhere. The Kesten kids were still too little to go to school, so between a rotation of babysitters and their grandma, someone was usually there. The half-finished houses that normally had a hive of workers, hammers clapping and saws roaring, sat in a state of limbo. Everyone had disappeared. Nothing. No one. All gone. Bye-bye.

CHAPTER

SIX

It took a lot longer than it should have—we practically tiptoed all the way there—but we made it to my house fine. The mood on the way was the same as when you're watching a scary movie, waiting for the jump scare. But the longer we waited for it, the more tense things became. And it never came, so....

We went to the slider in the back. Evan went to pull, grabbing the handle and getting in a ready stance. But as he was starting to lean into it, he stood upright, dropped his head, and turned around to us.

"Are any of the windows unlocked?" he asked.

"What?" Patricia asked. "Why? What's wrong with the door?"

I remembered before he said it: My parents put those stupid wooden rods behind the slider so you can't just yank real hard to pry it open. "Pretty simple, ain't it?" my uncle said when he came over and cut them for us. "Now...it might not *stop* a criminal, but it'll at least make em think another time or two about looking for easier prey rather than breaking the window here."

Yeah, thanks; Oakesville was such a hotbed of criminal activity.... (It was probably an excuse to come over and drink beer with dad.)

After assessing that ab-so-*lute*-ly no one was around, we walked around to the front of the house. On our way around front, we were all looking around every which way, as if we heard someone yelling our names, but it was just the anxiety, which, I had noticed, didn't serve the same purpose it once did. I used to get anxiety about missing assignments, and it made me want to crawl into my locker until everyone was gone. But since I had switched a few times, now was heightening my senses. I heard every *whush* and *shush* of the wind. Saw little specks in my peripheral vision that turned out to be far off birds crossing between my eyes and the sun. And I could smell Elizabeth and the other girls' deodorant, or whatever they put on. Every time the wind blew from her to me, I caught a whiff and couldn't help peeking over.

"The front door's open..." Birdie said.

"I think we left it that way," I said. No one moved for several seconds. "I'll go in first."

I wasn't feeling particularly brave, but I felt compelled to see if...I don't know. Just to see, I guess.

I walked through the already open front door, everyone else slowly spilling in behind me, one by one. Dylan was the last one in. He took one last look around and shut the door. Everything looked strangely the same. It felt like looking at a model of my house that wasn't quite to scale. Maybe everything was too small? Or maybe the hallways were a little too wide? Or the paint wasn't exactly the right shade? Familiar, but somehow wrong.

"Hey man, can we get a change of clothes, too?" Birdie asked.

"And likewise," Andy said, wiggling his thumb over his shoulder at the girls, "maybe a shot of deodorant?"

"Yeah," I said, without looking at them. "Upstairs, to your—"

"I'll check the rest of the house real quick first," Dylan said. "And we know where it is; we've been here a million times."

Without any arguments (not like he waited for one, anyway) he quickly and quietly jogged up the stairs and poked his head first, then his whole body into one room. A moment later he was out and doing the same to the next room. The other guys walked past me, thanking me under their breath, a few shoulder pats. Typical show-no-emotion-unless-it's-sports type of stuff. But in that moment, inside what used to be my house, alongside the girls who had cleaned up a little, I noticed how filthy we really all were. Our clothes and skin were dirty. Even the girls, cleaned up or not, had hard set faces. We almost looked like some kind of half human, half animal hybrid. I guess we might have been starting to feel that way, too.

As I went into my room to freshen up, I was overcome by the quiet, and how strange it felt to be in a house again. Back in the woods my eyes shot right to every sound I heard. Automatically. I would go instantly frozen, silent, and on guard if I felt something as simple as a shift in the wind. I was ready to turn and sprint at every second. We had developed another sense that, although meant life and death hours before, seemed useless here in this house. It made me wonder, even if we get out of this place, whether *any* place would ever feel like home again.

Oddly, as bad as I felt for myself, I also felt something new— empathy for the switchers. Not the folks who put the whole little hostile takeover thing together, but the ones caught in the middle.

Our switchers.

Us. Them. Whoever they are.

Dylan gave the all clear as we came back out of my room. He skipped the hygiene pit stop and was on his way back down the stairs, but stopped dead in his tracks about halfway down. His eyes shot wide open and he jabbed his pointer at the front, mouthing "Who. Is. That."

I turned—those senses kicking in, along with a welcomed surge of adrenaline—but only saw the side of someone's head darting into a blur.

Katie was out the door in the time it took me to blink.

CHAPTER

SEVEN

WE STARTED for the door after Katie, who was immediately followed by Dylan. By the time I broke the plane of the front door and got outside, I was just able to catch Katie running around the corner of my house. I ran towards the gap between the houses, bracing myself for a lot of running, but I came to a hard stop when I saw Katie had tackled a person, who was balled up, grunting in pain. Within seconds, everyone was out and gathered around.

Katie crab walked few steps back, then stood by the rest of us.

Dylan took a step forward, and with a scowl demanded, "Where did *you* come from?"

Evan pushed himself in front of Dylan. "*Mike?*" Evan said, in disbelief. Sure enough, it was Mike, cradling his hand that was still recovering from the collision with Andy's face.

As Mike started to stand up, Evan went to him, taking Mike by the arm attached to his good hand, and helping him to his feet. Then, to my surprise, once Mike was up, he gave Evan a hug. Not just a quick one, but they *really* hugged it out.

It felt weird staring at them, so I looked around. Everyone looked a little stunned, except Dylan. He stood completely still, scanning the area with his eyes, turning ever so slowly to take full stock.

"So, what's up?" Evan asked. "Are you okay?"

"Yeah, I'm alright," Mike answered.

"What's going on?" Andy asked. "What were you doing?"

Mike looked at Andy with alarm, knowing he was too hurt and greatly outnumbered if Andy decided he still wasn't cool with what went down behind the 7-Eleven. But as the seconds passed, and Andy didn't make a move, Mike relaxed. A little.

"Hey, man," Mike said. "Listen. About your eye and everything—"

"Don't worry about it," Andy said.

Mike wasn't sure.

"Seriously," Andy said, almost laughing. "We've got bigger problems. And Evan told me you were going through some stuff. We're cool."

Mike shot Evan a hurtful look. Evan shrugged uncomfortably. Mike looked at us, then, kind of shaking his head a little, back at Evan, and said, "Dude..."

"He was sticking up for you," Elizabeth said.

He looked at her with cold indifference. But then he looked down and thought for a few seconds.

"Whatever," Mike said. "Like he said, we've got bigger shit to deal with."

"That's not exactly what he said," Birdie whispered to me.

"Right," Andy said. "So, do you mind telling us—why all the sneakiness?"

"I, uh," Mike started. "Well, I seen you guys back there. Wasn't, you know, sure if it was the real you or those whatever they are." He hesitated to ask, but ultimately did: "Are any of you guys..."

"No," Evan said.

Mike shifted his jaw and gritted his teeth while he looked at us. Finally, he sighed and said, "Well how bout this? We got a spot in the wildlife reserve where me n some other people—who, ya know, made it through the attacks—are camped out. So long's were all cool, you guys can come."

"Did a lot of people make it?" Patricia asked, eyebrows raised, her tone of voice more a plea than a question.

"Nah, not really. I mean, some of the people who were here made it

303

through the attacks. But not too many people who *weren't* here made it back. The roads are useless. Well, I mean—they've got one side of 96 cleared for a stretch, but they patrol it pretty good.

"At first people who made it camped out in the neighborhoods. Some in houses, some in the yards. Things were getting kind of normal after a day or two, but then people started sneaking away after those people did *something* to them."

"*Switchers*," someone whispered.

Mike asked what switchers were. We told him. He didn't fully believe it right away, but Evan brought him around.

"Right around that same time, the people doin all this started stormin through lookin for certain people. Some people tried to fight back. Shit, that old man from the corner house over there—he probably took out close to a dozen of em before they finally got him."

"Mr. Miller?" I asked.

"If you say so. Anyways, stuff started gettin *crazy*, ya know, and so everybody who was still around went into the woods and made a little camp. Where I'm gonna go now. I already grabbed some food to bring back before I saw you guys." Mike kicked at a backpack on the ground that must have fallen off when he was tackled. He bent and picked up the backpack. As he threw it over his shoulder, he asked, "You comin?"

CHAPTER

EIGHT

WE FOLLOWED MIKE. Not because of the fresh deer meat he told us about, or because of the chickens and eggs they took from one of Michigan State University farms out in the middle of nowhere. Although that all sounded great after eating packaged food the last few days. Here's what it mostly came down to: the complete lack of people anywhere in the neighborhood made a compelling case *not* to stay there for the night. We knew someone who had survived *this* long, and they invited us to somewhere that at least offered a façade of safety.

On the way we asked questions in voices that sounded like we were negotiating our terms for officially accepting Mike's invitation.

"How do you even cook anything?" Dylan asked.

"Fire. Unless it don't *need* to be cooked, then, ya know, you just eat it."

"You said you have eggs and meat. What doesn't need to be cooked?" Patricia asked.

"Peanut butter. Spam. Tuna in a can. Fruit or veggies in a can. Just about anything in a can...."

"Seriously? You were breaking into other people's houses to steal from their pantries?" Katie scolded.

"Given the situation," he stopped walking (and so, then, did we) and paused for dramatic effect, "I don't think anyone minds." He resumed walking.

She didn't say anything, but her face showed her mind hadn't changed either—not *really*. We all got moving again.

Seconds later, Mike stopped and put up a hand for us to do the same. I held my breath, bent my knees just a little, and started scanning the area. But then I *heard* it. Right away it sounded like someone slowly turning up the radio on a station that was pure static. But, of course, no one had a radio on. It was the now-forever-unmistakable-sound of a plane approaching in the distance.

"Shit," Mike said. He pointed towards the street corner at the nearest suitable tree—a big pine that had been trimmed up two feet or so off the ground, and ran to it, yelling, "Under the tree—*now!*"

A sharp tickle went off in my stomach, igniting my engine. I ran as fast as I could and slid baseball style under the tree, rolling a few times at the end to make room for everyone who came in diving, rolling, and sliding in behind me. It took a few seconds before the sound got loud enough to indicate the plane was nearly over us. It came from behind us on the right side, passed almost straight overhead, keeping on a straight line until its rumble faded out of existence.

The forest was straight ahead of us, but from where we were, there was a gap of a few hundred yards of zero tree coverage. Had we left even a minute sooner, we would have been spotted by whatever that was.

"Haven't seen one of those in awhile..." Mike said.

"Maybe we oughta just stay put, guys," Dylan said, shrugging his shoulders. "If they're getting active, it's probably not a good idea to be out here."

"Yeah, no," Mike said. "I ain't taking no chances being seen, but I am going back." Andy and Patricia nodded, then we all agreed.

Except Dylan. "I'm telling ya—someone's gonna get hurt..."

"We gotta keep moving, man," Andy said. Dylan stared back at him with mistrustful eyes. Led by Mike, we walked almost half a mile down the road to where the tree line wasn't so far off. When we got to a good spot to cross over to the reserve, not far from our old middle school building, we looked around and listened a few seconds. There hadn't been any other action since that one plane, and we didn't hear or see anything else. We ran until we were well into the darkest part of the shade. Then we ran in a little farther. Until we came to a fence with a little sign posted halfway up it:

PRIVATE PROPERTY
Mich. State Natural Area

And right next to the sign, a large whole that had been cut, rolled open, and pinned in place. And I couldn't help hear Axl Rose screaming, "You know where you are? You're in the jungle baby. You're gonna *diiiii-iiiiiiiiiieeeeeeeee!*"

CHAPTER
NINE

THE PERFECT BODY-SIZED hole in the reserve's boundary fence had been there for a long time. Probably since our burgeoning collective of subdivisions was nothing but woods and cornfields. No one was sure if the sign was there first, or if MSU put the sign there rather than fix the opening. One of those chicken or the egg things, I guess.

We walked through the opening, following Mike. He led us no more than ten, fifteen minutes before the smell of fire-cooked venison streamed into my nose. Once we could smell it, we couldn't get there fast enough. I guess I couldn't speak for the others, but once *I* smelled real, fresh food cooking, I forgot about the dull headache that I'd had the last day or two. I forgot about the pain in my legs and feet. Hunger outweighed everything else. All I thought about was getting to where we were going, taking my shoes off, and eating my weight in deer meat.

We came to a tiny creek and followed it for about five more minutes. When I say the creek was tiny, I mean I could almost spread my legs and stand on both sides of it. I couldn't help but think about the river in the switchers' PO. It popped in my head automatically, but I didn't think about it for long.

"Right up there, everybody," Mike said. Then he yelled up ahead.

"Found some hungry stragglers! Don't worry, I know em—they're cool!"

We looked at Mike like dogs waiting for the *"go get it,"* and he nodded us off towards the fire with the meat hanging over it. But as I got closer, I saw they were using charcoal rather than a proper fire. Probably to minimize the smoke and not give their spot away to the patrolling airplanes.

It was mostly kids. By kids I mean grade school through twenty-somethings. A few bona fide adults were present, but they were clearly the minority. I saw a few faces I recognized, but most were new.

As we walked towards possibly the most delicious smell I've ever encountered, I stopped and looked behind me.

"Are you coming, Evan?" I asked.

He hung back, talking to Mike. "In a minute. You guys go ahead."

I turned and kept walking. I looked over my shoulder and saw Evan inspecting Mike's damaged hand.

CHAPTER
TEN

EVERYONE WAS COMFORTABLY GATHERED around one of the fire pits. There were several spread around a communal area in the middle of all the tents. The entire crew at this camp was, as Birdie put it, "About half-a-dozen dozen." Or six dozen, if you're anyone but Birdie. Dozen is a weird word.

Most folks were finishing dinner around dying charcoals. "Why do you use charcoal instead of wood?" I asked.

"Easier to light. Makes less smoke. Not visible from as far away. Easier to smother to put out. Better for—"

"Point made," Dylan said, getting up and walking away.

"What's his deal?" Mike asked Evan.

"He's always like that."

"Not usually *this* bad," I said.

"No one is really themselves right now, huh?" Katie said, staring into the graying coals.

"What's he doing?" Elizabeth asked.

"Looks like he's smoking a cigarette," Patricia mumbled.

"He's so *cool*," Birdie joked under his breath.

Me and Andy giggled, to Birdie's surprise, while Dylan disappeared into the trees.

Elizabeth finished chewing her last bite of the first freshly cooked anything she'd had since this began. Her face started asking the question before she got the last bite down, forcing her to put her head down and reset. She cleared her throat and asked one of the older people sitting around our pit, probably a mom of one of the kids, "How's everyone doing?"

"How do you mean?" the woman asked. She was probably forty or so but looked older from the dirt stained lines on her face. She looked at Elizabeth like she asked her a riddle or something.

"Health-wise. You know, is everyone healthy? Anyone injured?"

"No injuries to speak of. Though there *is* a nasty little bug that has been going around the last few days."

"Do you have medicine?" Elizabeth asked.

"We do. No shortage of over-the-counter pills around here. Some prescription ones, too. But it doesn't seem to do much bringing temperatures down or breaking their fevers."

"Oh no, I'm sorry to hear that," Elizabeth said, pausing. Then, "Where are the sick people now?"

"We quarantined them. They're in their own tents a little bit downwind of us."

And that was the end of the conversation. Darkness was spreading, and most folks were quick to get to their tents before the light was gone. No one thought much of what was said.

Until the next day.

CHAPTER
ELEVEN

I woke several times in the night—sometimes from forest sounds, but mostly from stress dreams—but fell back asleep, deep and hard, almost as fast as I awoke. Almost like a kid on Christmas Eve, I couldn't stop my mind from thinking about what tomorrow would bring.

At the first hint of light, the whole crew came alive together. While some yawned themselves awake, others set to making a new stack of coals in the barbeque pit in preparation for breakfast. Others retreated into the woods in small groups. One small group grabbed some buckets and plain white t-shirts and began walking towards the creek. Hardly anyone spoke as they began their day.

"Whatcha doin?" I asked one of the kids holding a bucket and shirt.

She looked at me confused, like *what a stupid question*. "Uh...getting *water*."

"From the creek?" I asked.

"*Yeah*." The edges of her lips curled up, but not in a smile. More like the face someone makes when they're constipated.

"What are you going to do with it?"

"Drink it."

"Is that safe?" I asked. We'd drank water from streams and rivers, but that was in places where there wasn't city pollution, and the water wasn't the color of diarrhea.

"We filter it," she said while holding up the shirt, "then we boil it," she said, gesturing towards the pit.

I was going to ask a follow up, but she shook her head and walked away before I could. I watched as her and her friends made their way to the creek, but my attention switched over to the tents that were on the fringe of the camp. The tents with the sick people in them. Someone was moaning in distress.

My fellow travelers were sitting around the pit, with empty cups, save for the instant coffee grounds. They heard the noise, but not all of them responded to it, besides turning their heads. Except Elizabeth. She stood and took a few slow steps toward the tents. She stopped and looked at me, her eyes sad and curious, then started taking more meaningful steps towards the distress sounds.

"Whoa, wait up," I said, tripping as I stood. "I can, uh, come with you or whatever—if you want me to."

She smiled. Kind of. Her mouth was smiling, but the rest of her face wasn't feeling it. She stood sideways from me, waiting for me to join her. When I got next to her, we heard the moan again. Louder this time. Followed by a hacking cough, capped off with a pathetic whimper.

Elizabeth wrapped her hands around my elbow and pulled us closer together. I momentarily forgot what we were doing, until she exhaled in a pained way that sounded, to me, like a sink being turned on and off in a distant room. Between her selfless compassion for others and how pretty she was, I realized—embarrassingly late—I was staring at her and dragging my feet like an idiot. We held eyes for a moment, then her face softened, and she looked, once again, like the girl in the flowery dress back at the hole, before all this really got going. Her anxiety-riddled face was gone, replaced with a kind, knowing smirk. She gave my arm two quick squeezes. "Come on," she said, just above a whisper. She pulled my arm to pick up the pace, then let go of my elbow. And the moment was over.

Trying not to look desperate, I let her get a step or two ahead of me before matching her pace, trying to play it as cool as I could.

One of the adults, another mom by the look of her, was already at the tent, peeking in through a small opening in the zipper flap. She was talking to whoever was inside, but I couldn't make out the words.

"Hello?" Elizabeth said, startling the woman some.

The woman returned her attention to the person in the tent for a few seconds, then zipped the door back up. She took a little time taking the two of us in before she said, "Yes?"

"Sorry," Elizabeth said. "I was just wondering if there's anything we can do to help?"

She kept her eyes on us but spoke over her shoulder, "I'll be right back, Natalie. You rest, sweetie." She motioned for us to follow her as she hurried away from the tent, and so we did. When we were safely out of earshot from the medical area, the woman said, "Some of the people are getting sick. At first it seemed like it was just a cold or something." This appeared to cause her great pain, and she had to compose herself. "But it just keeps getting worse. Raging temperatures. Constant aches. Migraines."

Immediately, an awful thought crossed my mind. In an attempt to hopefully rule out my concern, I pointed to the back of my head and asked, "Is it a certain part of the head that hurts?"

The woman was barely holding back a sobbing fit, but the urge disappeared with my question. Different emotions spun behind her eyes like a roulette wheel. Her head went at an angle as she said, very slowly, "Back of the head. Low down. Almost down to the neck. Why?"

I felt like a trap door had opened beneath me. I tried to hide it and thought for a moment I had.

Then she said, almost in an accusing voice, "*Why?*"

CHAPTER
TWELVE

I SAID SOMETHING LIKE, "I dunno. No reason. Just trying to be helpful." I could tell she didn't buy it, that much was obvious. But she didn't press me, either. She just went and got some water, then went back to the tent to care for her child.

But when she was gone, Elizabeth, who stayed cool in front of the mom, dropped the act and asked, "What do you know that you're not telling her?"

I took a few deep breaths while I weighed out which words to use.

"I think it's spreading," I said.

"What?" she said. "What her kid has?"

"The parasite," I said, voice trailing into a whisper on the last syllable.

"I don't..." but she couldn't finish her thought.

"We should talk this over with the group. See what they think."

She opened her mouth to answer, but only nodded, slowly at first, then more rapidly.

CHAPTER

THIRTEEN

I WALKED with Elizabeth back towards our group. Some were sitting, others standing by the warming pit of coals, waiting for water for coffee to boil.

"Hey Andy," I said. I tried to sound casual, so as not to attract unwanted attention from the rest of the camp. "Can I, uh, talk to you for a second?"

Wiping his tired eyes, he said, "Yeah, what's up?"

"Mmm, maybe over here. Only take a second."

"Can a guy get some coffee first?"

"Andy." Elizabeth said his name like he was a puppy going for a treat before getting the command to do so.

He looked at both of us, eyebrows raised. "Yeah. Fine." He slapped his knees and stood up with dramatic effort.

As we moved away from the rest of the group, I heard a few of them ask Elizabeth, who stayed behind, what was going on.

We were walking, walking, walking, when Andy stopped me and said, "Dude. Not to be a jerk or anything, but—*what?*"

I tried to talk, but words eluded me. I looked around with my mouth silently opening and closing.

"I think you need coffee more than I do," he said. "C'mon. It's on me," he said with a smile. He put a hand on my shoulder, nudging me back towards the group with him.

"It's *here*," I said.

He stopped. "What is?" Then, panicky, he looked at his watch.

"No, not that. Maybe *because* of that..."

"Kurt: I need you to take a breath and make some sense, bud."

Now the rest of the group was watching with mounting interest. I bit my lip and took a breath.

"The parasite. The sick people—I don't think they're sick. I think they're infected."

"They said that, or you said that?"

"I said—"

"*Well, how do you know?*" There was emotion in his voice, but not anger.

I gave him the Reader's Digest version of what I knew about the parasite's symptoms, about the people-in-question's very specific headaches. Andy didn't look convinced, but he wasn't arguing either.

"Well," he said, thinking. "Okay...uh...then, uh...*man*."

"I know," I said.

"Do *they* know?" he asked.

"Didn't seem like it."

"I don't know, man. Do we...do we tell them?"

I looked at my feet and shrugged.

"Damn, dude," he said.

"I know..."

CHAPTER
FOURTEEN

I WASN'T sure how to deliver the news to the rest of our group. First, I'd have to find a clever way to separate them from our new friends. Fortunately, Andy had that part covered.

"Hey! Whaddya say we make ourselves useful?" Andy said, walking up to the group.

Everyone looked at him with their go-on-I'm-listening faces. I tucked back in next to Elizabeth. She gave me a cute little smile while biting on her lower lip. Then I glanced over at Birdie, who gave me the hubba-hubba eyebrows. What a dork—albeit a perceptive dork.

Andy continued. "Let's go collect wood, or...do...*something* helpful."

"Oh, you don't have to do that," one of the grownups said.

"I feel kinda antsy," Andy said. "I just wanna set my mind to a task."

"I s'pose if you just *want* something to do...."

"C'mon, guys—grab your stuff," Andy said, grabbing his bag and walking away without waiting.

"Where's he going?" Patricia asked the group.

"Not far," Elizabeth said. "*C'mon.*"

With a few grunts and groans, everyone got up and followed.

We hadn't walked more than 30 seconds when Andy turned and

stopped us, using a crossing guard gesture. He started looking around. "Where's Evan?"

"Oh, I think saw him at Mike's tent a little while ago," Katie said.

"Which one is Mike's?"

"That one," she said, pointing. "The tannish one with the blue rain cover."

"Alright," he said. "I'm gonna get him real quick. And Mike might be helpful with this, too."

"What can that one-handed asshole help with?" Dylan scoffed.

"About half of what a two-handed asshole can," Birdie mumbled.

Dylan closed his eyes, taking a deep breath and stretching his neck.

"We got it," Elizabeth said, moving away from me. She grabbed Birdie by the arm: "Come on, hot shot. You and I can quick go get Evan and Mike."

Birdie shrugged happily and followed Elizabeth to Mike's tent, while Dylan ground his teeth together and stared him down, shaking his head in slow motion.

A few minutes later we were all together for our "wood gathering" session, or whatever those people thought we were doing. *We don't even need wood.*

Andy didn't waste much time. As soon as we were far enough from the camp, Andy simply said, "Okay, Kurt. Tell em."

"Bah...what?" I said, caught off guard. "Oh. Yeah, so..." and I told em everything I had heard about the parasite's symptoms, and how those symptoms were manifesting themselves in the "sick" people at camp. Then I said it. "I think the parasite is here."

Silence.

I couldn't believe it. No one looked shocked or even the least bit dismayed. They looked like they were doing mental math, maybe, but no obvious signs of mental distress. No disbelief. They just silently stood there, letting it soak in.

Except Dylan. He started to say, "No, it—" but immediately caught the rest of the sentence and swallowed it back down. Mike jumped in and asked, "What the hell are you talking about?"

It took a minute to get Mike caught up, but, after looking at Evan for reassurance, he seemed okay about it all. Well, not *okay*, but—you know what I mean....

THE PEOPLE at camp had the gist of what was happening on the surface —the invasion, the illness—but they didn't know what was happening outside of what they could see right in front of them. Only here, right now. The other points of origin, the whole time-travel-body-swapping thing, and all that stuff were totally and completely out of sight and mind.

The sun was now officially up, casting an otherwise beautiful orange glow from just below the treetops, as if the sun had just come alive somewhere deeper into the forest.

From what Katie and Evan said, we had maybe two hours, give or take, before the last window opened. Then—who knew?

And, almost like she read my thoughts, Katie said, "Hey *guys*? I've been thinking about the last switching window. What's going to happen and—"

"*What* the...?" Mike gasped. "S'that...that the..."

As I spun to see, my heart turned to brick.

There it was.

I say 'it' because it wasn't really a him anymore. Not *just* him. It was the parasite, looking curiously at us through the tired eyes of an early-elementary aged little boy, dressed in dirty clothes, with mussed up hair. After taking us in, its left shoulder convulsed a few times. Its knees bent and straightened. It tipped its head back and over. Its chin was almost touching its left shoulder. Then all its muscles tightened and contracted for just a second, shooting its head upright again, causing the group to startle and jump back a step.

My eyes darted to see what it looked at—a tall, dead tree, whose leafless branches shot out in every direction but down. It's dried-out bark covered in patches of bluish-gray fungus.

The boy's parasite-controlled body stood straight as it turned to its left and rigidly began walking towards the tree.

"What's going on?" Mike asked. His breathing was shallow and rapid. "What's-ee *doin*? What's happening?"

"We have to kill it," Dylan said. "Before it spreads. We *have* to."

"*What?!*" Mike said, "We don't even know who that is."

"If he's not from this camp, we don't need to tell anyone. We just need to take care of it. *Dammit*. Then go looking for more. It'll spread fast if we don't," Dylan said.

"It's true," I said. "Not that that's what we should do, but that *is* what they said they have to do over there."

"Who's 'they'?" Mike asked, his voice going up an octave.

"The switchers," Dylan said. "What do you hunt with out here?"

Mike couldn't say anything. He just stood there, looking at Dylan, his uncooperating mouth frozen as he tried to speak.

"*Hello?*" he said, waving his hand in front of his face.

"Uh," he said, searching his mind for his sanity. "A, uh...hunting... a bow and crossbow back in my tent."

"Go grab em," Dylan said.

"He can't go back there looking like that," Elizabeth said. Mike's face was riddled with confusion and anxiety.

"I'll get it," Evan offered.

"No," Katie said. "That would be weird. Mike, you should get it. Evan, you can go with him; they've seen the two of you together enough. If anyone asks, tell them we're going to try to go hunting to help out. That'll give us a lot of time before anyone starts wondering where we all are."

Evan nodded. "Come on, man," he said, putting a gentle hand on Mike's neck. "It's gonna be fine, alright? Let's go."

Once Mike and Evan were gone, Birdie asked, "So who's gonna do it?" He looked like a little kid who couldn't find his mom at the grocery store.

We looked amongst ourselves, waiting for a brave soul to volunteer and remove the burden from the rest of us. Except Katie—she was looking at the ground just out in front of her, eyes searching back and forth as she gnawed on the end of her thumb. "Maybe," she said. "None of us will have to."

"What do you mean?" Elizabeth asked, head cocked, mouth hanging slightly open.

Katie looked at me. "Do you know how long it takes before the parasite will spread from that boy out to everyone else?"

"It'll climb the tree, kill the kid, and start from there. But I don't know how long it takes. Couple hours. Couple days. I'm really not sure."

She nodded and thought some more.

"Do you know how long from the time a person gets infected before the parasite takes over and they...become like *that*?"

"At least a day. Probably a few," I said. "Why?"

Mike and Evan were close by, making their way back to us. Katie waited for them to rejoin us before she continued.

"The crossbow here should, ya know, do the job," Mike said, holding the weapon over his head. "I should take the shot. You guys'd probably miss, and I don't want to waste these." He dropped a bag of arrows (what do you call that, a quiver?) to the ground and held the crossbow out for someone to grab.

"Hold that thought, Mike," Andy said. Mike tilted his head and gave an inquiring look. "Katie said it might not be necessary."

"How so?" Evan asked.

CHAPTER

FIFTEEN

"SUPERPOSITION," Katie said.

"What do you mean?" Evan asked.

"Superposition," Katie calmly repeated. "It's a theory in quantum mechanics—"

"How do you know stuff like that?" Dylan barked.

"What do you mean?" she asked.

"You're a switcher, aren't you?" He leaned in and his eyes narrowed. "You wouldn't know about stuff like that. Guys, don't listen—"

"*Dude!*" Elizabeth said. "She's not a switcher, she's just really really smart."

Dylan looked at us guys. "Hey, guys. Come. *On.*"

"I know what superposition is too, Dylan," Evan said. "It's not a big deal."

"Yeah," Birdie said. "Even *I've* heard of it."

"Where'd *you* hear about it?" Dylan asked.

"NPR," Birdie answered.

"Why do you listen to NPR?"

"*Mm*-mm. Why *don't* you?"

"Hold on, guys," Patricia said. She turned and looked at Katie. "In the interest of time, I have to ask you two questions. If I miss anything, let me know. First, does anyone know *what* is going to happen once the last window closes? Second, what about the timing of everything? I mean, if we can figure out when it opens *and* how long, we won't know how much time that passes *while* it's open. Not with our stupid watches that stick while it's happening."

"Oh!" Birdie said. "We could use my watch." He held up the back of his wrist, showing off an oddly large digital watch.

"Hey!" Dylan said, grabbing Birdie's arm for a closer look. "Why do you have a digital watch?"

"I *like* it," Birdie said.

"But you called out windows opening before," I said. "How'd you do that, then?"

"Huh? *Oh.* Yeah, I have another, uh, *non*-digital watch," he pulled his arm away from Dylan, "that Andy's switcher gave me. But now that it's almost over and I'm with you guys, I just wanted to wear mine again. The other one's in my bag." He reached behind him and patted the bottom of his backpack.

Katie walked over to Dylan. "Can I see it?" she asked.

"Sure," he answered, shoving the watch in her face.

She ignored the personal bubble invasion, saying, "Your watch. It's fast. Birdie..." Katie said, a flash in her eyes. "Have you adjusted your analog watch at all since the first window opened?"

"No."

"Have you changed the time at all on your digital watch?"

"Nope. Why?"

"Because the time kept going on the digital watch when it stopped on the analog watch..."

"*Shoot*," Birdie said, shaking his head. "That's why it's slow." He slung the bag off his shoulder. "Hang on, let me fix it a second." He knelt on one knee and began unzipping his bag.

"Wait," Katie said. "I think I have an idea..."

CHAPTER

SIXTEEN

WHILE KATIE, Evan, and Birdie talked and drew with sticks on a creek bed, the rest of us sat around in a circle, just out of listening distance.

"They've been over there a while now," Dylan said. "I think we should be talking about what *we're* gonna do here pretty soon?"

"Don't you think that's what *they're* doing?" Patricia said with an almost accusatory tone.

"That's what I'm talking about," Dylan said. "Why's it that Evan, Katie, and Birdie have all the say?"

"Evan's *real* smart, man," Mike said. "Like, *genius*-y smart."

"So's Katie," Elizabeth said.

"Nah, not like Evan," Mike said, making Evan smile. Mike continued: "Smart, sure, but—"

"No, seriously," I said. "I talked to Evan's switcher. He even said Katie's the brains."

Evan's smile vanished as his lips twisted together towards the side of his mouth.

"*No shit?* Wow," Mike said, looking impressed. Until he looked at Evan, then he went back to poker face.

"What about Birdie, then?" Dylan complained. "He hasn't switched at all? I'll bet he did at the beginning and his switcher's been here ever since. Evan's switcher is out there somewhere on the other side of the same stick, trying to get back to here. So's Katie's. And even if Birdie isn't a switcher, he's obviously—"

"Hey, leave him alone," Elizabeth said. "Birdie's actually pretty smart, too. We took stats together at the high school this past year. He got close to, if not over, a hundred percent."

"He comes over to my house a lot after school until his mom gets home," Andy said. "I've seen him do his math homework. Watching him go through his math homework was like watching someone write a letter. *Whoosh.*"

"Particularly with statistics and probabilities," Elizabeth said.

"*That's* probably why he hasn't switched. He's too valuable to send out into the field. Unlike some people," Patricia said.

Dylan looked at us and grunted. Then he turned and walked away from us. But just before he turned, a grin went up one side of his mouth with a humorless giggle. I figured he either left to, I don't know, calm down or pout. Or a little of both.

I waited until I couldn't hear him stomping away, and even then I whispered, "You think there's anything to what Dylan was saying?"

"Nah," Andy said at full volume, brushing the idea away with his hand. "Birdie could tell when I wasn't me. I think I could tell if he wasn't him. Dylan's just being extra special right now. Pretend he's not here."

"Yeah, I guess," I said. "I dunno—I guess, if I'm being honest, I'm a little worried, too. This close to crunch time—I'm anxious to have a plan. Ya know?"

"Well," Elizabeth said. "Doesn't look like you'll need to wait much longer. Here they come."

CHAPTER

SEVENTEEN

WE STOOD as Katie and Evan walked over, side by side, Birdie trailing a few steps behind—eyes wandering, looking generally distracted. Not atypical of Birdie. Katie and Evan looked energized. Almost happy. But Birdie's attention was elsewhere. I followed his eyes. That parasite-controlled kid had lodged himself way up near the top of the tree. He'd already clamped his mouth into the dry splintery wood. His eyes were open. He looked nonchalant—the same look in his eyes he might've had when he was watching tv.

"Alright," Katie said. Her voice snapped me back into the moment. She took a breath and continued, "When the window opens, it's going to be a matter of getting in the right place. We have to be in the right place at the right time. So basically, when the window closes, if we're where we're supposed to be..."

"What?" Elizabeth said.

"Well, it's tricky," Katie said with a strained forehead. "When the window closes, we will end up in one of two places: our PO at the moment *just* before the first switching window opened, or the switchers' PO at the exact moment the last window closes. All the time between the first and last window—and the plane of existence in which it passed—will ripple and fade out of existence completely or keep going as a new timeline. Am I making sense?"

No one said otherwise, but no one showed any signs of comprehension either. Myself included.

"It all comes down to superposition," Katie said. "Basically, it's the theory that something can exist in two places at once, but not permanently. When the last window closes, different things might happen."

"Different things to different people, possibly," Evan added. "So, based on what we know, we believe that whoever is *here* when the window closes for good will go back to our PO."

"*If...*" Katie said.

"Yeah—if." Evan nodded. "*If* you switched. At. All. Then being in this newly created timeline will send you back to where the first window opened, at that old house behind the 7-Eleven."

"*Or...*" Katie said.

"Right," Evan said, "Or you'll cease to exist, or exist solely in this newly created timeline."

"Yeah, so...there's a pretty big difference between those options," Patricia said.

"Right," Andy said, shrugging, "but that's what we got. So...."

"Pretty much," Katie said. "And if we're right, then the switchers must know that. So, we need to make sure they can't switch us back over there. Then wait it out."

I started to worry that I might randomly switch in the last window and get stuck in the switchers' parasite-infested PO. That made me think of something Evan's switcher told me about my seemingly random switching—it's not as random as it seems. I missed a whole weekend the first time I switched, and the switchers were building devices the whole time. They had some kind of prototype to work from.

I dropped to both knees and dropped my backpack on the ground. I unzipped it and dumped it out upside down. I started spreading everything out. A few snacks, water bottle, some socks and underwear, and not much else.

Hmm...

"We only have the one device, right?" I asked.

"Yup," Birdie said with a grin, patting his pack.

"Are we sure about that?"

"Whaddya mean?" Andy asked.

"Evan's switchers said there's probably a simple reason why I was switching when I wasn't supposed to. I've thought about all the crazy reasons it might be happening, but I haven't thought about the simplest one: there's another device somewhere. I thought maybe I had it, since I was the one it was affecting, but I don't see it."

Andy looked around at everyone. "Check your bags!"

Everyone dumped their bags, the girls a little more carefully than the boys. Nothing. We checked the bags of the people on both sides of us, just to be sure. Nothing.

"What about Dylan's bag," Patricia said.

He'd left it when he walked away in a huff.

Andy turned and looked for him. "Dylan! Where ya at, man?"

Silence.

I grabbed his bag.

"What are you doing?" Birdie asked.

"Playing the piano, Birdie," I barked.

"Huh?" he said.

I dumped the bag out close to the ground with a few shakes, then dropped it next to the pile. A couple plastic water bottles, a few packs of cigarettes, lighters, change of socks and underwear. A few granola bars and whatnot. Nothing interesting. I picked up the bag to put the stuff back in before Dylan came back. No harm no foul.

But the bag seemed a little too heavy to be empty. I patted it and felt something on the inside, like a small portable radio or something.

I opened the bag and found an awkwardly sized pocket on the inside, maybe big enough for a small pencil box or something. I opened it.

"What're you doing?" Andy asked me.

I held up a just-a-second finger, then used the same hand to fish out a rectangular box. It was some kind of machine, Frankenstein'd together with what looked like household appliance parts.

"What is that?" Katie asked.

329

Birdie scooched through Evan and Katie. "Hey," he said. *"There* that is."

CHAPTER
EIGHTEEN

"THERE *WHAT* IS?" Katie asked.

"The original," Evan said.

"We stashed it back where we found it after we made a copy," Birdie said. "I thought The Alliance blew it up."

"Obviously not," Mike said.

"Heh," Birdie hummed, smooshing his lips to the side while he bit his cheek.

"What's the deal with it?" I asked.

"Birdie found it in the basement of the house behind the 7-Eleven," Evan said.

"Yeah," Birdie said. "Remember when Andy and I went down there? *That* was down there."

I looked at Andy. His face looked frozen in a funny way. Except his eyes, they were moving around while he put it back together in his head. "Yeah, that...that's right," he said. "I went in after him. By the time I got down there, he'd been there a minute."

"I already found it when I yelled up to you guys that I was okay," Birdie said. "Lights started going off just after I got down there. It was under the stairs, sitting up against the wall. I went over to look at it. Just before Andy started down the stairs, I picked it up."

"Yeah, and he had it when I got down there," Andy said. "He was sitting on his knees, kind of holding it in his lap. I was about to ask him what it was, but I passed out. Or thought that's what happened."

"Yeah," Birdie said. "I got up to help him and the device fell on the ground. He got up quickly, though. Like nothing had...well, you know what it looks like when someone switches. Anyway, he said, 'Where is it?' and I figured he meant the thing I was holding onto—the device. I turned and looked where it had fallen off my lap onto the ground. It wasn't lit up anymore, so I thought, whatever it was, I'd broken it. But I picked it up and gave it to him anyway."

"Then you ran out of the house like it was on fire," I said. "What was that about?"

"Oh yeah. Andy—or his switcher, rather—told me to. He said, 'Run out of here saying...*something* happened to me. Something that'll freak out Mike and Evan so they'll take off.'"

"He told you to say *something* happened, so you literally said *something happened?*" Mike ridiculed.

"Worked," Birdie said with a shrug. "*Aaaaaa*-nyway, he had me take the device back to my house. Said to leave it by the front door for him to get later, and act like nothing at all happened when I got home. Just act normal and he'd come by and give me a thumbs up if everything was fine. And he did. So, I thought everything was cool.

"The next day he came over to my house. *Early.* Then we went to get you guys. I stayed on my bike in your driveway. He took the device out of his bag and went and stood under your window, looking at his watch. After a little time went by, he looked up from his watch and the lights on the device turned on again. He messed with it a little. Then he put it away and went to your door. When he rang the bell, Kurt's mom answered in her robe. She was telling Andy it was too early to come over, and Kurt was still asleep, and all that. Then Kurt came running out of the house. Crazy, huh? He switched you while you were asleep and switched you back when you were asleep. Stole you from your own body, inside your own house, and you didn't even know it. Kinda the perfect crime, huh?"

"You guys," Katie said. "My watch is doing it again. We gotta turn those off."

"Easy-peasy, this one's already off," Birdie said, waving it in the air.

I jostled mine around, back and forth in my hands. "Guys," I said. "Hey, uh—I'm not sure what I'm doing."

"It's not that different from the other one," Evan said. He started walking towards me.

"I'm closer; I got it," Birdie said. He set his device down on top of his bag and came to help me.

"Birdie," Dylan yelled from behind Mike and Evan. "Stop."

Birdie completely ignored Dylan and kept walking, stopping next to me.

"Birdie!" Dylan commanded. "Don't. Touch. The device."

Birdie answered back. "*Dude*...we have to make sure," he paused as he squatted down next to me and grabbed the device, "that the switchers don't—"

Birdie was suddenly rocked back onto his butt, dropping the device in front of him between his legs. He stared down at his chest, in shock, at the small arrow sticking out.

While we weren't paying attention, Dylan snuck behind Mike and Evan, grabbed the crossbow that Mike must've set down at some point, and shot Birdie with it.

"I told you to stop," Dylan said.

CHAPTER
NINETEEN

"WHAT ARE YOU *DOING?!*" Andy yelled. He rushed to Birdie's side, while Dylan quickly reloaded.

"What I came here to do," Dylan said. "Get away from the parasite. Now Kurt—I see you looking at that device." Dylan's switcher pointed the crossbow at me. "Don't be stupid."

"If you kill any of us, your friends'll get stuck in your PO," Katie said.

"That's why I didn't kill any of my friends' switchers."

"I just don't understand how you could do this to us. To anyone," Elizabeth said.

"Spend enough time in my PO. It'll make sense. Besides, you got a few bright bulbs here. Maybe someday you'll get a chance to switch out to a new PO."

"We wouldn't do that," Patricia said.

"Yeah," Birdie strained. "You dick."

"No need for name calling, young man," Dylan sarcastically shook his head.

"This looks bad," Andy said, looking over Birdie. "We have to switch him or he might..."

"Oooh," Dylan said. "Yeah, that's not gonna happen. His switcher is on the naughty list."

"What the hell does that mean?" Andy asked.

"He was aiding the enemy. That's a no-no."

"Yay me," Birdie said, followed by a wet cough.

"Besides," Dylan continued. "He wouldn't have come, anyway—not without his kid somehow being able to come, too."

Was that his kid he was giving the dad voice to in the supply room?"

I gathered my thoughts around our present situation, and asked Katie, "So, if he dies *here*, what happens when the last switching window closes?"

"I— I don't know for sure—I..."

Keeping his weapon up, Dylan started moving around the group, in my direction.

"What are you doing?" I asked.

"Well, I can't leave the devices with you, can I? Even the shitty one that hardly ever works right. I had it in Kurt's bag, but every time he bumped the damn thing it switched him."

The sound of planes rumbled somewhere far off. Dylan frowned.

"Calmly put both devices in my bag and give it here, please and thank you."

There was a brief silence, during which nobody moved. The planes were getting steadily louder.

"*Now!*" Dylan yelled.

"Fine," Andy said. "I'll give em to ya."

"Easy..." Dylan said.

Andy grabbed Birdie's device, then walked over to me and grabbed mine off the ground. He stuffed them into the backpack, taking no care in the process.

"I said *easy*, dammit," Dylan complained.

"Oh yeah, sure thing," Andy said, a little too casually. Then, without even zipping the bag shut, tossed it with a high arch, slow-pitch softball style towards Dylan. Dylan watched as the bag sailed through the air, lowering the crossbow to brace for the catch.

Then Andy made his move.

CHAPTER
TWENTY

ANDY WAS at full sprint before the bag reached full altitude, closing the roughly twenty-foot gap between them at a breakneck speed. Dylan caught the bag and tried to lift the crossbow to get a shot off on Andy, but Andy was too quick. He put his head down and spear-tackled Dylan, who managed to get a clumsy shot off, sending an arrow safely over our heads and into one of the trees. Andy crawled up onto Dylan's torso and pinned him down. An eerily familiar sight, but, again, like a negative of a photograph.

The planes were close and, from the sound of it, would be overhead at any minute.

"Evan!" Andy shouted. "Switch him back. *Now!*"

Evan ran over and began hitting buttons on Birdie's device.

"It's not working," he said. "Oh, wait. Here." He picked up the old device.

He pushed a button, and reality faded to black.

CHAPTER
TWENTY-ONE

I FELL to my knees in my adult body. Gunshots were going off somewhere.

"Kurt?" a man's voice called.

I looked around. It was old Evan. He grabbed me and pulled me behind a tree.

"Are you hit?" he asked, looking me over frantically.

"No," I mumbled. "I don't think so." I checked myself. *All good, phew.*

We were in the woods. The Rebels were advancing towards a sturdy little hut with a door. I instantly recognized it. We were just outside the switchers' compound, or base, or whatever.

"They switched me by accident," I explained. "What are we doing here?" I looked down. "And why do I have a gun?"

Evan's head went back slowly, then dropped to his chest as he exhaled his frustration. He didn't have to answer. I knew. The rebels were attacking the switchers, and at just the right time.

Well, not for the switchers, I suppose. Sucks to be them.

Evan began looking back and forth between me and the ensuing battle. I couldn't tell what was going through his mind. Maybe whether to stay or abandon me. Whether or not I should join the fight. But then he said, "Go hide. Get somewhere safe. This isn't your fight."

"Like hell," I said. "Switch me back!"

"You'd have to use one of the devices inside, and I'm not—"

"Let's go." I said, surprising both of us. When you have nowhere else to go, fear is a hell of a motivator.

I could see he didn't want me to come, but he said, "Come on. Stay behind me."

I'm totally fine with that.

The gunfire calmed for a moment, then picked up heavily again for several seconds.

When it slowed, he stood, took a deep breath, raised his weapon and moved from behind the tree. I didn't have time to think about what he was saying before he started squeezing off rounds. When he stopped, he said, "Last chance to turn around." Then he started walking towards the hut without waiting for a response.

"Are you sure I can switch in there?" I asked.

"Let's find out," he called back over his shoulder.

Gun in hand, I whipped around from behind the tree to follow behind Evan. I saw people—most wearing black fatigues, but not all—lying on the ground. It froze me for a second. Mentally, anyway. I was still behind Evan, close enough to reach out and grab his shoulder.

"Kill anyone in black that comes at us," he said without looking at me. "When we go in, tuck in somewhere in the middle of the pack and watch your ass."

I worried that I might get confused for Alliance, but I looked down and realized that my switcher had changed into street clothes since my last visit.

Within seconds of receiving my instructions, the Rebels dispatched the rest of the remaining Alliance fighters.

"Wait!" one of the Rebels ordered.

Almost as if they were waiting for this cue, another small group charged out of the door. They were taken out immediately, save for one or two in the back who retreated before making it all the way outside.

"*NOW!*" the voice commanded. And with that, the Rebels converged on the hut, squeezing in two, sometimes three at a time. I hurried to make sure I wasn't part of the last group in, but didn't push too hard to get up front, either.

Moving in this river of angry bodies, the doorway swallowed me whole, and I descended back into a place I'd hoped never to go again.

CHAPTER
TWENTY-TWO

I saw the large elevator doors had been pried open, and rebels were destroying the elevator. The wave of Rebels broke through a wide set of heavy double doors, and I kept my feet moving to not get trampled. It felt disturbingly like the last day of school. The doors led to the top of a staircase like you might see in a parking ramp, only with no visibility to the outside. Partway down the rows of stairs, the wave came to a halt. The group up front was working on taking down another wide set of doors at the bottom of the staircase. It didn't take long after a few *bangs* and *booms* for the doors to give way. The line moved only a step or two, then halted at the sound of gunfire coming from inside.

Shots were returned for a few seconds, then stopped. My ears were ringing, but I ignored the *weeeeeeeeeeeee* sound and pressed on, stepping over a few Rebels and more-than-a-few Alliance on either side of the doorway.

As we moved down the hallway, I tried to remember which way was what. But everything looked the same—not to mention the alarm lights were blinking on and off—and I had no idea where we were, or where we were going, so I stopped thinking about it and followed for the time being. Each time we came to an intersection of hallways, the Rebels split up to sweep as much of the compound as possible. Once one large group, the Rebels had split into many smaller teams. Evan's team rounded a few corners but found no one.

"Could that have been all of them?" one of the Rebels asked.

"Maybe..." Evan said.

"They have a place they go when there's trouble," I said. "It has revolving doors. They might be in there."

"What kind of place?" Evan asked.

"I don't know. Some kind of bunker. A panic room or shelter or something. I didn't actually—"

I was distracted by a door. It had no knob. There was nothing written on or near the door. Only a keypad next to it.

"Hey, hey, hey," Evan said, snapping his fingers. "Focus. Where is this place?"

"Uh," I said, thinking about which way I approached the door the first time. "That way!"

"Good," he told me. Then to the others, "Let's go give em a taste of their own, eh?"

What does that mean?

They started jogging down the hallway. I started too, but only at half-speed. I let them all get ahead of me, then hung back when the hallway doglegged to the right.

I didn't like the way Evan said, *give em a taste of their own.* He smiled like a crazed person as he said it, and the other rebels didn't smile so much as bare their teeth. Whatever the plan was, these people were determined to a lifetime of war, one way or the other. And I wanted no part in it.

When the group disappeared around a corner, I backtracked to the knobless door. To the lab. The switching lab. I closed my eyes and tried to remember the path of the hand that opened the door last time I was here. I was in a wheelchair, and I watched the guard enter the passcode. It was right in front of my face and I had a close look.

I tried something.

A red light illuminated above the keys.

I tried something else.

Red light.

I thought again. Tried again.

Red light.

I looked down at my feet. Slowed my breathing. Closed my eyes and thought. Hard.

Up-down-left-down. I tried another combination.

Green light.

The door whirred and clicked. Then it went ajar.

I lifted my weapon, kicked the door open, and took a knee.

"This lab's full, dammit!" an annoyed voice said. Footsteps clopped towards the door. "Go to the emergency—"

It was some kind of doctor-looking person, who, when he saw me—particularly my gun—jumped a little and threw his hands up.

"Don't shoot. You don't understand. We—*Stephens?*"

I ignored the man's recognition of me, focusing on the people in the weird lab chairs. It was the guys (minus Lt. Berder—and me, of course), the girls were there now, and a few others I didn't recognize, all barely conscious and strapped down. "I'm not letting you switch those people."

But then an awful thought occurred to me: if I want to safely switch back—yep, watch is still stuck—I'll have to kill this guy. I didn't think I was prepared to do that. The only other option then was to wait and guard my friends' safety until the window closed. *But then, I'll be stuck—*

"Look out!" a voice called from the doorway. *Evan's* voice.

While I was thinking, I lowered my weapon and took my eyes off the doctor, who had pulled a handgun.

A shot went off and I crumpled to the ground. Then another shot rang.

CHAPTER
TWENTY-THREE

I FELT FOR THE SHOTS, for any pain. There was none. I looked up and saw the doctor lying on the ground. If he wasn't dead, he wasn't trying to get his gun that was right next to his hand.

"Get his gun," Evan wheezed.

They were both shot, though Evan seemed to be in better shape. But not by much.

I stood and went to the doctor. I almost expected him to grab my ankle like the bad guy in a scary movie when everyone *thinks* he's dead, but then—*gotcha!* But the longer I stood there, the larger the puddle of blood got. I kicked the gun a little way from the body before picking it up. Just to be safe.

"I need you to help me," Evan said.

"How?"

"Switch me."

"But then—"

"I'm *dying*," he begged.

I heard voices down the hallway: "It was this way, *come on!*"

I ran to the door and shouldered it closed. A few seconds later I could just barely hear people banging on the door outside.

"No," Evan said. "Let them in. You don't know how to do it."

I thought as fast as I could. While I thought, I looked around. I saw a digital clock that had a timer counting down. It showed just over 2 minutes. *Must be how long the window will stay open.* Then my brain clicked into gear.

"How do I do it?"

"What?"

"I want out, you want out. I'll do it."

Evan frowned at the wall while he thought. "Fine." He talked me through the steps, pointing at this and that. His words were coming slower and softer every other sentence. I helped Evan onto the empty chair I assumed was meant for the dead fella. I thought about strapping him down, but didn't think it would matter that much. He wasn't going anywhere.

"You have to identify the target you're switching. Grab that," he said, pointing at something that looked like the result of a small boom box having a baby with a large controller from a remote-control car. "It's the control for the device. It's more accurate than those half-assed ones you guys have." He pointed towards something on the ceiling. It looked kind of like a TV satellite. "You'll be able to see...the target through that lens. You point...and click...and there you go."

I looked up at the timer. Only 35 seconds. Evan was breathing very slowly. Every exhale sounded forced and shallow.

I quickly ran up to Dylan and slapped him on the face a few times.

"Hey," I said. "How old are you?"

"*Mehm-teen,*" he barely managed to open his mouth, his eyes rolling in their sockets.

Andy was next to him. I went through the same routine.

"*Thirty—*"

Heard what I needed to hear. Moved to the next chair, asked the same thing.

"What are you...doing?" Evan asked, grimacing.

"Checking something." I went down the line of chairs, asking them all how old they were. Luckily, they were all conscious, but had enough drugs—no one was in a position to lie. Me and Dylan were the only PO foreigners in the lab. A quick check showed seventeen seconds left on the timer.

I grabbed the controller, dumped Andy to the ground, hopped in his seat, and targeted me, Dylan, and the others in the sight.

"No," Evan whispered. "*NO!*"

He raised his gun at me.

15...

Shit! Why didn't I take his gun?!

14...

I put my thumb over the button.

13...

I started to push down.

12...

But Evan fired his gun, scoring a direct hit in my chest.

11...

Evan's hand dropped.

10...

His gun fell to the ground from his hand, as did the controller from mine.

9...

I felt both too much pain to move and too weak to get up anyway. I was dying. Fast. I could feel my energy draining out with all the blood. The banging outside the door intensified.

8...

I thought about home—and started crying.

7...

The banging on the door stopped all at once—and my vision began fading from the edges in.

6...

The door whirred and opened, with Lt. Berder running in looking like he had literally been dragged through hell.

5...

"Kurt?"

4...

"I just wanna go home, Birdie" I said, sobbing and hopelessly covering my wound—Lt. Birder was kneeling over a chart laying beside the dead doctor.

3...

"I just...wanna..." but I didn't have the breath to finish.

2...

Birdie stood, sprinted to me, grabbed the controller....

1...

My arms fell to my sides—and everything went black.

CHAPTER

TWENTY-FOUR

After everything went black, I felt an odd numbness. Slowly, the blackness turned white. I could hear sounds. People talking. My friends' voices. And someone else's. But they might as well have been speaking Klingon—I couldn't make out a recognizable syllable. The blind whiteness began turning into colors. No shapes or even discernable colors. Just kind of a tie-dye that moved and changed and danced to a beautiful rhythm that lacked any discernible melody. Slowly, the colors took form, becoming shapes. People. Trees. The moon. Tall grass. A light brown brick building. A small old red house. And the sounds were a conversation we'd had before....

I was back in my PO! Not just my PO. My time! The place and time before *it* happened. Where this whole thing started. I kind of faded into it like how some songs come on with the band in full swing, the volume slowly rising until the sounds begin to work together and make sense. Mike was standing near Evan, who was holding Andy. Me and Dylan were standing by each other. Birdie was out of sight, presumably in the basement of the house. As everything came into focus, the talking stopped. Evan let go of Andy.

"What're you doin, Evan?" Mike yelled.

"You don't remember?" Evan said.

"*I* do," Andy said.

"Me too," Dylan said.

"Are we home, guys?" I asked.

"I think so," Andy said. He touched his face and winced.

"God, it feels good," Dylan said, looking at his hands. "I've been over there awhile, man."

"Yeah, I kinda figured," I said.

"Hey!" Mike yelled at us. He cradled his hand over his stomach, turned to Evan and said, "What the hell's goin on, man?"

Evan's face strained as he tried to figure out how to explain it.

"*Birdie!*" Andy said. He ran to the front door of the house and called to Birdie, told him not to touch anything and to come up immediately.

"Is it," Birdie started. "Is it...safe?"

"Yeah, dude," Dylan yelled. "Douche-tard ain't gonna do nothin."

"What did you call me?" Mike said, starting towards Dylan.

Evan tried to interject, "Mike don't—"

"Hey Mike!" I said. He stopped and looked at me. "Instead of picking on someone, let's have some real fun."

"What're you talkin about?" he said, his eyes narrow with resignation.

"I have an idea. I think you'll like it."

"Oh?" he said. "Hold on. Wait. What's going on?" he said, shaking the confusion from his head.

Birdie came out of the house. Slowly. Like a groundhog wary of its shadow. I popped a few tears when I saw him but stopped myself before it got out of control. I could tell he didn't remember anything, which meant he didn't make it. Then I couldn't tell what the tears were for: Birdie dying in the in-between world the switchers created, or just being happy to see him now. I guess it was both.

"What's your brilliant idea?" Mike asked.

"Anyone still got any money on them?" I said.

TWENTY-FIVE

I took the money we scraped together—mostly change from our earlier purchases—and went inside the 7-Eleven.

"Forget something?" the cashier asked, looking up from one of the store's magazines, which was conspicuously tucked inside a different magazine.

"Yeah," I said, slapping the change down on the counter. "I forgot something my dad asked me to grab."

"What's that?"

"Some lighter fluid."

He glanced over the magazines, barely, before putting his wall back up, saying, "We're not supposed to sell lighters to kids..."

"I know. But it's for my dad. And," I countered, "it's not a lighter."

The cashier put the magazine on his chest and squinted at me.

"He gave me the money I used in here a minute ago to get something for myself, but said I could only have it if I brought him back some lighter fluid."

"*Really?*"

"I don't wanna go home without it," I said, trying to squeeze as much desperation out of my face and voice as possible. "Please don't make me..."

The cashier put his magazine down, looked at me sideways a second, then stood up with an annoyed grunt and grabbed the lighter fluid from the back shelf. "Alright, listen," he reached across his body, over his shoulder, and grabbed a small tin with his free hand. The inside magazine slipped an inch. "I'm gonna set this down on the counter. Then I'm gonna finish reading my magazine," which he tapped back into place on the counter. "Leave the money there, but don't. I mean DO. NOT. Take the lighter fluid. Got it?"

"Wouldn't dream of it."

"Good."

He set the container on the counter and put his magazine wall back up.

I left the change on the counter and walked away with the lighter fluid.

Duh.

CHAPTER
TWENTY-SIX

I WENT AROUND BACK and wiggled the can at Mike.

"What's that for?" he asked.

"Isn't it obvious?" Birdie mumbled. We all looked at him with smiles the joke hadn't warranted, which caused him to raise an eyebrow before averting his eyes.

"It's for the house," I said.

"What do you mean?" Mike asked.

"Let's burn it down," I said with a shrug.

He looked at me like I was speaking a foreign language. Then he smiled and a single laugh shot out of his mouth, but he quickly got serious again.

"You're joking," he said.

"Mike," I said. "I know you have a lighter on you. I know you like to light things on fire. Let's get rid of that stupid old house. It'll be fun. Then maybe they can build an Arby's there or something."

He looked around at all of us, very nervous like, and said, "You're just trying to get me in even *more* trouble."

"No, I'm not. Give me your lighter, Dylan—*I'll* do it too."

"You *are* serious," Mike said.

"Here," Dylan said, tossing me the lighter.

"Listen man," I told Mike. "Let's do this together and then maybe we can all be cool with each other. Whaddya say?"

Mike shrugged at Evan, pulled his lighter out of his pocket, and flicked it to life.

"Let's rock!"

CHAPTER
TWENTY-SEVEN

I WENT into the house first, Mike followed behind me.

"You guys are crazy," Mike said. "You *know* that, right?"

"A lot of things worse than being a little crazy," I replied.

"If you say so." He said it exactly the same as he did when we first ran into him by my house. It sent a chill through me.

I could hear Birdie quietly questioning why we were doing this, and Andy reassuring him it would be okay.

"Careful, man," Dylan hollered.

"Yeah, yeah," I said. "I got it."

"Meh-meh-*meh*," he mocked.

"That kid ain't too bright, is he?" Mike said.

"He's...I dunno—he's Dylan." I really didn't know what to think. Could I blame him for decisions he won't make for years? If we end up in the same predicament, that is. And even if we don't, is he just that kind of person?

I noticed the old carpet felt gross and spongy in spots, so I focused on finding a dry spot close enough to the door and started pouring the can of lighter fluid out into one concentrated puddle.

"Whoa," Mike said. "Don't bogart the lighter fluid. Let me spread it around a little."

I reluctantly handed him the can. He took out a pocketknife. "Let's get right to the point, huh?" he said. Using only his good hand, he put the tin on the ground, held it steady with his foot, then stabbed the knife into the can and twisted it, creating a quarter-sized hole. He put the knife away and, staying low with the can, walked a trail of fluid through a doorway into what I assumed was the kitchen area, and vanished out of sight. I heard the can drop onto the floor in the other room and a few seconds later he was back, lighter in hand.

"You ready?" he asked, flicking his lighter to life once again.

"Hold on," I said. "It's probably not a good idea to put the flame right on the fluid."

"How else ya gonna do it?" he said, in a bully's voice. It didn't faze me in the least anymore.

"Hmm..." I said. "Oh! I got it." I ran to the doorway. "Who's got that cigarette butt?"

"What cigarette butt?" Dylan said.

"You guys said *I* didn't remember," Birdie mumbled, then he lightly backhanded the front of Andy's shoulder.

"Huh?" Andy said. "Oh yeah!" He reached into his pocket and delicately pulled the remaining half of a cigarette out of his jeans.

"Give it here," I said. He walked it over and put it in my outstretched hand. I took a step back into the house. "We'll use this," I said holding up the slightly bent cigarette fragment.

Mike's lower lip jutted out as he nodded in an I-guess-that'll-work way. Then he asked, "May I?"

I handed him the cigarette and moved onto the front steps. He lit it, took a couple deep drags. "Ugh," he said. "Whose nasty-ass discount smokes are these?"

I assumed it was rhetorical and watched him carefully, ready to bolt.

"Gross. Alright," he said with a grin. "Ready?"

I thought, *I've literally never been more ready for anything in my life*, but only gave a single nod.

Mike got into a baserunner's stance and held the lit cigarette at arm's length. He took one deep breath, held it in, and dropped the cigarette into the puddle.

CHAPTER

TWENTY-EIGHT

WE RAN AWAY from the house. I stopped a few steps short of the back of the 7-Eleven. Mike stopped when he ran into me. For a second it looked like nothing was going to happen.

"Maybe the cigarette went—"

Poof!

We heard the *woosh* of a flame being born. Then we saw a thin stream of smoke start out the door. Within seconds, the inside of the old house was illuminated. Within a minute, the whole living room floor was crawling with flames.

"Guys," Birdie said in a panic. "Guys, we gotta get outta here. We can't be here. We'll get in trouble."

He—as he sometimes did—had a point.

"Let's go to the hole until other people show up," Andy said. "Then when a crowd gathers, we can come back and act all surprised."

Mike laughed. "You guys really *are* crazy."

"C'mon," Birdie pleaded, already on his bike.

"Alright buddy," I said. "Lead the way."

Birdie looked at me in disbelief.

"Well?" I said.

A smile crept up on one side of his mouth, then disappeared.

CHAPTER
TWENTY-NINE

By the time we got to the hole, the outside of the house had just started to catch fire. Smoke plumed out of every opening. We could smell it. It gave me an uncomfortably familiar feeling. I had to remind myself that *we* were in control this time. But it was hard convincing myself.

After we heard the sirens in the distance we agreed to wait until the fire truck was parked and the hoses were out before we went back, which didn't take long.

"Alright," Evan said. "Shall we?"

CHAPTER

THIRTY

WE RODE BACK, weaving slowly through tree stumps and construction equipment. We got as close as the firemen would allow—a few steps in from the parking lot.

While everyone watched the flames engulf the house, Andy leaned over and whispered to me, "What about the switchers that made it over?"

"I don't know, man," I said. "Hopefully the Rebels stopped most of them."

"And if they didn't?"

"Yeah, I don't know."

"Hey guys," Dylan said. "Look who it is."

I didn't turn right away; I was lost in thought, troubled by Andy's question.

"I know them," Birdie said. "They were in advanced stats."

That got my attention.

It was the girls, looking no worse for wear. They rode their bikes together. I hardly noticed the other two; I couldn't take my eyes off Elizabeth. They were walking towards the crowd that had gathered to watch the spectacle, but their eyes were on the fire reaching for the night sky.

357

When she looked away from the house, I waved at Elizabeth. She looked at me, smiling without actually smiling. She nudged the others, saying something and pointing towards us. They came our way.

"Hey," I said.

"Hey," Elizabeth said.

I looked away, a bit nervous. I caught eyes with Birdie. He gave me the hubba-hubba eyebrows. *Birdie's always gonna be Birdie.* The thought brought me inexplicable joy. *Probably a blessing he doesn't remember.* I gave him the hubba-hubba eyebrows right back. He smiled and turned back to the fire.

"Did you all...?" I fumbled for an end to the sentence.

"Yeah. You guys?" she asked.

"Mike and Birdie don't remember."

"Of course Birdie doesn't—" she stopped mid-sentence, thought, said, "Probably just as well."

"Right," the thought of Birdie dying was awful, but also surreal since I was looking at him. We went through so much, it's almost like he's a living memory.

"What about all the other switchers?" she asked.

"Hm? Oh," I let out a long sigh. "I don't know."

She nodded. Then she asked, "Katie doesn't think the ones that didn't make it can come back anymore, but what if they do? How would we even know if they did? And what about the ones that *did* make it through?"

"I don't know," I said.

She looked down and twisted her lips.

"Hey," I said, slipping my hand into hers. "We'll cross that bridge if and when we come to it."

She locked her fingers into mine and squeezed my hand.

"Do you think everything will be okay?" she asked.

"If something isn't right...we'll know it when we see it," I said. "But everything feels good right now. Maybe we just focus on that?"

She smiled at me for a long moment. Then she kissed me. Just a quick one, but it sent a shock through me like I had switched again.

When she pulled back, all I could do was look at her with a big dumb grin on my face. She laughed a little and put her head on my shoulder.

Together, we watched in silence as the house fell in on itself. And for the first time since *it* happened—maybe ever—I was excited for the future.

THIRTY-ONE

S<small>INCE THEN</small>, I haven't noticed much out of the ordinary. But things have gotten a little weird lately, you must admit. I'm not saying there's anything to get excited about. Not yet.

My warning to you is this. I don't know exactly when in time the window opened in our switchers' PO, but I do know this: Every day I look more and more like the man I saw in the mirror at the lab. So much so that sometimes, early in the morning, when I'm struggling for my first clear thought of the day, I'll look in the mirror and won't recognize myself. And in that moment, I'm there again.

Keep your eyes, ears, and mind open.

Beware of people who make you uneasy and you can't put your finger on why. You might not know what to look for, but you'll know it when you see it.

G<small>OOD LUCK</small>,
   Kurt (& Elizabeth) Stephens, Michigan, 2022

ACKNOWLEDGMENTS

Special thanks to TJ Tranchell for editing, Kirk Ross for the art, Joshua Marsella for formatting, Jennifer Soucy for your notes (and introducing me to TJ), and Brandon Scott for your support (and for introducing me to Josh). You guys are great friends and extremely talented individuals, and this book is here in large part because of you. Thanks also Mike Draft, JoAnn Collins, Nate Williams, Joanne Beltran, Angie Schuart, Ross Freeman, Justin "Smitty" Smith, Paul Brogan, Jason Tieri, Pamela Dail Whiting, Mike Breymann & Cristina Calcagno, Sal & Jane (my parents), and to my wife and kids.

Lastly I'd like to thank John Bellairs for writing the first books I'd ever fall in love with, and to my elementary school librarian, Mrs. Creegan, for introducing a hyperactive, reluctant reader to something dark and weird. It made an impression.

ABOUT THE AUTHOR

Christopher Tallon lives in west Michigan with his wife and kids. He loves camping, playing guitar, and hosting *CREATIVE OPS* (A Podcast for Creative People). Before working from home as a writer, Christopher worked in construction, served overseas in the military, and taught middle school English in Grand Rapids, MI. *Switchers* is his debut novel.

Visit the website: www.christophertallon.com
Follow on Twitter, Facebook, and Instagram: **@TallonWrites**

ONE FINAL NOTE

Thanks in advance for leaving a review, posting about the book on social media, and/or anything you might do to help spread the word about my book. You're awesome.

Made in the USA
Columbia, SC
03 October 2022

68281576R00221